PRAISE FOR THE NOVELS OF ROWAN KEATS

When a Laird Takes a Lady

"The magnetic attraction between Aiden and Isabail is intense and sensual, c[illegible]s. Keats's ability to re-c[illegible]-thenticity to this nov[illegible]-sional characters and [illegible]

[illegible]y

"Keats serves up a powerful story. . . . She not only weaves the era's history, intrigue, and power plays into her plot, but also creates a wonderful, passionate romance." —*RT Book Reviews*

"A story that reels the reader in . . . and complex, intriguing characters who touch the heart."—The Romance Dish

Taming a Wild Scot

"Get ready for a rich, exciting new voice in Scottish historical romance! Rowan Keats captures all the passion and heart of the Highlands as she expertly weaves a wonderful tale of passion, intrigue, and love that you won't want to put down. I'm already looking forward to the next book in what is sure to be a must-read series."
—Monica McCarty, *New York Times* bestselling author of *The Hunter*

continued . . .

"Keats's debut sets the stage for a rising star of medieval romance. She seamlessly weaves an unusual romance with the intrigues and power plays associated with the era, greatly enhancing the story's emotional power."

—*Romantic Times*

"Lyrical writing . . . and a strong cast of characters will keep the reader engaged." —*Publishers Weekly*

ALSO BY ROWAN KEATS

The Claimed by the Highlander Series

Taming a Wild Scot
When a Laird Takes a Lady

To Kiss a Kilted Warrior

A Claimed by the Highlander Novel

Rowan Keats

A SIGNET ECLIPSE BOOK

SIGNET ECLIPSE
Published by the Penguin Group
Penguin Group (USA) LLC, 375 Hudson Street,
New York, New York 10014

USA | Canada | UK | Ireland | Australia | New Zealand | India | South Africa | China
penguin.com
A Penguin Random House Company

First published by Signet Eclipse, an imprint of New American Library,
a division of Penguin Group (USA) LLC

First Printing, December 2014

ISBN 978-0-451-47086-7

Printed in the United States of America
10 9 8 7 6 5 4 3 2 1

Chapter 1

Glen Storas
The Red Mountains, Scotland
March 1286

As the last rays of the setting sun gave way to purple dusk, Morag Cameron stared up at the roof of her cottage, where Magnus was replacing a section of straw thatching that had slipped away during the winter storms. "Surely you can't see much in the gloaming. Are you not coming in to sup?"

"Aye," he said, as he combed the bundles of straw with a stick driven with iron nails, ensuring the thatch was even and clear of debris. "I'll be but a few moments longer. Would you fetch me the hazel spars?"

She gathered up the thin strips of hazel wood he'd split earlier and climbed the ladder.

He took them from her with a quick smile. "Thank you, lass."

Leaning on the rungs of the ladder, Morag watched him work. Despite the coolness of the early March evening, he had shed his lèine from his upper body. His arms and chest were completely bare, and she was treated to a display of rippling muscles as he deftly twisted each of the hazel spars into thatch pins. He hammered the pins deep into the straw, securing the thatch, and then looked at her.

"Shall we eat?"

She nodded and descended.

He followed, hopping the last three rungs to the ground. The ropy contours of his back glistened with sweat, and she admired him when he stopped at the water barrel to wash straw dust from his hands and face. As water sluiced over his handsome face and trickled down the hard planes of his chest, Morag swallowed tightly. These were the hardest moments. The ones that wrung her gut with a mixture of longing and guilt. She and Magnus lived like a married couple—mending the bothy, living off the land, sharing every chore—but they were not wed. Magnus was not hers.

Indeed, he was not Magnus at all. He was Wulf

MacCurran, a renowned warrior and cousin to the laird. Rather than eating bawd bree with her, he should be supping at Dunstoras Castle with his kin, dining on venison, haggis, and fine wine.

Had he not lost his memories in a fierce battle last November, he surely would be.

Magnus shook off the excess water and slipped his arms back into his lèine. The loose linen tunic properly covered his flesh, belted at the waist, but did nothing to disguise the magnificence of his form. There was no hiding his broad shoulders and brawny chest, and the cream-colored cloth tunic ended at his knees, so his powerful legs remained exposed to her gaze.

He opened the bothy door and ushered Morag ahead of him.

The bothy was small—a single room just big enough to hold a wood-framed bed, a central cooking fire, Morag's upright loom, and a small table for preparing food—but it was tall enough to allow Magnus to walk about without grazing the roof, and it was a welcome warmth during cold winter nights.

She ladled stew into two wooden bowls, and they sat side by side on the edge of the bed as they ate.

Frowning, Magnus peered into his bowl. "You've made a fine meal, as always, but there's little here to sustain a man. I'll go hunting tomorrow. My work on the roof can wait until we add more meat to the stew."

Morag eyed the bucket in the middle of the room. "So long as the hole is repaired before the next heavy rain, I'll be content."

He shifted on the bed, his heavy leg pressing briefly against hers, and Morag's pulse leapt. A vision of him bearing her to the mattress, his lips locked on hers, sprang into her thoughts. She quickly buried the image, but not before her cheeks bloomed with heat.

It was an impossible vision. Not once in the four months he had lived with her had Magnus done more than kiss her. And even that kiss had happened only once. Five weeks ago, before he set out on a mission to aid a strange woman who'd knocked upon their door, he'd swooped in, given Morag the kiss of a lifetime, and then walked out.

Morag had spent the next few days pondering the deeper meaning of that kiss, wondering where it might lead. But when Magnus returned, everything had changed. He'd been withdrawn and thoughtful, consumed by what he had discovered on his journey. He'd found his kin while he was away, and learned the heartrending truth about the night he'd nearly died—that his wife and son had been slain by a murderer. One mere kiss meant nothing in the face of all that.

Morag was ashamed that she continued to dwell upon it.

But it had been a truly memorable kiss. Hot and passionate and full of sweet promise.

Magnus took the bowl and spoon from Morag's hands and stood. He washed the bowls in a mix of sand and water, then rinsed them and put them away. "I know it's your intent to work on your weaving at first light. Shall we retire for the night?"

Morag avoided his gaze. Better that he never know the direction of her thoughts . . . which at the moment had naught to do with weaving. "Aye."

He banked the fire and blew out the candle. Darkness settled over the room, relieved only by the golden glow of smoldering coals in the fire pit. She untied her boots, removed her overdress, and slipped under the blankets. Magnus waited until she was lying with her back to him; then she heard him remove his lèine and join her on the bed. Not touching. But near enough to sense each other's warmth.

This was how all their evenings ended, sharing the dark together in silence. Morag wanted more, and under different circumstances she would have asked for it . . . but her respect for him held her back. He was the most honorable man she had ever known. If he needed time, then she would give it to him. And if he never showed an interest in another kiss, she would accept his decision. Sadly, but willingly.

Morag closed her eyes.

She owed that much to the man who'd once shown her more kindness than a shunned woman had the right to ask for. . . .

Dunstoras Castle
July 1282

"Morag Cameron," declared Laird Duncan, staring down at her from his high-backed chair on the dais, "you are hereby banished from the village of Dunstoras, never to return, save to trade your goods and buy supplies on faire days. You may gather whatever belongings you can carry on your back, but by evenfall you must be gone from these walls. Do you understand?"

Morag glanced across the crowded great hall at Peadar, still hoping he would break his silence and speak for her. The young blacksmith knew the truth—that Tomas had wooed her with tireless devotion, promising her the sun and the moon and eventually, a lifetime of happiness at her side. She'd given Tomas her maidenhead the night he'd whispered that vow in her ear, believing him to be a man of his word. How wrong she'd been. The next morning, Tomas had put her aside with callous disdain, denying he'd ever made such a vow. But Peadar had heard his brother's promise to wed her—he had the power to put an end to this mad pro-

ceeding, if only he would tell the laird what he knew. But he did nothing. He stared at his hands, refusing to look up.

His silence was an unexpected knife in her gut.

She'd thought him a very different man.

In the months following Tomas's betrayal, Peadar had proven himself an able friend, offering a sympathetic ear to her woes and a shoulder to cry on. They had become lovers only recently—after her heart had mended and the future once again held promise. He was kind to her, and respectful, and she had begun to believe that a marriage could be built on such a foundation. Until last Sabbath. That was when Tomas had discovered their alliance and accused her of seducing Peadar—as she had once seduced him. All lies, of course. But Peadar had not refuted his brother's words.

Tears sprang to her eyes. What a fool she'd been.

She was no wiser than her mother, offering her heart to a faithless man. No one would speak for her. Her father was gone, her mother dead. She was a Cameron among MacCurrans, and without Peadar's support, Tomas's hateful words were taken as truth, even though they were merely jealous ranting.

She was alone.

Morag blinked rapidly to clear her eyes and faced the laird. She'd pled her case to him and Brother Francis as passionately as she could . . . to no avail. The testimony of Tomas and his friends had been too convincing. To them she was a fallen woman, a woman who incited brothers to lust over her and then fight over her. But she was not that woman.

She stood straight. "I understand."

"Then begone."

She turned toward the accusing faces of the villagers—faces she'd known all her life. There was not a kind eye to be found in the room. Struggling to hold her head up, she crossed the wooden floorboards to the door. The crowd parted to let her pass.

How would she survive outside the castle walls? It was summer now, thank God. The nights were warm and there would be berries to pluck. But come winter she would suffer badly.

When she reached the bothy she had once shared with her mother, Morag packed a bag with as many of her personal belongings as she could—clay pots, wooden bowls, steel spoons, and clothing—and stuffed another bag full of woolen spools. She slung one bag over each shoulder and then tried to pick up her loom. But it was heavier than she thought. And awkward.

Morag dragged the loom out of the bothy and down the lane, leaving a trail of twin grooves in the dirt. She headed toward the small wooden bridge that spanned the burn. Once she crossed, she would be out of the village. Unfortunately, it would not be an easy goal to reach—some thirty or forty villagers had lined up on either side of the lane, each with at least one rotted vegetable in hand. They meant to see her off with a vengeance.

Had she been willing to relinquish her loom, she could have made a dash for safety.

But weaving was all she knew. She had no skills to work the land; nor did she know how to make ale or uisge beatha. To have any hope of survival, she needed this loom. Morag stiffened her shoulders, bowed her head, and tightened her hold on the wooden frame. She would not leave it behind. No matter how difficult the trial.

As soon as she came within range, the villagers began calling her names and pelting her with their spoiled vegetables. Neeps and parsnips and onions, mostly. A few were soft, leaving juicy remains clinging to her clothing and face and hair, but most were hard at the core and delivered bruising blows. Not as brutal as a stoning, to be sure, but painful nonetheless.

"Jezebel!"

"Whore!"

A neep hit her in the face, and Morag stumbled.

Her fingers slipped, and she lost hold of the loom, the frame slamming to the ground. Fearful that a vindictive soul would stomp on the wood and break it, she scrambled to regain hold of it. Her pause allowed a volley of projectiles to hit her from every side, and Morag had to bite her lip to stop from crying out. Her legs wobbled, and her resolve took a beating. She was about to drop to her knees in the dirt when she felt a sturdy hand grab her elbow. Suddenly there were no more vegetables, and the crowd's jeers fell silent.

Morag looked up at her savior.

It was Wulf MacCurran, the laird's most formidable warrior. Taller than all those around him by a full head, the laird's nephew commanded respect by his very size. He'd clearly been out hunting—two fat capercaillies hung from his belt, and he carried a long ash bow in his free hand. He likely didn't know she'd been banished.

"You ought not to aid me," she said quietly to her protector.

"She's been cast out," said Tomas, pushing through the crowd to the front.

"Aye," Wulf said. "That I can see. But the lass will face difficulty enough on her own. There's no need to punish her further. Get along home, now, the lot of you."

The big warrior did not often involve himself in village disputes—he spent most of his time training in the lists and providing for his young wife and bairns—so his words this day carried a great deal of weight. With disgruntled expressions but nary a complaint, the crowd dissipated. Even Tomas dared not contest Wulf's judgment. In no time, Morag stood alone with Wulf in the lane.

"Thank you," she said. "You've eased my lot considerably."

He slung the bow over his shoulder, then took one of her bags and the loom from her hands. "There's a clearing in the forest a league from here that would make a fine spot for a bothy. If you work hard, you can build it before the heavy frosts come." He led the way across the bridge.

Morag stared after him in stunned disbelief. Build a bothy? By herself?

An image of a wee bothy in the woods lept into her mind, and hope sweetened the air in her chest. Why not? She scrambled to follow the big warrior. She was able enough. And the supplies necessary lay freely around her. All she needed was a small room with a fire pit—she could expand it over time, if that was her desire.

Wulf shortened his strides to allow Morag to catch up.

"Why are you aiding me?" she asked warily. There had to be a reason.

He shrugged. "A man does not stand to watch a woman suffer."

"Even a woman branded a harlot?"

He halted and looked down at her. His eyes were a brilliant shade of blue that stood out against his sun-darkened skin. "You can live your life as others see you, lass, or you can live your life as you see yourself. Are you a harlot?"

She shook her head. "I am a weaver."

"Then be a weaver," he said, marching forward through the bracken.

Morag followed him. "That is certainly my intent. But who will buy cloth woven by a harlot?"

"'Twill not be easy to make your way," he acknowl-

edged. "You may need to trade farther afield. But if you craft the finest cloth in the glen, even those who vilify you will eventually come 'round."

"I already craft the finest cloth in the glen," Morag said matter-of-factly.

He smiled as he helped her over a moss-covered fallen log. "Then make your cloth impossible to resist."

Morag chewed her bottom lip. When her father—also a weaver—had walked out, never to return, he'd left behind almost everything he possessed. Including his notes on creating dyes. Her mother had kept them, convinced they would eventually draw her husband back to her. An unrequited longing. The notes lay in a bundle at the bottom of Morag's bag, still tied with a yellow ribbon. But they need not remain that way. Her father's cloth had been renowned throughout the Red Mountains, the colors unparalleled. If her cloth came close to matching his . . . ?

They trudged in silence for a while, wending a path up rocky hills, down grassy gullies, and through the thickest part of the forest. When they broke from the trees into a wee meadow filled with wildflowers, Wulf stopped and set her loom down.

"This is it," he proclaimed. "The loch is over yon brae, and the auld broch is a half league to the east."

Morag slowly spun around. Her imagination built a bothy with a pretty thatched roof and a painted door. It was perfect. "Thank you."

"I'll be by every other Sunday to do the heavier chores," he said. "Until you're settled."

"I'm grateful for your aid," she said. "But do not risk your uncle's wrath on my account."

Wulf shrugged. "Laird Duncan often has opinions that do not match my own. I follow my honor."

"And your wife? Would she not be concerned to hear you offering your services to me?"

He smiled. "Nay. She'll be of like mind to me. Elen is a practical lass. She'd see your loss as a loss for Dunstoras. There are too few weavers of any skill in the glen." He pointed to the edge of the tree line. "Come. We'll build a small shelter there to keep the rain off."

It took them the better part of the day to fashion a lean-to that could weather a strong wind. By the time the sun slipped below the tops of the trees, Morag had a roof, a pallet, and a cooking pit. Wulf had given her plenty of advice on how to structure the bothy, and had even begun the task of gathering stones for the base.

"I must be off, lass," he said, slinging his bow over his shoulder once more. "Will you fare well?"

Morag grabbed his hand. "Aye, I will. And I've you to thank for that. You've aided me more than you'll ever know this day, and I doubt I'll be able to return the gift."

He gave her a serious look. "Survive, and that will be gift enough."

Then he set off across the meadow.

Morag watched him until the verdant shadows of the

woods swallowed him. He'd given his time and advice without asking for anything in return. He'd accepted her without judging. And he'd spoken of his wife with kindness and respect. What a truly intriguing man. Had he not already been wed, she might easily lose her heart to Wulf MacCurran.

Morag listened to the deep, even breaths of the man sleeping beside her in the bed. She had learned to call him Magnus—a necessary chore while Tormod MacPherson had held the glen, pledging to slay all MacCurrans—but in her heart, he was and always would be Wulf.

When she found him down by the loch, beaten and bloodied and near death, saving him had not been a conscious choice. Aye, the risks were great. But no greater than the risks he'd taken to support her when she'd been shunned. MacPherson's men had stormed her bothy several times, never quite believing her tale of being wed to a lame farmer. Thanks to Wulf's lost memories and the name he had assumed, that story had been impossible to dispute, and eventually the soldiers had ceased to bother them.

Morag sighed and rolled onto her back.

Wulf's naked heat was only an inch away, a powerful temptation. She threaded her fingers together and laid her hands carefully—and safely—on her chest.

In some ways, things had been easier when MacPherson had commanded Dunstoras. Certainly she'd been less tormented by guilt. Healing Wulf and avoiding trouble had been all she worried about. But MacPherson and his army had vacated the glen a month ago, and the MacCurrans had returned to the castle, welcomed by the new owner, Lady Isabail Macintosh. Wulf ought to be living there now, surrounded by those who called him kin. But he'd chosen to stay with her, and no amount of discussion had thus far swayed him to change his mind.

She drew in a deep breath, savoring the warm, male scent that was uniquely Wulf. A mix of earth and spice that reminded her of sweet sage.

Perhaps she hadn't tried hard enough. Lord knew, she dreaded the day he would depart. But she knew well that he wasn't hers to hold. He never had been. All those Sundays when he'd stopped by to help her, he'd been nothing but respectful and friendly and eager to return home. It was *she* who had waited with anticipation for his arrival, *she* who had begged his opinion of her new cloth designs, *she* who had lain awake at night wishing she were Elen MacCurran.

Genuine sorrow pinched her nose tight. Terribly unfair, the fate of his wife.

A better woman would force Wulf to leave. Drive him away with cruel words—back to his kin. But she could not. Hurting him, even for his own good, was simply not possible. Not after all the kindness he'd shown her, not after all the counsel he'd given her.

Morag put her fingers to her lips.

Not if it meant losing a chance for one more kiss.

Chapter 2

Morag sat back and studied the cloth taking shape on her vertical loom. She ran her fingers over the soft pattern of green, blue, black, and red threads. The hues were aligned in neat vertical and horizontal bands of varying widths, and the result was every bit as unique and lovely as the fine twill weaves her father had been renowned for.

She gave a low sound of satisfaction and resumed her task, wending the woof swiftly through the warp, lifting and lowering the four heddle sticks as needed. She wove four threads of black wool, then twenty threads of blue.

Wulf had left the bothy immediately after breaking their fast to snare a hare for their supper pot. A good thing, really. His presence wreaked havoc upon her concentration. Instead of carefully tracking the thread counts, she found herself dwelling on the faint curve of his smile, or the splendid contours of his manly shoulders, or the rasp and rumble of his deep male voice. But market day was fast approaching, and a half-finished cloth would not buy them oats for their bannock or candles to burn after dark. Fortunately, with him gone, the cloth on her loom called to her, daring her to bring it to life.

Twenty threads of black, twenty-four of green, four of red.

Each spool of wool that fed her loom was dyed by her own hand, using the tinctures her father had developed, and watching the vivid pattern emerge sent a wave of pure joy washing over her. There was nothing so rewarding as seeing the image in her head take shape on the rack.

With a sigh of contentment, she threw herself wholeheartedly into her weaving.

So lost in her design was she that when the door to the bothy crashed open, Morag fell off her stool.

Heart pounding, she scrambled to her feet and faced her intruders. Two armed strangers stood in the doorway, garbed in the tunics and trews of Lowlanders. She'd spied many such men in the glen when Tormod MacPherson had held Dunstoras Castle for the king, but his mercenaries had departed weeks ago, replaced by Highlanders loyal to Isabail Macintosh. Without taking her eyes off the intruders, she sent a quick prayer skyward. Now would be a fine time for Wulf to return.

"On what authority do you enter my home unbidden?" she demanded, doing her best to tame the quaver in her voice. Chances were poor that they held any authority at all, but she could hope.

The larger of the two men answered, "My own."

Morag could see little of his features, just a halo of bright sunlight around the dark silhouette of his form. But there was no disguising the threat he posed. She tossed aside her shuttle and grabbed the long-handled broom leaning against the wall. Not the most intimidating of weapons, but it was the only thing within easy reach. "And who might you be?"

"My name matters not," he said. "Yield and your life will be spared."

Morag swallowed tightly, her throat suddenly dry. A cotter living off the land was rarely in possession of coin, so there was only one other thing these men might be seeking from a woman alone in the woods . . . and she wasn't willing to give it over. But her hopes of besting two armed men in a battle of strength were slim.

She steadied her grip on the broom.

There was still a slight chance they could be persuaded to leave. "What is it you seek? I've no coin, but I'll willingly give all the food and water that I have."

The leader stepped closer, and his features surfaced out of the gloom. A pockmarked face, long tawny hair, and an ankle-length dove gray cloak. He carried his weapon with the unconscious ease of a hardened soldier, but it was the cold cruelty in his eyes that made Morag's heart sink. In his mind, her fate was already sealed.

"We've no interest in your food," he said. Signaling to his cohort to go left, he advanced another step.

"Food is all I'm prepared to give," she said firmly. The bothy was small—a fact she often rued, but not today. The door was a mere four paces away, but the fire pit and a heavy iron cauldron lay between her and escape. "My husband will return anon. You'd best be away."

He grinned. "Your husband? You mean the strapping lad with the lame leg?"

Her heart flopped. Dear Lord. Had they already encountered Wulf? Laid him low in some shadowed part of the wood? "You won't want to vex him," she said, her palms suddenly cold with sweat. "His tolerance for lackwits is low."

A snort of laughter filled the bothy. "We watched him hobble up yon hill. He won't be so difficult to best."

Morag breathed a sigh of relief and banished the image of Wulf falling victim to a well-placed sword with the same determination with which she had built this bothy. Stone by stone. Thatch by thatch.

Wulf had regained most of his strength these past four months. He was a far cry from the badly injured man she'd dragged home from the edge of the loch last November. While it was true that his left leg hadn't fully recovered, he was yet a formidable warrior.

"Give me the broom," the pockmarked man coaxed, stretching out his hand, palm open.

Morag slapped his fingertips. Hard.

"He'll be sore enough to discover that you've given me a fright," she warned. She would not be able to keep them at bay for much longer. If only she knew when Wulf would return. How long had he been gone? One hour? Two? "But if you harm me, he'll not quit until he sees me avenged."

Morag jabbed her stick toward the leader, urging him to step back. He held his ground. His eyes were not on the broom, but on her face, and Morag knew he was gauging his best moment to snatch the broom from her hands. She pulled back sharply, terrified of losing her weapon.

"Get thee gone," she snarled.

Her only hope of escape was to run. Backward was not an option—the roof thatching was thick and firmly attached. Wulf had seen to that once he was on his feet. So it had to be forward. But was she sufficiently fleet of foot to round the fire pit and elude the two men?

And what would she do if she miraculously succeeded?

She had no plan for such an event. No hidden weapon, no place to hide.

Morag bit her lip. Foolish lass. She'd never truly worried about brigands and thieves. In the beginning, Wulf had kept a watchful eye upon her and ensured that her part of the forest was well protected. Under MacPherson's rule, she'd been so occupied with Wulf's recovery that escape had never crossed her mind. These days the glen was a quieter place, but Lady Macintosh's men were too busy with repairs to the keep and the village blackhouses to be riding regular patrols.

Her gaze flickered to the open door, and back to the pockmarked man.

He smiled. "Too late for that, lass."

Without further warning, he stepped toward her, grabbed the broom, and yanked it away, skinning her palms. Tossing the stick aside, he thrust a hand into her long black hair, snaring a sturdy hold. Then he pulled her to his chest with a forceful tug.

Tears sprang to her eyes, but she did not surrender her freedom willingly. Fighting with wild desperation, she raked her fingernails across his face and dug into his eyes with her thumbs. The mercenary loosened his hold on her. Morag bolted for the door.

Praying that Wulf was somewhere nearby, she screamed his name.

"Wulf!"

Wulf stared at his reflection in the calm, sunlit loch. It was a handsome enough face, pleasantly square and even. And it was familiar. Comfortingly so. But he struggled with the knowledge that it belonged to a man he didn't really know. He'd adopted the name of Magnus when he'd awoken with no memories, but Wulf MacCurran was his true name. He was cousin to the laird and father to a fine lad, but four months after an attack that had left him near dead, he still could not remember one moment of the life he'd led before waking in Morag's bed.

Dipping a hand, he scattered the image and scooped up some water.

The water was icy cold as it slid down his throat, despite the hint of spring in the air.

The Fates had reunited him with his clan last month, which should have brought peace to his lost soul. Instead, it had left him more unsettled than before. Nothing about Dunstoras was familiar, even though he'd been assured by all that he and his family had roomed there before the hateful night that stole his life away. So he had returned to Morag's bothy. Chopping wood, hunting for food, and repairing her home gave him purpose—a purpose that seemed more in line with his inner beliefs than living in a castle.

Wulf abruptly pushed to his feet, his hands fisting. He attempted a smooth stand, but his left leg betrayed him, quivering in protest. The hare hanging from his belt swung wildly as he stumbled. It was a lean offering for Morag's stew pot, but he'd been lucky to snare anything this close to the bothy after MacPherson's army had decamped. Two hundred men trudging east toward MacPherson land had scattered the wildlife far and wide.

He stilled the swing of the hare and retraced his steps along the pebbled beach.

With his hunt complete, logic suggested he return promptly. The sooner the rabbit was in the stew, the more savory it would become. But of late, Morag had been staring at her loom with wistful intent. Cloth was her primary offering on market days, but the looks of longing he'd caught on her face told him weaving was more than simply a trade for her. She drew pleasure from it. If his presence caused her to forgo her weaving, she'd come to resent him in time. And resentment was not the emotion he wished to cultivate in his lovely, dark-haired benefactress.

But how long should he stay away?

He glanced up.

It was midday now, the sun high in the sky. Was

the morning enough? It was hard to know. Although she rarely sat at the loom while he was present, when she did, she displayed an incredible talent he could barely fathom. Changing colored threads without pause, moving sticks up and down, and sliding the shuttle from one side of the loom to the other at blurring speed clearly required a quick mind and nimble fingers. The cloth that developed at the top was, to his mind, a miracle.

His feet turned in the direction of the bothy.

One peek inside the hut would settle the issue. If she was yet enthralled in her weaving, he'd grab a bannock and some cheese, and head back into the wilds.

At the bottom of a woodland hill, about two furlongs from the bothy, he paused and frowned. In the soft mud of the path, the print of a boot heel was clearly outlined. It was too small to be his boot heel and too big to be Morag's. And given the heavy downpour of last eve, such a crisp print could only have been made that day.

Wulf's gaze lifted.

There was no sign of movement in the trees, but his heartbeat quickened anyway. Morag was alone. And he'd left his sword hidden in the woodpile behind the bothy.

He set off at a run.

Or as close to a run as he could manage. His left

leg proved uncooperative, wobbling with every stride and sending shards of excruciating pain to his hip with every attempt to hold his full weight. He was forced to slow to a hobbled jog, and even then the pain was biting. Still, he made it to the clearing in good time, pausing at the edge of the trees.

The door to the hut hung open, the interior a dark shadow.

The open door was not, of itself, a bad omen. Morag might simply have chosen to partake of the sunshine and the unusually warm day. But he could not hear the *clack-clack* of the loom in operation; nor could he hear her humming, as she was wont to do when busy with a task.

He skirted the clearing until he reached the back of the bothy, then quietly dug between the stacked firewood for his long sword. Wrapped in several layers of burlap to protect it from the elements, the bronze-hilted weapon was exactly where he had left it. It settled into his palm with an ease that made his blood sing. Even in the absence of his memories, one thing remained true—he was born to be a warrior.

The sharp crack of wood on wood reverberated inside the bothy.

Wulf's grip tightened on the sword. 'Twas not the sound of something falling, but the sound of something thrown with great force. But as ominous as that sound was, it did not prepare him for what he heard next.

"Wulf!"

His heart sank into his boots. The raw desperation in Morag's voice could not be mistaken. She was in dire straits. Oblivious to the cramps that shot up his leg, Wulf ran for the cottage door at full speed. When he entered, it took precious long moments for his eyes to adjust to the dimness. Masking his inability to see well, he halted just inside the door, planted both feet wide, and challenged his opponent with cold, lethal intent.

Morag made it as far as the table before the smaller of the two mercenaries grabbed her skirts and whipped her off balance. She collided with the table, then spun sideways into the wall. Pain exploded in her skull, and black spots filled her vision. The dirt floor rose up to meet her and she hit it hard, all the air in her chest expelling with a low moan.

A guttural roar of fury came from the door of the bothy. Both mercenaries spun around at the sound, and Morag took advantage of their surprise. She rolled under the table. As she did so, she caught a glimpse of the mighty warrior filling the open doorway. Her heart leapt. *Wulf.* He'd come for her, just as she'd prayed. But this was a version of Wulf she hadn't seen since the night he was attacked and left for dead—bristling with rage, every muscle pumped and ready. His lips were a grim slash on his face, his eyes dark with lethal fury.

Having drawn the mercenaries' attention away from her, he wasted no time.

Wielding his bronze-hilted sword like it was an extension of his arms, he swung the huge blade with such speed that it hummed in the air. The first mercenary went down midstride, never having met Wulf's steel with his own. The pockmarked leader had better luck. He parried Wulf's next swing with his sturdy short sword, the sharp blades sliding along each other with sparks a-flying.

In terms of sheer power, Wulf had the edge. He delivered a series of heavy strikes that pounded his opponent's defenses and forced the man back, leaving him less and less room to maneuver.

But the mercenary was aware of Wulf's weak leg. His swings were calculated to extend Wulf on the left side, and eventually his strategy gained him the edge he needed—Wulf's leg buckled slightly, allowing the mercenary to escape the torrent of blows. He ducked to the right and put the table between himself and Wulf.

Morag found herself staring at the man's trew-clad legs.

Remembering the sharp yank on her hair, she felt for the wee knife she kept at her belt. A mere three inches long, and dull from cutting yarn, it was hardly a reliable weapon. But if she could aid Wulf at all, it would be worth the effort. Wrapping her fist firmly around the short handle, she drove the blade into the mercenary's calf.

He howled.

But instead of hopping away or pausing to pull the small blade free, as she expected, he shoved the table toward Wulf and grabbed for Morag. Hauling her to her feet, he yanked her to his shoulder and laid his sword blade along her throat.

"Stand down or she dies," he said to Wulf.

Wulf did not lower his weapon. He slowly walked out from behind the table, keeping a wide gap between them, and studied the mercenary with icy calm. "Step away from her now, and I may be persuaded to spare your life."

The mercenary snorted. "Let us not waste words. Whether the girl lives or dies is up to me. If you value her at all, you'll lay down your weapon."

Morag stared at Wulf. Although she knew there was a chance she would die, she did not dwell on it. Balancing her weight carefully on one leg, she lifted her other boot slightly to hint to Wulf what she was about to do. Then she kicked backward, aiming for the wood-handled knife she'd planted in the mercenary's leg.

Wulf surged forward at precisely the same moment. When the mercenary flinched from the sudden jab in his leg, Wulf knocked the sword from the man's loosened grip with a solid strike of his pommel, narrowly avoiding a cut to Morag's throat. Morag ducked clear and darted for the farthest corner of the bothy.

That should have been the end, but the pockmarked man refused to yield.

He feinted to the right, picked up his fallen comrade's weapon, and attacked Wulf anew.

It was a pointless effort. Wulf was larger, stronger, and clearly angry. As their blade edges slid against each other, he hooked his quillon on his opponent's crossguard and yanked the weapon free of the man's grasp. It hit the iron cauldron with a loud clang and slid into the fire pit.

Even swordless, the pock-faced man's resolve did not waver. He yanked his hunting knife from the sheath at his belt and took a slice at Wulf's arm. The blow landed true, and blood bloomed on the sleeve of Wulf's cream-colored lèine.

Wulf responded swiftly.

With a rueful but determined expression on his handsome face, he swung his sword one last time and took the man down. The wretch finally met his end. He stiffened under the blow, then collapsed, the light of life fading from his pockmarked face. As the fellow dropped to the ground, Wulf spun to face Morag. The look in his eyes was fierce, but protective, and her pulse fluttered.

"Are you injured?"

"Nay," she said, easing away from the wall. Now that the danger was over, her arms and legs quivered like jelly.

He stepped over the two bodies and crossed the room with strong, purposeful strides. Fool that she was, she could not help but admire the play of muscles in his powerful legs as he gained on her. Few men were blessed with such a vigorous form.

Wulf halted in front of her, only inches away.

As serious as she'd ever seen him, he ran a callused thumb over the crest of her cheek.

Then he cupped her head in his large hands and slowly tugged her forward. His lips found hers in a passionate embrace that turned her world upside down. It was the kiss she had been longing for—hot and wild and dangerous—but it was also the kiss she knew should never happen. There was no chance for a life with Wulf. She was a woman branded as a harlot, and he was cousin to a laird and father to a bright young lad. His time with her would be brief; of that she was certain. Just long enough to break her heart, if she let him. But all her carefully reasoned thoughts took wing as his mouth slid roughly along hers. Instead, yearning mixed with wonder and breathlessness mingled with joy.

For a blissful moment, Morag simply surrendered to the sweet friction of their joined lips.

There was nothing she wanted more than this man and this kiss. The sureness of his hands, the manly scent of his skin, and the sheer wonder of his firm lips on hers almost made her forget the two dead bodies lying on her floor.

Almost.

With a soft moan of regret, she flattened both palms against the solid planes of his chest and pushed. Had it been a matter of strength, her efforts would have been for naught—Wulf's power far exceeded hers. But the moment he felt her resistance, he broke off the kiss and stepped back.

Morag pointed to the fallen men. "Even mercenaries deserve a burial."

Wulf shrugged. "Not when they prey on women."

"Aye, even then. Take them outside."

"For you, I will." He reached for the body of the pockmarked man, then said, "This is a fine cloak for a simple soldier."

"I noted the same myself. Perhaps he stole it from some other hapless soul."

He unpinned the cloak from the man's neck and handed her the cloth. "Or perhaps he's no simple soldier."

Morag took the cloak, eyeing it for bloodstains. There were several small ones, but overall the cloth was clean. It was a fine, tight weave, brushed to a smooth finish. Not made in Dunstoras, likely. There were only three skilled weavers in the glen, including herself, and none of them made such simple but elegant cloth. Morag folded the cloak and set it aside.

Wulf heaved the body over his shoulder and headed for the door.

"What's that?" she asked sharply, as a black-and-gold crest bobbed in front of her eyes.

He stopped and turned around. "What is what?"

She darted forward, pointing to the man's sark. "This sigil. I've seen it before. On the night you were nearly killed. One of the men who attacked you wore it."

Wulf frowned and lowered the man to the ground. "Are you certain?"

"Aye. I'd forgotten it till now, but I saw it clearly in the moonlight as they rode away."

He crouched and fingered the crest. "It's not familiar to me."

"Perhaps the laird would recognize it."

"Perhaps."

Morag saw wariness creep over Wulf's features. He returned to the castle every few days to visit with his son, Jamie, but save for that, he preferred to avoid his kin. "This is the first clue we've had to what happened that night," she urged softly.

He took his knife and cut the crest from the dead man's sark. "Aye, and I'll follow it to its bitter end, have no doubt."

"So you'll go to Dunstoras?"

"Aye," he said, pushing to his feet. "And you'll come with me."

"Nay," she protested. "You know I'm not welcome there save on market day."

He sent her a long, quiet look. "I cannot leave you here alone."

"I've lived alone in these woods for over four years."

"And today was very nearly your last. I'll not hear your nays. You'll come with me, and that is all there is to be said."

Wulf spoke softly, but Morag did not mistake that softness for leniency. The set of his shoulders and the look in his eyes told her he would not give, no matter how long or how vociferously she argued. But walking into the village and facing the accusing eyes of her detractors made her stomach heave.

She met his blue-eyed gaze and nodded.

It seemed they both had reason to make this visit to Dunstoras a short one.

Chapter 3

The inner close of Dunstoras keep bustled with the quiet energy of souls replete with a midday meal. Villeins went about their tasks with purpose, but their paces were languid and their smiles frequent. Only a few short weeks after their return to the keep, few signs remained of the hardships the MacCurrans had endured as an outlawed clan.

Wulf placed a hand on the small of Morag's back and guided her toward the stairs to the donjon. Even though he remembered nothing of his life within these walls, he felt a stir of pride when he gazed upon the tower. It was both a practical keep capable of withstanding a siege and a visual pleasure, with its pale gray walls pointing to the heavens.

"The laird will likely be inside," he said.

Morag halted abruptly, a frown upon her face.

"I cannot simply march up to the laird and speak my piece."

"Aye, you can."

She shook her head. "I've not the right to be heard."

"Your right is assured. You are with me."

"That may have worked at the gate," she said. "But the laird is no weak-kneed lad to be cowed by a fierce stare. He knows I've been cast out."

Wulf turned his fierce stare on Morag. "You have news of importance. He will see you."

"Then you go. Speak with him first. If he agrees to hear me, send a lad to fetch me. I'll wait for you in this very spot."

Wulf frowned. This very spot was a muddy patch in the middle of the close. Unprotected. Vulnerable. "Are you certain? I am reluctant to leave you alone."

Morag did not falter under his steely gaze. "I'm certain."

"Then I will bow to your wishes." He scanned the close. There were no obvious dangers to Morag—no glaring matrons, no rood-wielding holy men. "The laird will want to hear the tale from your own lips, but first I must find him."

"Perhaps he's lingering in the donjon after the midday meal?"

"Perhaps." Wulf drew Morag into the shade of the stable. He cupped her chin, forcing her gaze to meet his. "Remain here in the shadows, and like as not you'll go without notice until I return."

She sighed. "Just be quick."

He dropped his hand, gave her a short smile, and jogged across the close to the donjon. He had no intention of remaining in the keep any longer than was necessary. Inside, a dozen gillies were cleaning away the tables after the midday meal, but other than that the hall was empty. Not a sign of the laird to be seen.

Waylaying a young lass on her way to the kitchens with an armful of soiled linens, he asked, "Where might the laird be?"

She pointed to the stairs. "He and Niall went up a few moments ago. To the solar."

She turned away, clearly thinking he knew where the solar might be. Which he had, only a few months past. But no longer. Since his return, he'd limited his exploration of the keep to the great hall and a chamber on the third floor. "Where is the solar?" he asked.

She halted and turned back to him, a furious blush in her cheeks. "I'm so sorry, Master Wulf. I forgot for a wee moment. On the second floor, at the end of the hall."

He tossed her a smile of forgiveness, then took the stairs two at a time to the second floor. Niall answered his knock.

"Now, there's the lad we need," the lean soldier

said, opening the door wide. "We could use your help with the plans for the new wall."

"I've a better topic for discussion," Wulf said, entering the well-appointed room that served as a retreat for the laird and his family. High-backed chairs placed before the fire, colorful tapestries on the walls, and sweet-smelling rushes on the floor lent an air of warmth and welcome. To those who belonged.

He dragged his gaze away from the room's comforts and crossed the planking to a table where Aiden was bent over a sketch of the castle's defenses. He tossed the sigil under the laird's nose. "What clan does this represent?"

Aiden straightened, staring at the black-and-gold symbol with a frown. "The head of a bear on a broken shield? I know not." He picked up the scrap of cloth. "Why do you ask?"

"We were attacked by two men this morn, and one wore these arms."

Both Aiden and Niall stiffened at the word *attacked*.

Niall asked, "Since their identities are still a mystery, I assume neither man survived?"

Wulf shook his head. "They would not surrender."

Aiden offered the scrap to Wulf. "'Tis likely they were simply thieves."

"Nay," disputed Wulf. "Morag spied those same

arms on the night the queen's necklace was stolen." The same night his wife and wee son were slain. But he couldn't bring himself to utter those words.

The laird gave the sigil a second look. "She's certain?"

"Aye. She's in the close, if you wish to query her accounting of that night."

Aiden nodded. "That I will. But first we must determine to whom the sigil belongs."

"You're of a mind that it belongs to the man in black," guessed Niall.

"Wulf chased the murderer out into the night," said Aiden, his fists tightening on the cloth. "Is it not likely that he was felled by the wretch? This is the first real clue we've had since we found the black wolf cloak. Fetch Lady Isabail's herald and we will plumb the bottom of this well of deceit."

Morag was not one to fidget.

She knew her own mind and rarely had reason to debate the wisdom of her actions. But today she stood in an uncomfortable spot. The path past the stables was a popular route for villagers seeking baked goods from the keep kitchens. As yet another pair of women passed her by with furtive glances and heavy frowns, she shifted her weight from one foot to the other. Why had she promised Wulf she would remain? The terms of her shunning were clear—she was permitted to live in the glen, but she was not to visit the village or the castle save on faire days, and then only so long as was needed to trade her cloth for necessities.

Morag hollowed out a spot in the hay pile and leaned against the stable wall.

The other problem with her chosen spot appeared a moment later. Tomas the bread baker strode past her, heading for the kitchens. The burly young man failed to notice her in the shadows until he was nigh on past her. Then he drew up short, a shocked expression on his face.

"What are you doing inside the keep?" he demanded.

Morag held her ground, although every instinct told her to run. "I've accompanied Wulf MacCurran on a matter of some urgency."

He scanned the close. "A fine story, save there's no Wulf about to verify its truth."

"He's gone inside to fetch the laird."

"You grow bolder with every lie," he scoffed. "Get thee gone before I call for the warden."

Morag straightened and faced the young man she'd once hoped to wed. "If ever there was a bold liar, Tomas, it was you. It was your viper-tongued falsehoods that led to my shunning."

His hands fisted and his face boiled red. "They were not falsehoods. You lay with me and then you lay with Peadar. You fucked my brother not three months after you swore you loved me."

Amazingly, his words still cut deep, even after all this time. They were a bitter reminder of how young and foolish she'd been, and how misplaced her faith. Tomas had melted her heart with honeyed words, a crooked smile, and a whispered vow of marriage—only to spurn her the very next day, gloating over how easy she'd been to gull. Taking solace in Peadar's arms had been another mistake, but it had been Tomas who had shattered her girlish illusions. "'Twas you who spurned me, Tomas. After I lay with you and spoke those words, you told me you'd never wed me. Indeed, you said you'd have nothing further to do with me."

"Because you're a whore."

"Nay, I was simply a foolish girl charmed by a man who only wanted to slip his cock between the legs of every girl in the village."

His nostrils flared. "You took payment."

"I took nothing," Morag refuted strongly. "You gave me that brooch as a gift—*before* I slept with you."

"You are a lying quim," he snarled. "And the warden will support my claim."

"What's going on here?"

Morag spun around. A lovely blond woman stood immediately behind her, having just exited the stables. It was a woman she recognized, having last seen her a month ago, looking rather bedraggled. Nothing like she looked now. Today her hair was elegantly coiffed and her dark burgundy gown was unstained and wrinkle free. "Lady Macintosh," she acknowledged, offering a light curtsy.

The lady's cool blue gaze bored through her for a moment; then she nodded. "Morag, is it?"

"Aye."

Lady Macintosh turned her attention to Tomas. "And you are the baker's journeyman."

"Aye, your ladyship," he said, bowing. "Tomas."

"What seems to be the difficulty? Your raised voices can be heard clear across the close."

Tomas responded before Morag had a chance to speak. "This . . . person . . . is not to be within the keep walls save on faire days, by order of the laird."

Lady Macintosh's eyebrows rose delicately on her face. "Truly? The current laird made this ruling?"

"Nay," Tomas admitted. "The old laird."

The lady smiled nicely. "Then I shall take this situation in hand personally, and resolve it. Thank you, Tomas. You may return to the kitchens."

He hesitated, clearly interested in adding to his arguments, but the lady's dismissal left him no options. He bowed and departed.

"I owe you a great debt," the lady said quietly. "Were it not for the aid you lent me that night, all of this"—she waved her hand at the keep around them—"might belong to the Comyns, and young Jamie would likely have lost his life."

Morag stood a little taller. There was truth in the other woman's words. "You needed water and food to continue your journey. Any good soul would have done what I did."

Lady Macintosh's eyebrows soared. "In the dark of the night? To complete strangers? I think not. And you did more than provide me with food. You gave me Wulf."

Morag snorted. "Have you met the man? None can make him do aught that he does not desire to do."

"True," the other woman agreed. "But that night his desire was to please you, and you were in favor of aiding us."

"His desire was simply to recover his memories," Morag said, shaking her head. "As it is now."

"Nothing was simple about that night," Lady Macintosh said with a chuckle. "Will you accept my thanks for your help?"

"Of course, your ladyship."

"Please," the lady said, a faint frown forming on her brow. "Call me Isabail. You've seen me at my worst and shown me a kindness I can never repay. I should welcome your friendship."

Morag glanced around, hoping no one had heard. "Nay, my lady, I cannot. I am shunned for promiscuity. It is beyond inappropriate for me to address you at all, let alone so familiarly."

"So Tomas's tale is true?"

Morag grimaced. "Less true than he would like to believe. But the outcome is the same. I am indeed shunned."

"What brings you here, then?"

"I came with Wulf."

Isabail took Morag's arm. "Then I suppose I must drag you before the laird for retribution, or at least appear to. Come along. Let's find Wulf and Aiden."

Morag allowed herself to be tugged across the close to the keep stairs. Appearing reluctant was easy—she truly had no desire to meet the laird. Laird Duncan had been a harsh man, given to raging tirades. His son was likely not much different.

As they entered the dimly lit tower, Isabail paused to glance around the great hall. "He must be in the solar." She took a step toward the stairs, then abruptly changed direction and headed for the large central hearth, where a lad sat diligently cleaning and polishing a set of bone-handled dirks.

"Jamie," she called to the boy.

He looked up, and Morag's heart took a tumble. She knew that face almost as well as she knew her own—it was a thinner, younger version of Wulf's. A wave of guilt hit her hard. There could be no doubt—this was Wulf's son.

A bright blue gaze met hers. "Aye?"

Isabail pulled Morag forward. "I thought you should meet the woman who saved your da's life."

He shot to his feet, looking solemn.

Morag swallowed. It was her fault this boy had been without his father for so long. Allowing Wulf to return to her bothy after he rediscovered his kin had been a mistake. A selfish mistake. "I'm sorry for your losses," she murmured, her throat dry.

He nodded. "I've you to thank that my da did not die along with my mum and wee brother. I'm grateful to you."

Morag flushed. How wrong it was to hear thanks spilling from the boy's lips. Aye, she had saved his father's life—and at some risk—but that was months ago. Wulf was healthy now, and he should be living in the keep with his son. "He's still healing," Morag said. "But he's a strong man, and he'll return to his duties anon."

"Aye," agreed Jamie, though his gaze dropped as he spoke, hinting at doubt.

He didn't quite believe his da would come back to the keep, and who could blame him? Wulf had lived at the castle for only a fortnight after he was reunited with his kin. The failure of his memories to return, even under constant daily reminders of living among his family, in the home where he'd been raised, was a sore point.

"Well," said Isabail as the silence grew uncomfortable, "let us leave Jamie to his work and seek out the laird."

The women skirted the gillies sifting through

the rushes for bones left by the hounds and climbed the stairs to the second level.

"He must miss his da," Morag said.

"I expect so," Isabail acknowledged. "But he doesn't let on. He's a quiet lad."

"He's had a rough time of it."

Isabail nodded. "His mum and brother poisoned, his da missing for months, and a madman taking him prisoner at knifepoint. And yet he seems to be doing well. Niall has taken him on as a page and swears the lad will soon make the transition to squire. He learns quickly and is diligent."

They paused before the last door in the hall. Isabail knocked and then entered without waiting for a response. The door swung wide and Lady Macintosh ushered her into the solar.

Inside, four men stood in front of the fire.

They all looked up as the ladies entered, halting what must have been a lively discussion—the laird had his arms folded decisively across his chest, his brother was red faced, and Wulf wore a thunderous look that did not bode well for his opponents.

"Please continue," Lady Macintosh invited. "It would appear you've yet to reach a consensus."

Niall threw up his hands. "Because your husband refuses to see reason."

"I am the one who stands accused of a crime I did not commit," the laird said simply. "If anyone should go to Edinburgh, it should be me."

"You are still a wanted man," Niall argued. "The king has allowed Isabail to give your clan a home, but he has yet to pardon you. You cannot walk through the gates of Edinburgh without a care. And as fortunate as I've been in freeing men from dungeons lately, I doubt even I can fetch you home from Castle Rock."

Lady Macintosh took a chair before the fire and waved Morag into another.

Morag held back, uncomfortable. The solar was as fine a room as she had ever seen, the walls draped in tapestries, the oak chairs carved in patterns of ivy leaves and thistle. A flagon of wine stood on the table next to a platter of sweet delicacies that included candied fruit and tablet. The laird and Niall wore fine woolen tunics atop their lèines, looking every bit as elegant as Lady Macintosh. Even the herald, Sim, held his brat at his throat with a large silver brooch.

She did not belong here.

She tried to catch Wulf's gaze with a small wave, but failed.

His attention was locked on the laird.

"And why, dare I ask," said Isabail, "are we contemplating a return to Edinburgh? I've just unpacked my belongings."

"I finally have a means to identify the man in black," the laird said. He offered his lady the sigil Wulf had cut from their attacker's clothing. "Sim is not familiar with the sigil, but he believes a royal herald will know the mark."

"The king's marischal grants arms," Sim said. "If the badge is of his making, he'll know its owner."

"Which is why I must speak with him," the laird said. "I must know with whom this man is aligned."

"There's a price on your head," Niall said sharply. "You cannot approach the marischal."

"How do we know this badge has anything to do with the man in black?" Isabail asked, peering at the sigil.

Wulf answered, "Morag saw these same arms the night the queen's necklace was stolen."

All eyes swung to Morag.

Isabail frowned. "Was it not dark?"

Morag nodded. "Very. The clouds were thick that night and I had little chance to see details. But as they were riding away, the clouds parted and the moon shone on one man's shoulder as the wind pulled at his brat."

"There you have it," the laird said. "If not the man in black himself, then a liegeman."

"Even so," said Niall, "your likeness hangs on every pillory post in the kingdom. The king's men will arrest you on sight, and that would risk more than your life. The king is unaware that you've wed Lady Macintosh; if he discovers your association—"

"All is lost," Aiden finished flatly. He spun away

from the table and stalked to the narrow window. "Yet the man in black *must* be found."

"Then I'll go to Edinburgh," Niall offered.

"Nay," said Wulf quietly. "I'll go."

Niall shook his head. "You've not yet recovered from your injuries."

"After breaking him out of Lochurkie, you're as notorious as the laird himself," Wulf pointed out. "My lame leg will not endanger our cause. I'm not going into battle, just calling upon a royal herald."

"My apologies, cousin," said Niall, grimacing. "'Twas not my intent to cast a slur. You held your own at Tayteath. I am sworn, to protect the clan. It is my duty as a Black Warrior to go."

"If the goal is to make quiet inquiries and return with facts that will prove our innocence to the king, I am the wiser choice."

"You are not completely unknown," pointed out Niall. "The men who attacked Morag this morn were sent by someone."

"Aye," said the laird. "Someone knows you are alive and likely fears the tales that you could tell."

Morag stared at Wulf. He returned her stare, as calm and deliberate as ever. It was true. The men had come for *him*—and he knew it. That was why he would not allow her to remain at the bothy.

Wulf shrugged. "There's no reward for my capture. I'm still the better man."

Aiden shook his head. "I'm not convinced."

Wulf stood taller. "I do not beg your permission, laird. I claim the right of vengeance. If that sigil leads to the man who murdered my wife and wee lad, it will be *I* who discover the filthy cur's name. I am owed that right."

Silence fell in the room. The tone of Wulf's voice was colder than Morag had ever heard it. He never spoke of his family, and she'd feared he had no attachment to them, but that clearly wasn't true. There was a depth of bitterness in his words that could be caused only by pain.

After a lengthy moment the laird heaved a sigh. "You are indeed owed the right. Go to Edinburgh with my blessing. Take the wolf cloak we discovered at Tayteath, as well. Leave no stone unturned in your efforts."

Morag frowned. "Of what import is a wolf cloak?"

Isabail glanced at her. "'Twas the garment worn by the murderer on the night the necklace was stolen. We found it in the possession of his accomplice, Daniel de Lourdes."

Morag's memories of that night had narrowed to a few vivid details, and she could not recall if she'd seen such a cloak. But it was definitely possible.

Aiden and Wulf shook hands. "Bring me the bastard's name," Aiden said.

Without a glance in Morag's direction, Wulf gave a short nod, spun on his heels, and left the room.

She swallowed tightly, suddenly hot with discomfort. Her right to be in the laird's presence had just left. "Was there aught else you required of me, laird?"

Aiden looked at her. Truly looked at her. Morag shivered, certain that his gaze saw more than her face and the clothing she wore. His cool blue eyes seemed to bore right into her soul, laying bare her every sin.

She held her breath.

"Nay," he said finally. "You may go."

Morag made her best attempt at a curtsy and strode from the room, her head held high.

"Magnus!"

He halted midstride and turned to face Morag. Her face was unusually pale, her freckles vivid against her fair skin. "You should call me Wulf," he said.

The hand that had been about to touch his sleeve dropped away. A coolness stole over her expression, and she nodded.

Regretting the pain caused by his words, Wulf added, "I can deny the past no longer. Those two men came for *me*. They came for Wulf MacCurran. And until I put name to the wretch who laid me low, you will forever be in danger."

She nodded. "I understand your need to go to Edinburgh. I wanted to wish you Godspeed on your journey."

"There's no need. You will be traveling with me."

"Nay," she protested. "I've goats to tend and cloth to weave. I cannot leave the bothy."

"You can, and you will. It's not safe for you to remain."

She frowned heavily. "Did you not hear me?"

"The danger is real," he said. "The only other choice would be for you to live here in the keep while I am gone."

A hint of color returned to her cheeks. "That's not possible."

He nodded. "Which is why you will accompany me to Edinburgh. You've several bolts of cloth woven, so we will travel under the guise of tradesmen bringing the cloth to market."

"And what of my goats?"

"I'll have someone fetch them." He grazed a thumb over the flush on her cheeks. There was danger in bringing Morag with him, but it should be a quick journey, and he felt more at ease knowing he would be there to protect her. "You'll like Edinburgh. It's a lively town."

Her eyebrows lifted. "You remember Edinburgh?"

He stiffened. "Aye," he said slowly, realizing it was true. "Without difficulty."

"A good sign, surely?"

It should be. Save he still could not remember

when he'd last been to the burgh or what had led him to visit. "Perhaps."

As they exited the stairwell, Morag's gaze slid across the great hall. "Will we bring Jamie along as well?"

Wulf watched his son diligently attack a spot of rust on a dirk. The lad's sandy hair shook with the ferocity of his endeavors, and Wulf was struck with a pang of pride. Jamie was a fine son, coming into his own under Niall's skillful tutelage. He deserved to continue his lessons with a doting uncle capable of teaching him the fine art of swordsmanship. Not to be shackled to a man with a lame leg and no memory of him.

"Nay," he said abruptly. "We'll travel faster with two."

Morag was silent for a moment, and he felt the censure of her thoughts. But she wisely did not question his decision. "When do we leave?"

"At first light."

Another frown settled on her brow. "And where will we pass the night?"

He grabbed her slender hand in his and tugged her toward the door. "The hay in the stable will make a soft bed."

"Surely there is a chamber assigned to you?"

Aye, there was. The same chamber he'd once shared with his wife and sons. But sleep eluded him in that room, and he chose not to spend the night there. "Come," he coaxed. "We'll rest better outside the watchful eye of the laird."

Clearly dubious, Morag allowed herself to be drawn forward. "Is rest truly what you had in mind?"

He grinned. "What else?"

In truth, although he had enjoyed teasing her about such things, he had never stolen more than a kiss. Not because he wasn't interested in more—God knew he thought about it often enough—but because she'd known only disappointment from the men who'd previously courted her, and he did not desire to be another disappointment. He wanted to offer her a whole man, not a half.

"Naught else," she tossed back sharply. "We'll be lucky to pass a good night in a bed not our own."

A flush rose in her cheeks as she realized she'd implied an intimacy between them. He caught her gaze and held it with his own, allowing the grin to slip away. "We'll make the best of it, lass."

Chapter 4

Ten bolts of cloth. Morag frowned as she packed them in the back of the cart.

It was a telling tale that she had so little to show for her winter efforts. Last year she attended Saint Finan's Fair in mid-March with fourteen—a far better offering. The hours lost to healing Wulf before yule were worthy ones. It was the hours lost since that gave her pause. Cloth was her only means of trade, and she would feel the pinch of her idle hands before the first harvest.

She glanced over her shoulder at Wulf. A heavy mist had settled in the glen overnight, and even though the sun had risen, fog still blanketed the keep. She could hear others working in the close, but she could not see them.

"Perhaps I am better to sell the cloth in the village," she said to Wulf. "They know the quality of my work here. If the buyers in Edinburgh are not as discerning, I may not earn the coin I'll need to see me through the summer."

He covered her hand with his big one and squeezed. Warm, reassuring . . . and gently coaxing. "We need to play the part of tradesmen. If we've nothing to trade, our journey will raise suspicions."

She sighed and pulled away, covering her bolts with a tarp.

"If you take a loss by waiting to trade in Edinburgh, I'll make it up to you."

"Do not make assurances you can ill afford to keep," she chided him, scrambling into the seat of the cart. "You have other commitments deserving of your coin."

Wulf stared at her, his arms folded over his chest. "I make no vows that I cannot prove true."

"That's your pride talking," she said. "Let's be off. We've five days of travel ahead of us. We'll see naught of Edinburgh with you standing there."

"You've mastered the nagging tone of a goodwife, I see," he said, leaping up beside her in an easy bound. Only a slight stiffness betrayed the weakness in his left leg.

"Not yet," she retorted sweetly. "But be assured I will apply myself to the task with great determination."

He took the reins in hand and encouraged the pony to set off. The cart rolled forward with a series of creaks and groans, the hard plank seat biting into Morag's rump.

"What are these leather straps on the seat?" she asked.

He leveled a look at her. "My sword. I've fastened the scabbard underneath."

"Is it really necessary to bring a weapon along? Do you anticipate danger?"

"'Tis possible," he admitted. "The crags and corries of the Red Mountains likely hide an outlaw or two. There may be fools who think robbing a cart headed to market will glean them an effortless bounty."

A vision of parting with her cloth at knifepoint leapt into Morag's thoughts, and a bloom of anger burned in her breast. "No one should benefit from my labors but I."

"We're in agreement then," he said. "The sword stays."

She'd no doubt resent the leather strap chafing her bottom within the hour, but she nodded. "The sword stays."

As they approached the keep gate, a solitary figure waiting patiently in the early-morning mist became visible—young Jamie. A fine layer of moisture clung to every hair and fiber of his clothing. The lad had a small bundle in his hands and a resolute expression on his face.

Wulf pulled up.

"I cannot take you with me," he said to the lad. "Not this time."

"I know," Jamie said. He took a step toward the cart and offered Wulf the bundle. "My training is paramount. I'm to begin swordsmanship on the morrow."

Wulf took the package. "What's this, then?"

"Uncle Niall says you're going to Edinburgh to hunt for the man who poisoned Mum and Hugh."

Wulf frowned. "Uncle Niall says more than he should."

"Since you've no memory of our kin, I thought you could take those with you," he said, pointing to the bundle. "To keep your will strong."

"My will to avenge them does not suffer from my inability to remember them," Wulf said strongly. "Rest assured, the man in black will pay."

Jamie nodded, his expression easing. "Take them anyway."

Wulf unwrapped the bundle to reveal a delicate silver locket and a small wooden horse.

"You gave that locket to Mum the day Hugh was born, and you carved that horse for Hugh last summer."

Wulf stared at the two objects for a long moment, then lifted his gaze to his son. "I'll take proper care of these and return them to you with the name of our enemy. I promise you that."

Jamie stepped back. "Godspeed, Da."

As they continued on, Morag took the locket and toy horse, wrapped them carefully, and tucked them into the front of Wulf's lèine, next to his heart. For the first time she understood the value of his lost memories, and how vital it was that he retrieve them. Jamie's mother and brother deserved to be remembered, especially by a man who had clearly loved them.

They passed beneath the gate and headed south down the glen. Wulf's attention was on the path and the route ahead. But Morag kept glancing back, watching the figure of young Jamie MacCurran disappear into the mist.

The first three days were uneventful—long days in the cart broken up by occasional walking over rougher patches of terrain and even longer nights under the stars. Wulf's leg did not fare well, growing ever stiffer with the long bouts of inactivity.

By the third evening, when they rolled into the bustling burgh of Perth, the muscles in his thigh were knotted so tight, he could barely breathe. He reined the cart to a halt before a small hut displaying an ale wand, and slid to the ground, gritting his teeth. Sharp pains drove up his leg to the scar that ran from his hip to his inner thigh.

"Why are we stopping here?" asked Morag. She eyed the steady stream of men who were ending their workday by paying for a ladle of ale.

Wulf gripped the side of the cart with a white-knuckled hand as he waited for the pains to subside. "The alewife will know who is willing to take in travelers."

Her brows rose. "No sleeping on the ground tonight?"

"Not if we can find lodging." Wulf pushed away from the cart and walked carefully to the alewife's open door. The toothless old woman stood in the open doorway with a barrel of ale at her side and a long-handled scoop in one hand.

"Ha'penny a ladle," she mumbled, holding out her hand.

He dropped the split coin into her palm and accepted the full ladle. The brew was dark and bitter, but it slid down his throat with a smooth kick. "A second for my wife, if you will?"

She gave him the ladle and he brought it to Morag, who drank deeply.

"My weary wife and I seek lodging for the night," he said as he returned the ladle. Her gaze sharpened, and she gave him a thorough review before turning her attention to Morag. "Where ye be from?"

"Braemar," he said.

She frowned and sold another ladle of ale to the lad behind him before she answered. "Take the next wynd to yer left, three doors down. The widow Uma might be willing to take ye in."

"My thanks," he said. Determined not to limp,

he turned slowly and walked back to the cart. Taking hold of the pony's harness, he tugged.

Morag said nothing until they turned down the wynd. Once they were out of sight of the alehouse, she said quietly, "Rub the leg as you walk. 'Twill warm the muscle."

Annoyed that she'd seen him favoring the leg, he ignored her comment. "We'll eat, sleep, and get an early start in the morn."

"Nay," she said.

He stopped and turned. "What did you say?"

"This is the first time I've been in a burgh. I want to walk about, meet people."

"And who will watch your cloth while you go about? These people are strangers—they'll take what's yours without a care."

She scowled at him. "Let us meet the widow Uma. If she seems an honest woman, we can leave the cloth with her. I did not agree to travel all this way so I could see the inside of a bothy."

Although the dull ache in his leg continued to plague him, Wulf considered her words. Walking would be good for his leg, and would likely help him sleep. "Fine."

He knocked on the wooden door of the third hut, and took a step back when a small elderly woman answered the door. No sense intimidating her.

The widow Uma was indeed willing to take them in for the night. She offered a bed and a bowl of stew for supper. Their bed was a plump straw mattress as sweet-smelling as any in Dunstoras Castle, and Wulf gave his approval of the arrangements with a soft grunt. The widow did seem to be a trustworthy sort.

When the cart was unpacked and their bellies were full, Wulf and Morag set out for the village square. Market day at Dunstoras was a busy event, but nothing compared to a trade day at one of the richest trading burghs in the kingdom. Perth was a thriving inland port that drew ships from the continent, as well as goods from the numerous craft guilds.

Even with the sun on the wane, the stalls in the square were a hive of hawking merchants, craftsmen, and fishmongers. Many of the stalls were down to their last few items for trade, but that didn't dampen Morag's enthusiasm. She insisted on peering into every stall, eyeing the goods with lively reactions ranging from awe to surprise.

"Spanish silk," she said breathlessly, running her fingers lightly over the material.

He grumbled. "Had I the coin to drop for luxuries, I'd spend it on a jug of French wine."

He bought two pastries from a baker and handed her one. They were cold and not near as tasty as they'd have been earlier in the day, but a delightfully buttery treat nonetheless. He retrieved a crumb from the corner of Morag's mouth and offered it to her on his finger.

She grinned and licked it off.

Wulf swallowed tightly, a hot jolt of desire bursting in his loins. But Morag was oblivious to the moment—she had spied another interesting stall and scurried away. He drew in a slow, deep breath, shook off the edgy feeling in his gut, and followed her.

A cloth merchant's stall still had a good number of bolts for sale, and Morag was peering at each of the offerings with a critical eye.

As he came up behind her, she whispered, "Not to be prideful, but none of these is as good as my own."

He agreed. The colors were duller, the weaves looser.

"How much for this one?" Morag asked, holding up the corner of a red-black-and-yellow cloth.

"Three shillings a yard."

"What?"

"Ye heard me," the merchant growled. "Buy or move on."

Morag took a decisive step back. "I definitely will not buy at that price. That's—"

Wulf grabbed her arm and dragged her away before she could enrage the merchant. The plan was to make a quiet trip, attracting little notice. Causing a furor in the market would not be a good start.

"Can you believe that man?" huffed Morag. "Three shillings. He's a thief. The cloth wasn't even properly waulked."

They stopped in front of a leather goods stall displaying purses and gloves. The glover looked up hopefully as Morag picked up a pair of heavy men's gloves. "Now, this is fine work. And just your size, I'd guess."

Wulf pried her away from the gloves, leaving a disappointed vendor. "Only men of arms have need of such gloves," he said.

She took his right hand and turned it palm up, running a finger over the thick calluses on his thumb. "You could use such gloves when you practice with your sword."

The effect of her touch was instantaneous. Sweet, burning desire surged through his groin, and for a brief moment he imagined all the places such a touch might lead. Wild, wonderful places. Then he shook her hand free of his. "A peasant doesn't own a sword," he reminded her. "And therefore has no need for gloves."

She heaved a sigh and continued to the next stall. The sun was nearing the horizon and the daylight was growing dim. Several of the merchants were packing up what remained of their goods.

This time the stall she paused before was rented by a hammerman. Metal goods ranging from fire pokers to cups were strewn across the display. The hammerman was wrapping his wares in burlap and placing them in a large woven basket.

Morag was drawn to a brass spoon with a smooth bowl at one end and a leather loop threaded through a hole at the other. She picked it up and held it to the last golden gleams of daylight. The handle was etched with a knot pattern that closely resembled the one on his sword.

"How much for this?" she asked.

The hammerman glanced up. "Three pence."

"Oh." Morag held on to the spoon for a moment longer, then laid it back on the display table. "'Tis lovely. A bit too fine for the likes of me, though. Good day to you."

Then she turned and offered her hand to Wulf. "Shall we head back?"

"Aye." He threaded her arm through his and together they strode back to the widow's house.

Unwilling to burn any more of their hostess's candles than necessary, and knowing they intended to make an early start the next morning, Wulf and Morag settled in quickly for the night.

In the dim light of the banked fire, Wulf watched Morag remove her overdress, leaving only a white linen sark covering her generously curved body. She combed out her long black hair, as she did every night, and stretched out on the mattress, her back to him. It was the same routine they'd followed for the past four months. And it had the same effect on him—slowing his heart to a heavy thud in his chest, shortening his breaths to unsatisfying gulps, and creating a throbbing ache in his groin that demanded to be eased.

But, as always, he held his needs in check.

Theirs was an odd relationship. Like a husband and wife, they shared a bed, but without any of the intimacy such an event normally entailed. In the beginning it had been because of his injuries, but of late it was his honor that held him back.

It certainly wasn't a lack of desire.

He'd spent many a night lying next to her, listening to her soft breathing, inhaling the sweetly feminine scent of her body, and envisioning every kiss he would bestow should he ever have the good fortune to truly bed her. Not every night, thank the stars. In the beginning, his only concern had been to heal. But as his injuries lessened, he'd begun to notice the gentle curves and delicate beauty of his benefactress. Normally, an unspoken admonition was all it took to tame his wild thoughts, to ruthlessly shut out those hot, sweet dreams. But not tonight.

Wulf stretched out beside Morag and stared up at the thatched roof. The mattress was not wide, but he made a point of ensuring no point of his body touched hers. His imagination refused to let go of the thoughts that had seduced him since Morag had licked the pastry crumb from his finger. The wet heat of her lips on his skin continued to torment him. Every taut muscle in his body urged him to snatch her to him and make real those vivid dreams he'd had since becoming aware of her as a woman.

Of which there were hundreds.

But taking her was impossible. With his past life lost and his leg a lame appendage, Morag deserved better. She deserved a man who could leap to her defense, not hobble. She deserved a man who knew his purpose in life and could be a full and willing partner.

He was not that man.

Not yet.

But the identity of the man in black was the answer to his prayers. If he confronted the wretch who had slain his wife and son, who had brought the king's wrath down upon his clan, and who had ambushed him in the wood and left him for dead, his memories would return. There could be no doubt.

He had failed his kin, and the loss of his memories was God's punishment for that failure. Vengeance fulfilled was the only way to reclaim his life.

And give him the right to court Morag.

He rolled over on his side, away from the warm woman whose beauty called to him with every waking moment. Memories he might not possess, but steely determination he had in spades.

Morag was shaken awake by someone before dawn. Darkness yet prevailed, but she made out the thin figure of Uma crouched beside her. Her face was impossible to see, but the angry tone of the old woman's voice was unmistakable.

"If ye're thinking to rob me," she said, "I'll have none of it. You'll pay me what you owe, or I'll be calling for the bailiff."

Morag sat up, shaking the grogginess of sleep from her head. "Rob you? What do you mean?"

The old woman rose to her full height, gray hair hanging in a long braid over her brat-covered shoulder. "Yer man is gone, flown in the night. The cart as well."

Morag's heart flipped. "That's not possible."

"See for yourself," she said, holding out her hand. "But first ye must pay me for the lodging and the food."

Scrambling to her feet, Morag cast about for her belongings—the burlap bag containing her meager supply of clothing and the bolts of cloth she'd left at the foot of the bed. Neither remained. Only a single ocher-colored gown lay on the mattress, neatly folded beneath her boots.

All else was gone. Including Wulf himself.

But there must be some explanation.

"You are mistaken," Morag told the widow. "He would not leave me here. He's merely attending to a task."

Uma snorted. "Why take the cart then?"

Why indeed? 'Twould be faster to walk than to

harness the pony for a short jaunt across the village. "He surely had his reasons," Morag said with a confidence she did not truly feel. After all, why would he insist on her accompanying him if his intent was to abandon her? "Let us give him some time to return before assuming the worst."

"I'll give you till the bells of St. John's ring at terce," Uma said darkly. "If he's not returned by then, you'll be facing the bailiff."

Morag forced a smile. "That's very fair."

She slipped the gown over her linen sark and quickly braided her long black hair, tying the end with a piece of wool twine. The widow warily watched her every move, no doubt expecting her to make a run for the door. When her boots were laced and the wrinkles were brushed from her gown, Morag faced her hostess.

"I'd like to look outside. Will you accompany me?"

Uma tightened her brat around her shoulders and nodded.

The old woman opened the door, and together they advanced into the lane. Dawn was breaking, and to the east the sky was a dark purple. The only people moving in the streets were those fetching water from the well. As Uma said, there was no sign of Wulf or the cart.

Morag took a deep breath of cool air and slowly let it out. If Wulf did not return she'd require some sort of payment to satisfy the widow. But what? She had no coin or possessions. Glancing at her feet, she grimaced. The only thing she owned worth trading were her boots—which were almost new. Going barefoot in winter was not an option, however.

Beneath her boots the cart tracks were frozen in the mud. Why worry? Wulf would return.

Morag took the widow's arm and led her back to the bothy. "Let me put the fire on and brew you some tea while we wait."

The old woman accepted her help, but warned her, "There'll be no tea for you until you pay me."

"I can wait," Morag responded agreeably.

She had just poured boiling water into a wooden cup lined with tea leaves when the sound of a creaking cart came to a halt outside the door. Moments later Wulf stepped into the bothy, filling the space with his large body. In his hand he held two steamy pasties.

He offered one to Uma and gave the second to Morag with a smile. "Are you ready to depart?"

Morag stared at him until the smile faded from his face. "Is all well?" he asked.

Did he truly believe a pasty made up for her rude awakening? Wretch. How dared he be so blithe?

"The good widow is seeking her due," Morag said. "She was about to take me before the bailiff."

"Och, now," the widow said, her mouth half-filled with pasty. "I promised to wait until terce, and I live by my word."

Wulf pulled the purse from the front of his lèine and presented the old woman with her coin. "Thank you for opening your home to us, Widow Uma. May I hope we'd be welcome on our return journey?"

"Aye," she responded happily. "As long as I have no other lodger."

Wulf pointed to the door. "Then shall we make way, wife? The hours pass swiftly and we've a long day ahead."

Morag snatched her multihued brat from her bed and tossed it over her shoulders. Then she bade the widow good day and marched out to the cart. Without a word to Wulf, and without taking his proffered hand, she climbed onto her seat and stared stoically ahead.

He climbed up alongside her.

"You're fasht with me," he said. "But I merely rose early, packed the cart, and fetched you something to break the fast."

"You should have woken me."

"Aye," he said softly. "I can see that I should have. Will you accept my apologies, lass?"

Morag wanted to say yes, but her chest was still painfully tight. She'd gotten a taste of what her life would be like when Wulf was truly gone, and it stung. But she couldn't tell him that. Over the past four months she'd come to rely on him. Not just to chop the firewood or snare the rabbits, but to wake her with a quiet smile and a pair of fire-warmed boots. To share a brief meal before settling in to the morning chores. When she'd peered down the wynd in both directions and seen no sign of him, a chill had settled around her heart. The chill of truth. Wulf was not hers. He belonged to Dunstoras and to young Jamie, and one day very soon he would realize it.

"I will," she said. "But not now."

He leaned over and tied something to her belt. "When you're ready, then."

Morag glanced down. Hanging from her belt was the lovely brass spoon she'd admired in the market the day before. The smooth bowl gleamed gold in the morning sunlight, the knot pattern just as fine and delicate as she remembered. Hot tears sprang into her eyes. As gifts went, it was inspired. A perfect combination of practicality and beauty. And it brought a sweet ache to her chest that he'd taken the trouble to hasten back to the market at first light to surprise her with it. Even though he'd frightened her half to death.

"Thank you. I shall treasure it." She lifted her watery gaze to his and smiled. "I trust you drove a hard bargain?"

"I paid only the price I was willing."

"As it should be."

And that was the last word she uttered until they arrived at North Queensferry many hours later.

Chapter 5

Wulf merged the cart into the line of pilgrims returning from Dunfermline Abbey. Three dozen or so. Some rode fine horses, one rode in a small curtained carriage, but most were on foot. Despite the lateness of the hour, the cold winter wind, and the anticipation of a lengthy wait for the ferry, an air of contentment hung over the crowd.

"We'll pass the night in the north village," he said to Morag. She hadn't spoken to him since early that morn, but the silence that lay between them was quietly content. With Morag seated beside him, her shoulders loose and her lips curved in a soft half smile, he managed to forget—for a time—all the troubles that haunted him.

"Will they have room for us all in the village?" Morag asked, her voice a little husky from lack of use.

"Not beds," he said. "But for a ha'penny we can sleep beneath a roof that will hold off the rain."

She glanced up at the heavy gray clouds. "'Tis a bitter night for wet weather."

"Aye," he said, as the cart inched forward. "But there will be hawkers with food as well. Queensferry is very hospitable to travelers."

"How long will it take to cross the firth?"

"A half day. The boat is slow and stops at the isle of Innis Garbhach, about midway, to avoid rough seas."

"And when we reach the shore, how long before we arrive in Edinburgh?"

"We'll be in the city before they close the gates," he said.

"You must have visited often to know the route so well."

He glanced at her. "I accompanied the old laird a number of times on his visits to the king."

"You remember that?"

"I do," he said, surprised. "Though when I attempt to call the laird's face to mind, I cannot." Frustration replaced the mild pleasure of his vague memories. Would the mists of his mind never clear?

Morag brushed a cool hand over his cheek, and he lifted his gaze to her face.

"Your memories will return," she said.

"I am not so certain as you."

"You must be patient."

That coaxed a half smile to his face. "Patience is not one of my virtues, I fear."

"Nor mine," she said. "That confessed, I wish to discuss a matter with which I've been remarkably patient."

Her tone implied a level of criticism, and Wulf's brow rose. "Oh?"

"Your wounds have been healed since yule, and yet you've made no attempt to bed me."

Wulf coughed. Although her voice was low it carried well on the night air, and it was almost a certainty that some of the pilgrims around them heard her words. "Such a topic is best saved for a moment alone."

"Your kisses suggest a strong desire," she continued in her usual forthright way. "What stops you from acting on it?"

"Morag," he continued.

"Is it my ill repute?"

He shot her a hard look. "I do not let others choose my companions."

"Is it a religious choice, then? Do you think my body unclean?"

"Don't be foolish," he snapped. "You are a beautiful woman. Any man would be honored to share your bed."

"Then why do you spurn me?"

They finally arrived at the headland that overlooked the Firth of Forth, and Wulf steered the cart to the left, heading toward the simple wooden frames that offered cover for waiting pilgrims. When the cart was halted, he laid the reins on the seat beside him and faced Morag squarely.

"I do not spurn you," he said firmly. "An honorable man does not tread lightly with his intent."

"What role does honor play in this?" she asked dryly. "I am not the woman you will wed."

"Why not?"

"You cannot present a woman branded as a harlot as the new mother to your son," she said quietly. "He would be shamed."

He stared at her. "A man cannot be shamed by the actions of others. Only his own."

She sighed and shook her head. "I know the way of the world. What we have will soon come to an end. Why can we not simply enjoy our nights together?"

Wulf cupped her chin in his hand. Her skin was cool and delicate. "Have faith, lass. I will not treat you ill."

She smiled and covered his hand with hers. "My faith in you has never been in question."

Her words rang with sincerity, but the sadness in her eyes robbed the moment of any pleasure. All faith aside, it was clear she did not believe they had a future together. And he could not offer a credible argument that would prove her wrong. Until he regained his memories and his life, such a future was impossible. All he offered was the danger of faceless assailants.

He leaned in and kissed her gently on the lips. Her skin was petal soft, her feminine scent a lure so strong it brought a sweet ache to his chest. But he did not succumb. He ended the kiss quickly and pulled back. "When the moment is right, we will be together. Not before."

Then he dismounted the cart and offered a hand to Morag. She eyed his hand for a long moment, clearly debating whether to accept his aid. In the end, she slid her fingers into his palm and took advantage of his strength to descend. Practicality over stubbornness.

"Don't mistake this for the end of our discussion," she said once she had both feet planted firmly on the ground. Her brat had fallen off one shoulder, taunting him with a glimpse of the pale skin that dipped into the neckline of her gown. "I am a woman of great purpose when need be."

A smile rose to his lips. "True words indeed."

Annoyed that he saw through her ploy so easily, she tugged her hand free of his and tightened her brat. "Get on with you. Find us a place to lay our heads for the night."

"For you, lass," he said gently, "anything."

Crossing the firth was uneventful. The winds were mild and the waves low. Although she peered into the depths with great intensity, Morag saw nothing of the selkies rumored to inhabit the waters. She and Wulf were soon back in the cart and on the last leg of the journey to Edinburgh. Her excitement over the trip had worn thin after so many hours riding in the cart, and with the rhythmic rocking, Morag found her eyes drifting shut.

"Lass, wake up."

The warm pillow beneath her head moved a bit, encouraging her to wake. "Hmm?"

"Look up," Wulf murmured in her ear.

Morag pushed away from his shoulder and sat up. "What is it?"

He pointed. "Edinburgh Castle."

Her gaze tilted up, following his finger. High above them on a massive rock outcrop stood a mighty stone fortress. Dark stone against a pale gray sky. It was an awe-inspiring sight, and her heart beat heavily as she gazed upon the formidable walls. "Is that the king's flag?" she asked, spying a gold pennant with a red lion rampant flying atop the tallest tower.

"Aye."

"He's in residence then?"

Wulf nodded. "If you're fortunate, perhaps you'll catch a glimpse of him."

Allowing her gaze to drop, Morag shrugged. "I've no desire to see the king. Such a grand life is beyond my reach and thus beyond my interest."

He arched a brow. "Surely you are curious about

the man who garnered peace with the war-loving Norse and resisted the demand of the English king to pay homage?"

"So long as taxes remain bearable," she said, "what the king does matters not."

"You say that now," he said, chuckling. "But women are forever sighing in lovelorn devotion when he passes them by."

"He's handsome, I take it?"

"So the women say."

"Handsomeness is not the best measure of a man." Morag eyed the open width of the south entrance as they approached. A pair of armed guards stood on either side of the wooden barbican, querying all who dared to pass beneath the portcullis. Most were permitted entry, but as she watched, one man with a small herd of goats was turned away. "Have we the proper writs to enter?"

"Leave the talking to me," he responded.

As the line of people slowly moved forward, Morag threaded her fingers and placed her hands in her lap. Even a slight tremble might betray her nervousness, and she did not want to be the reason they were turned away. But it was difficult not to worry. The laird of the clan MacCurran was outlawed, as were all Black Warriors, and if they failed to pass inspection at the cow gate, she and Wulf might find themselves chained in the bowels of the mighty keep on Castle Rock.

Wulf halted the cart alongside one of the two guards. "My wife and I have come to trade in the market."

"Name?"

"Wulf Cameron of Braemar."

The burly soldier stared at him, then let his eyes drift over to Morag and the cart. "What goods do you trade?"

Leaning back, Wulf lifted the tarp covering the bolts of cloth. "The finest woolens in Scotia."

The soldier grunted. "Let's see your papers."

Wulf pulled a folded parchment from the front of his lèine and handed it to the man. Morag sat still as a pole, trying not to fidget as the soldier received the parchment. What was written on the paper, she had no notion. But it must have satisfied the guard, for he folded it and handed it back to Wulf. "You have leave to enter."

Morag released the breath she was holding, as calmly as she could.

When Wulf had driven the cart under the portcullis and farther up the hill toward the main street, she whispered, "Wulf Cameron? Where did you get papers to uphold that claim?"

"Lady Isabail's herald."

"But it's a lie."

He shrugged. "She holds a number of secrets from the king, not the least of which is that she wed my cousin. She believes in his innocence and is as committed as we to seeking the truth."

Morag dried her damp palms on her skirts. "I can only hope the ruse never comes to light. It would cause her endless grief if we were discovered."

"Our visit will be short," Wulf said. "There will be little risk." He turned the cart onto the High Street that ran the length of the ridge extending east from the castle.

"What of my cloth? Will I truly be able to sell it here?" she asked. High Street stretched far into the distance.

"Aye," he said. "If you do not, the guards at the gate will be suspicious."

The cart fell into a deep rut and Morag was flung against Wulf's arm. She briefly savored his warm strength before pushing away. "So we'll stay a few days, at least."

"As few as we can," he agreed.

"Shall we seek out lodging first? Or the herald?" She allowed her longing for a brief respite to color her words. After five days of travel, a chance to wipe the grime from her face and hands would be most welcome.

"The herald," he answered. "The sooner we find him, the sooner I will have the name of the man in black."

Morag heaved a sigh. "Where then?"

"Beyond these burgages," he said, pointing to the left. "Down the third vennel, according to Sim."

They followed the public passageway down the hill and found themselves in a small courtyard surrounded by a half dozen whitewashed bothies. Wulf reined the pony to a halt and eased out of his seat. The hours that had passed since the ferry had already stiffened his leg.

He nodded toward the sign hanging in front of one of the bothies—a square board painted with a trumpet. "This must be the place."

With a stiff gait, he crossed the courtyard to the door and knocked.

The door was opened by a plump woman wearing a dun-colored gown and a white brèid over her hair. "Aye?"

"I'm seeking Marcus Rose," Wulf said. "I've an introduction from a fellow herald." He held out a sealed parchment.

She took the parchment and closed the door.

A moment later, a tall, thin fellow in a saffron tunic and dark hose opened the door. His hairline had receded substantially despite a youthful face. "Sim sent you?"

"Aye." Wulf pointed to the cart. "My wife and I would beg a moment of your time."

Marcus frowned, but after a moment he opened the door wide and beckoned them both inside. "I'll have my Becca heat some tea."

The inside of the bothy was much finer than Morag's humble abode. A carved bed frame, four high-backed chairs before the fire, and a rug in the living area. No chickens or goats welcome here.

"What brings you to see me?" Marcus asked, as Becca added tea leaves to a pot of boiling water over the fire.

"This." Wulf handed the herald the sigil cut from their attacker's tunic. "Lady Macintosh's herald is unfamiliar with these arms and suggested you might be able to identify them."

Marcus took the scrap of cloth and studied it. He grew very still as he stared at the bear's head, and Morag was certain he was going to name its owner. Instead he looked up and shook his head. "I do not know this mark. Whence did you get it?"

Sitting back in his chair, Wulf accepted a cup of tea. "It was found on the body of a man slain by wolves," he lied smoothly. "We have been tasked with returning the possessions to his family."

"Indeed," Marcus said slowly. "What possessions might these be?"

"A very fine wool cloak and a Spanish sword," Wulf said. "Not a great legacy, but meaningful to a widow or son."

Morag was impressed by the ease with which Wulf spun his tale. Sincerity rang from his words, and were she Marcus she would have wholeheartedly believed their mission was to restore the cloak and sword to their rightful owner.

"Perhaps I could be of more aid," Marcus said. "If you left this with me, I could compare it to those recorded in the Book of Arms maintained by the marischal."

"That would be most helpful." Wulf downed the last of his tea and stood. "We'll return in two days hence to review what, if anything, you've discovered."

Marcus nodded. "The Book of Arms is wonderfully illuminated. I'm certain I'll find something useful. If not this exact sigil, then some other clue."

The sun was still high when they made their way back to the cart. Wulf helped Morag onto the seat, but did not join her on the bench. "Better for my leg to walk," he said.

"Shall we find an inn?"

He nodded. "Not in the High Street, however. We need a quiet spot, one less frequented by the king's guards. Perhaps in the north quarter, near the loch."

Not familiar with the burgh, Morag allowed Wulf to guide the cart down the narrow streets. But as they entered the long narrow wynd that bordered the loch, she frowned. No gardens or whitewashing here. The bothies were pressed tightly together, and most were in sore need of fresh thatching. The citizens in this part of town wore weary expressions and clothing grayed with age.

Wulf stopped the cart before a building displaying an iron horseshoe. "The blacksmith will know of a cottager willing to take us in."

He ducked inside the barn, leaving Morag in the cart. She glanced about, a tingle of alarm running down her spine. A blind man stood in front of the smithy, his hat in his hand. Two doors down, a woman leaned against a hewed post, her skirts hiked up to display an ankle. And across the wynd another man with a hood pulled over his head was selling a pair of women's boots that were clearly not his own.

Heartbeat quickening, Morag clasped the hilt of the knife at her belt and waited for Wulf to return.

With arrangements made to board the pony and store the cart, Wulf traded the dim confines of the blacksmith's barn for the gray chill of an early March afternoon. He immediately spied the empty seat of the cart and halted abruptly, his throat dry.

"Morag?"

"Aye." She popped up on the other side of the cart. In her hands was a cloth doll with one eye missing and a torn arm oozing dried grass stuffing.

He circled the cart to find a wee lassie at her knee. "Who have we here?"

"This is Saraid," Morag said, nodding to her soot-smudged young companion, who looked to be about six years of age. "Her da works for the tanner."

"The smithy says the tanner has rooms to let."

Morag smiled at the young girl. "That's what Saraid told me as well."

"But the odor in a tannery is near unbearable," Wulf said. "So we'll try the candlemaker instead."

Wulf unhitched the pony and walked it into the barn. While he gave the creature a good rub and saw it fed, Morag took a needle and thread from her pouch and mended the doll's sundered limb. Grinning broadly, the lass took the doll. She thanked Morag profusely and then darted off to resume her task of gathering piss pots from neighboring bothies. An unpleasant task, to be sure, but the urine was used by the tanner to finish his leathers.

"You've made a strong ally," Wulf said as the girl disappeared around the corner.

"Allies are useful in this part of town, I should imagine."

"True enough." He gathered the bolts of cloth and their sacks of clothing and led the way down the wynd. "Just keep your purse tucked close. Cutpurses learn their trade young."

Morag frowned and opened the drawstring on her pouch. "You don't think . . . ?"

He chuckled. "Nay, but be wary."

The candlemaker was a short man with a puckered scar covering a third of his face. He noted Morag's quickly disguised curiosity and pointed to his face. "An incident involving hot wax," he explained. "Happened when I was a wee lad."

"Listen not to that man," called his wife from across the room. "The truth is far more sordid and involves a fool too deep in his cups."

The candlemaker grinned.

He led them to the stairs beyond two great vats of melted wax. "Down the passage to the right. You'll need to launder your own linens."

Wulf nodded.

"How long will you need the room?"

"No more than a sennight. We've cloth to trade."

The candlemaker grunted. "Edinburgh is known for its cloth. You may not have an easy time of it."

Morag frowned. "What do you mean?"

"The weavers' guild will levy a tax on your goods," the portly man said. "The price of woollens made in the burgh will likely be more favorable than your own."

When Wulf spied the storm brewing in Morag's eyes, he nudged her up the stairs. "Thank you for the honesty, Master Toulie."

"I will not sell my cloth for less than I can at Dunstoras," she whispered to him as they climbed. "Ruse or no ruse."

"Let us see what tomorrow brings," he replied.

Morag opened the door to their chamber and groaned. "Why ever did I agree to accompany you on this madcap mission?"

He peered over her shoulder. The room was tiny, barely bigger than the bed inside. But it was not the narrow confines that drew her dismay—it was the stained, threadbare mattress hanging on drooping bed ropes, and the rank reeds upon the floor.

" 'Tis only for a few nights," he said encouragingly.

"A few nights passed in this room, and we'll spend a fortnight itching and scratching," she responded.

"Can you not set it right?"

She spun to face him. "I suppose I should be grateful that your faith in me is so great."

Wulf lowered his bundles to the floor in the passageway. "Tell me what you need, and I'll fetch it."

"A broom," she said. "And some dried feverfew to tuck inside that pallet. I'll not sleep with vermin, even for you."

He gathered her to his chest, relishing the soft warmth of her body against the uncompromising firmness of his. He planted a kiss on the top of her head, inhaling her sweet scent. "You are a fine woman, Morag Cameron."

She allowed herself to be held for a brief moment, then pushed at his chest with both hands. "Off you go, then. Tide and time tarry for no man."

Releasing her, he stepped back.

"And fetch the tarp from the cart." She rolled up the sleeves of her sark and lifted one corner of the mattress, her nose wrinkled in disgust.

Wulf set off in search of her demands. This was the Morag he knew and loved. Since the attack in her bothy, she'd been a wee subdued, a little less assured. But Morag with purpose was a force to be reckoned with.

He grinned.

God help the town of Edinburgh.

They set out for the High Street just before dawn, when the dark of night still held sway and the moon shone bright as a silver denier in the sky. The market was quiet but industrious—vendors of all sorts were laying out their wares by torchlight. Fishmongers from Leith with their baskets of conger and garvie, bakers with steaming bread rounds and buttery pastries, shoemakers with footwear of every size, and farmers with sheaves of grass and the bruised remains of last season's neeps, leeks, and apples.

Morag spied samplings of almost every good she could imagine—and some she didn't recognize. Had she not her own goods to trade, it would have been tempting to investigate.

"There," Wulf said, pointing to a group of men arranging bolts of cloth on the flat displays of several booths.

Dodging a lad wheeling a barrel of pickled beets, they approached the cloth vendors. One of them, a reed-thin man with curved shoulders, paused as they neared. Eyeing Wulf's armload of colorful twills, he said, "Tuppence to display, and a tariff of one-third on all goods you sell."

"That's robbery!" snapped Morag, shocked.

"Take it or leave it." He addressed the comment to Wulf, ignoring Morag completely.

Morag opened her mouth to give the man a taste of her opinion, but Wulf grabbed her arm and tugged a warning.

"We'll take it," he said quickly. "Pay the man his tuppence, lass."

Her chest tight with bitterness, Morag dug into her purse for the coins and dropped them into the weaver's outstretched palm.

He marked off a narrow section of his stall with a sooty stick and went back to arranging his goods for sale. Morag peered at his woolens with a critical eye as she and Wulf placed her twills on the table. The man's were well made, with tight, even threads and a smooth brushed finish, but the colors were dull and lifeless. And the patterns lacked imagination.

But she said none of what she thought.

Best she learn to bite her tongue now. Later, when she watched him pocket twice the profit for goods of lesser quality than hers, she'd find it much more difficult to hold her wheesht.

"I must see to repairs on the pony's harness," Wulf said. "Will you fare well on your own?"

"Aye," she said. "There's little room for the both of us here. Go."

Morag used her small section of the display to best advantage, unraveling a portion of each of her ten bolts and spreading the patterns wide. Dawn broke as she set out the cloth, and the shoppers arrived not long after. In small numbers to begin, but within the hour the street was a-bustle with trade. Fresh food was the most popular item—most shoppers sought baked goods and produce. But a few wandered the full length of the street, exploring all the crafts for sale.

The sun burst free of the clouds, for which Morag was grateful. Standing in her booth waiting on a potential customer had chilled her to the bone. The sun did not completely banish the chill, but it warmed the skin of her cheeks and, combined with the thick wool of her winter brat, allowed her to smile at passersby with genuine enthusiasm.

Perhaps it was her smile that caught the eye of a round-faced man with a shiny bald pate and beardless chin. He was marching past the woolens, headed toward the silks and satins, when he abruptly stopped and looked her in the eye.

His expression was anything but pleasant, however. Until his gaze caught the vibrant colors of her patterned cloth. Then the angle of his eyebrows reversed, and his lips went from a grim slash to a soft circle. He stepped toward her, his pudgy hands reaching for the cloth. At the first touch, a groan of delight escaped the plump man's lips. "These are truly fine."

Morag's smile broadened. Finally, someone who could appreciate the quality of her goods. "Thank you, sir."

Her response shook him from his pleasurable reverie. The frown stormed back to his brow, and he glared at her. "A man should sell his own cloth. Where is the weaver who made these twills?"

Standing as tall as she could, shoulders back, Morag stared back. "I wove them."

The plump man lifted a corner of her blue-red-and-black cloth, peering closely at the weave. "Not possible," he proclaimed. "The threads are too tight and too even. A woman could not weave such a fine cloth. The task demands strength and finesse a woman does not possess."

"You err, sir," Morag said tightly. Anger was a hot bloom in her chest, but she kept it under control. The man, no matter how annoying, was still a potential customer. "I dyed the wool, I spun the wool, and I wove the wool. All of the effort placed in this cloth is my own."

He dropped the cloth and stepped back. "I've never seen you in the market before today. Are you a member of the guild?" His gaze shifted to the weaver who'd allowed her space to display.

The weaver shook his head. "Nay, Master Seamus. She simply paid her dues. I know not where she is from."

Master Seamus's dark gaze fell upon Morag again. "For all we know, you stole these bolts. Indeed, they look suspiciously similar to those crafted by Master Parlan, the head of the weavers' guild."

A lump of fear formed in Morag's throat. This was swiftly getting out of control. A small crowd had gathered, the other shoppers bending ears to the exchange with gleeful interest. "I assure you, I wove this cloth myself. My husband and I are from the north. We traveled five days to reach Edinburgh in hopes of selling the cloth at a good price."

Her words did not sway Master Seamus. He shook his head. "I am the king's wardrober," he said. "I cannot be associated with stolen goods. Let me see your papers."

Morag tried to swallow, but failed. "My husband has them. He'll return anon."

Seamus scowled. "Did you see this husband of whom she speaks?" he asked the weaver next to her.

"Aye."

He smoothed his hand over his bare chin, his frown still heavy. "I have purchases to make. If your husband returns afore those purchases are made, we'll resolve this matter quickly. Else I'll have no choice but to call the constable and have him handle the matter."

A cold trickle of sweat rolled down Morag's back. Involving the constable might well result in Wulf's arrest, should his MacCurran kinship come to light. This was truly a disastrous affair. But she could think of nothing to sway Master Seamus from his path of determined justice. "We've naught to fear from the constable," she lied boldly. "But I'm sure my man will be along rightly."

"Time will tell," Seamus said darkly. To her weaver neighbor, he said, "Watch her. She's not to leave until I return."

Then the portly wardrober turned and marched off.

Her stomach aquiver, Morag forced a smile and faced the small crowd of wide-eyed onlookers. "Come see the fine cloth that drew the attention of the king's wardrober," she said loudly, waving a hand toward her display of cloth.

None stepped forward at her bold claim, but her brazen words shamed them into moving on. Within a minute or two the throng had thinned to an occasional curious gawker.

Morag glanced at the sun, then down the street in the direction of the castle.

Where was Wulf? How long could it take to repair a harness?

Her gaze swiveled in the opposite direction, toward the silk merchants. No sign of Master Seamus, either, thank heaven.

But time was her foe.

If Wulf did not return shortly, all would be lost.

Chapter 6

Wulf dropped the harness off at the leather worker's, but rather than making his way back to the market, he set off toward Edinburgh's east gate. From the moment he'd entered the burgh yesterday, a memory had nagged him—the image of a well-kept cottage with a stone chimney. His thoughts were remarkably clear when it came to the layout of the city. Their failure came when he attempted to draw up any personal anecdotes. He could clearly visualize the mysterious abode at the far edge of the town and the route best taken to reach it, but he could not name its owner, nor why the abode was so easily brought to mind.

A visit was surely called for. But since he could not anticipate what dangers might lie in store there, venturing forth without Morag seemed the wisest course of action.

With his long-legged stride, he reached the southeast corner of the burgh in little time. The homes and their surrounding properties grew larger as he approached the city wall. Narrow wynds gave way to streets fashioned to accommodate carriages. Fewer pigs and goats wandered the lanes, and garden plots took on an ornamental air.

Turning left down a stone-walled close, he found himself in a small courtyard that fronted three thatched cottages. No one-room bothies here. Each of the three homes had a pair of shuttered windows to one side of a gaily painted door. One blue, one green, and one yellow. Although all three homes were similar, it was the one with the green door that captured his interest.

He knew this house.

He'd been here before; he was certain of it. Everything about the place evoked a sense of familiarity, from the fieldstone chimney rising up one side to the low wattle fence that separated it from its neighbors. Even the iron hinges on the door, shaped like clover, spoke to him.

Wulf stood in the shadow of the wall and stared.

All was familiar; that much was assured. But no other sensation surfaced—not the warm pleasure of friend nor the tense of dread foe. He truly had no notion of what lay behind that door.

And there was only one way to find out.

He marched up the path and knocked.

* * *

"My lord?"

William Dunkeld frowned. Was there any greater inconvenience than being interrupted while breaking the fast? Surely not. He slathered a generous layer of butter on his bread and slowly consumed it, refusing to look up until he was finished. But his enjoyment had fled. How could he be expected to savor his meal with someone hovering over his shoulder, nervously bobbing his head?

He speared the footman's gaze with his own, making his opinion of the interruption abundantly clear. But seeing the servant pale was not enough. Dunkeld pushed back his chair and stood up. Circling the table with his butter knife still in his hand, he crooked a finger at the hapless footman.

"Come."

The man swallowed, sweat beading on his brow. He stepped forward, reluctance in the tight features of his face and the shortness of his step.

"Put your hand on the table," Dunkeld said, pointing to the oak surface that still held the remnants of his meal.

The young man's whole arm shook as he did what he was told.

"What did the seneschal tell you about interrupting my meals?" Dunkeld asked, licking the remaining butter from his knife.

"Th-that it's not to be done," the lad stammered.

"And was I eating when you entered?"

"Aye, my lord," the footman said. "But the man who seeks to meet with you said this was a matter of great importance, and that you would be most upset not to be informed immediately."

"I see," Dunkeld said slowly, running a thumb along the dull edge of the knife. "Are you in service to the man seeking an audience, or in service to me?"

"You, my lord."

"Who, then, determines whether a matter is urgent enough to interrupt a meal?"

The young man's face fell. "You, my lord."

"Me," agreed Dunkeld. He gripped the butter knife tightly in his fist. "And I say nothing is urgent enough to interrupt my meal. Is that clear?"

"Aye, my lord."

Dunkeld encircled the footman's wrist, holding his hand firmly against the tabletop. He eyed the splayed fingers and flattened palm with calm objectivity. "What I am about to do is equal part punishment for disobedience and incentive to remember this lesson fully."

A fierce tremble rolled down the young man's arm.

To his credit, he did not dissolve into a mewling bairn begging for mercy. His predecessor had not been as worthy a fellow. Dunkeld identified a spot between two of the bones in the young man's hand as being the least likely to cause permanent damage and an inability to carry a steady tray. Then, without further ado, and before the young man's trembling made aiming the knife with accuracy impossible, he stabbed.

It took great force to pierce the flesh with a dull blade, but Dunkeld was a large man trained to the sword and seasoned by battle. The knife sliced right through the lad's hand and bit into the tabletop.

The footman shrieked with agony, and Dunkeld smiled. Lessons accompanied by pain were rarely forgotten. He yanked the blade free, and then snatched his linen napkin from the table and wrapped it around the lad's hand. "Have my surgeon see to that," he said. "And send in the man who so urgently desires to speak with me."

The footman's cries subsided to faint moans. He backed away from the table, his hand clutched to his chest.

Dunkeld reached over the bloodstained tear in the linen tablecloth and selected a choice piece of smoked herring from his platter. The oily fish was bursting with flavor, and he savored every bite. Everything about the day, from the brightness of colors to the pungency of scents, had suddenly gained vivacity.

Boot steps echoed on the stone floor as his guest approached the table. Dunkeld followed the fish with a chunk of aged cheese. Only when the boots were silent and his guest had waited for a full minute did he turn around.

The man was unfamiliar to him. Better attired than a peasant, but clearly not of noble blood—the fellow's hair was poorly cut and his boots were scuffed. Even his formal bow lacked finesse. "Marcus Rose, your lordship. Pursuivant in service to the royal herald."

Not a guest at all. A mere herald. "Who has sent you?"

"No one, my lord. I come on a matter I believe is of import to you and you alone."

Dunkeld popped a morsel of candied plum into his mouth. *You and you alone.* Those words gave him pause. It would seem this junior herald believed he had information of a rather secretive nature. "What price does this information carry?"

The armsman smiled. "I knew you would understand. A sovereign, my lord, and the information is yours. Upon payment, I shall never again mention what I know, not to anyone."

Dunkeld dusted leftover sugar from his hands. That he would guarantee. "How do I know this information is worth a sovereign?"

The herald shrugged. "I've named my price, and I'll now reveal what I know. If you agree it's worth the price I ask, then pay me. If not, perhaps I can be of further service in the days to come."

"Fair enough. What have you discovered?"

Rose dipped his hand into the front of his tunic and withdrew a remnant of cloth, which he handed to Dunkeld. "I believe you are familiar with this sigil."

Dunkeld stared at the black-and-gold bear's head. He did indeed know the symbol. It belonged to his longtime and faithful man-at-arms Artan de La Fleche. But Artan rarely wore the symbol, preferring to proudly display the arms of the house of Dunkeld, so it was surprising that this junior herald knew of a link between this sigil and him.

"Why would you assume such a thing?"

"It is the house symbol of a prominent French family from France, the Fougères."

Dunkeld tossed the scrap of cloth back at the herald. "This means nothing to me."

"The Fougère family resides in a great stone château east of La Fleche," the young man continued. "I know this because my uncle is his herald."

Dunkeld nonchalantly turned back to his platter of food and studied it, feigning an avid interest in what to eat next. But the food no longer held his attention. He had sent Artan to Dunstoras on a very specific mission, and it did not bode well that the only thing to return to Edinburgh was this scrap of cloth. Especially when that scrap of cloth was delivered by a herald—a man who by his very function spread word.

"I have no interest in your family history. Be specific. How does any of this concern me?"

"This sigil was given to me by a large man from Dunstoras who was making queries as to its origin. The man who wore this sigil is dead. I believe the large man was the one who killed him."

A tight spot beneath Dunkeld's breastbone burned like a hot coal. He trusted very few people in his life, and Artan was one of them. The man would willingly die for him—and it seemed he had. In and of itself a loss. Added to the recent loss of Daniel de Lourdes, his very handsome and talented lover, it was a heavy blow.

The young herald shuffled his feet in the rushes. "I am trusted by the man making inquiries. Should you desire it, I can ensure he never makes the connection between you and the sigil."

Allowing his anger to slip the reins with which he normally held it, Dunkeld swept the platter off the table with his fist, sending it and its remaining contents crashing to the floor. The hounds by the fireplace immediately rose and scurried toward the food.

The herald was wide-eyed. Surprised, but not yet afraid. He had no idea of the importance of what he had shared, or how far Dunkeld was willing to go to keep the information secret.

"Here's what you will do," he said. "You will return to your home, and you will immediately pack all your possessions—everything you own—and gather your wife and servants. When you have done that, you will return here to the castle and my men will find you a place to hide for a short time. This man must find nothing when he comes looking for his information."

The herald frowned. "But I cannot simply go into hiding, my lord. I have obligations."

Dunkeld conjured a reassuring smile to his face. Charm was a skill like any other—perfected by regular use—and years of playing false confidant to his brother made such a smile easy to shape. "Fear not. You are henceforth employed as a herald in my house. I will see your wife and family settled on one of my estates. You will want for nothing."

"Thank you, my lord." Relief washed the furrows from the herald's brow and he gave a short bow. "I knew you were a powerful man. It is my great honor to serve you."

"Go," commanded Dunkeld. "Settle your affairs quickly and return. This man must not have an opportunity to query you further."

He allowed Marcus Rose to scurry away, and then he swung to face the shadow near the door at the back of the room. A blond man stepped out of the corner, an elegant Englishman with a penchant for silk doublets. Today's doublet was dark green jacquard that shimmered in the candlelight.

"When he returns to the castle," Dunkeld said, crossing the room, "make certain no one ever hears from him or his wife again."

"Of course," the blond man said.

"It would seem Artan failed to kill the MacCurran warrior."

"For the second time," agreed the blond man. "Had he ensured the man's death last November, none of this would be necessary."

As true as the words were, they angered Dunkeld. Artan had run the man through and left him bleeding on the shore of the loch. Who could have guessed that a man suffering from such terrible wounds would survive? "Nay, the true fault lies with the clan MacCurran. They have stymied my every attempt at justice. Duncan MacCurran swayed my father from acknowledging me as his firstborn son. If not for the MacCurrans, I would be king." Dunkeld shook both his fists in the air as he felt his face turn red. "Heaven's blood! Why can I not crush the MacCurrans into dust, as they deserve? All three of Duncan's heirs yet live."

"But only one of them has the power to derail your plans," the blond man pointed out. "And he appears to be in Edinburgh seeking information."

Dunkeld scowled. "It makes no sense. He saw my face the night we stole the necklace. Why would he simply not reveal my involvement to the king?"

"Perhaps his vision is faulty." The blond man smiled. "Whatever the cause, it is moot. You may not have crushed the MacCurrans, but you have succeeded in tarnishing their reputation with the king. They cannot approach Alexander without irrefutable proof."

Dunkeld nodded, but the mystery of why the man was in Edinburgh asking questions still plagued him. For a man who lived by his wits, as Dunkeld did, knowledge was power. "Take care of the herald; then watch the herald's home for sign of MacCurran."

The blond man put a hand to the hilt of his sword. "I will slay him when he appears."

Dunkeld shook his head. "Not immediately. For the moment, just follow him. I would know if he's alone in the city, or whether he has come with kin."

The blond man nodded.

"As you wish."

Master Seamus returned all too soon.

The portly wardrober marched up to Morag's stall with two bolts of silk in hand, one a shimmering swath of white and the other a vibrant royal purple. "Well?" he demanded. "Can you produce your papers?"

She shook her head. "My husband has yet to return."

Seamus snorted. "Like as not, he's seen the guile is up and he's run for the gate."

She met his gaze evenly. "He will return."

"Well, he can retrieve you from the bailiff," the wardrober said. He waved a hand in the air. "Someone fetch the constable."

To her amazement, the weaver next to her spoke up. "I'm not certain that's necessary, Master Seamus. I've sent a lad for Master Parlan. As he's head of the weavers' guild, such matters are rightly his to settle."

The wardrober lowered his hand. "A guildsman ought to be policing the sale of merchandise with more care. Did you ask this woman's husband for his papers before allowing him to sell his woolens?"

"Nay. 'Tis the guard at the gate's role to check papers, not mine."

"I will not allow this woman to sell her goods until someone has verified her legitimate claim to the woolens."

"Perhaps I can help," came a deep voice from the other side of the crowd.

Morag looked up. The voice did not belong to Wulf. It belonged to a tall man with raven-black hair who pushed his way through the crowd and addressed Master Seamus with a rough smile.

"Causing my weavers grief again, Seamus? Have you naught better to do with your day?"

Morag stared at the black-haired man, her throat suddenly tight and dry. He hadn't changed much since she'd last seen him—he still had the same square chin and square hands. A few new wrinkles around his eyes, perhaps, but that would be testing the memories of a lass of ten. Master Parlan of Edinburgh was none other than Parry Cameron, the man who'd deserted his wife and run off to parts unknown when she was a child.

Her father.

"You're not doing all you can to prevent crime," Seamus said. He pointed at Morag. "This woman is selling cloth that is clearly not of her own making."

Her father's vivid green eyes turned to Morag. He studied her for a long moment without comment, then said, "What cause do you have to call her a liar?"

Seamus scowled. "A woman does not have the strength to weave such tight and even threads. See for yourself. The cloths she sells are some of the finest I've seen." He tossed Parlan a goading smile. "I'd say they're fine enough to rival your own."

The master weaver lifted one corner of Morag's cloth, rubbing the smooth texture between his forefinger and thumb. "They are indeed fine," he said slowly, a faint frown between his eyes. "The colors are a close match to my own, as well." He lifted his gaze and gave her another stare. "But I must disagree with your assessment that she's not the weaver." He held up his hands, palms forward to the wardrober. "What do you see, Seamus?"

Seamus squinted. "Calluses on the thumb and forefinger of both hands."

Parlan nodded. "From pitching the shuttle and lifting the heddle sticks. This woman bears the same calluses. You owe her your regrets for maligning her good name."

Seamus glanced at Morag, and she held her hands up for his inspection. He huffed and turned sharply away, marching away through the crowd. Not a word of apology was heard.

Morag's father fingered her cloth again. "May I ask what good name Master Seamus has so shamefully cast aspersions upon?"

"You already know," she said tightly.

His gaze lifted to her black hair, a mimic of his own, then returned to her face. "Tell me anyway, else I will not believe it."

"Morag Cameron. I am the daughter of Jeannie Cameron of Dunstoras," Morag confirmed, afraid to look at him too closely for fear that it would tarnish all her old memories. Finding her father again after all these years was not the boon she had imagined. The tale of his desertion was more romantic with his disappearance into thin air.

"How is Jeannie?" he asked.

"Dead and gone these past nine years," Morag responded coldly. Her mother had hoped right up to the end that her winsome Parry might return.

"A shame, that," he said. "She was a fine woman."

"Too fine for the likes of you," Morag agreed.

"I had to leave, and she would not come with me," he said. "But I do not expect you to forgive my actions." Parlan heaved a heavy sigh. "I'll leave you to the selling of your cloth. Perhaps we'll talk again before you leave Edinburgh."

Morag nodded sharply, unable to speak. She was close to choking on unanswered questions.

Then for the second time in her life, she stood silently and watched her father walk away.

A small, elderly woman in a blue gown and a snow-white headdress answered the door to Wulf's knock. She took one look at him, burst into tears, and ran back into the house, leaving the green door swinging in the breeze.

Wulf stood there, rooted to the spot.

It was not a typical reaction. Most women, even older ones, seemed quite willing to engage him in conversation. To the best of his knowledge, he did not often drive them to tears.

A moment later, a white-haired man with an equally white beard replaced the woman at the door. "Wulf? We had no warning that you were coming. Please forgive Eleanor. She still grieves."

Wulf let the awkwardness of the moment wash over him, then spoke candidly. "It is I who should make amends. It was not my intention to cause distress."

"Nonsense. Come in, lad." The old man opened the door wide and beckoned him inside.

Wulf shook his head. "I would be entering without right," he said. "I do not remember you."

The old man's face lost all expression. "Not remember me? Do you jest?"

"Nay, I do not. A number of months ago I was attacked and left for dead. Although I have recovered most of my good health, my memories of the past have been lost. I do not know who you are, sir."

The old man was silent for a long moment. Then he exited the house and closed the door behind him. The breeze caught at his fine red tunic, fluttering the hem of the heavy brocade.

"A part of me envies you," he said. He pointed up the close. "Let us walk while we speak."

Wulf nodded and accompanied the man down the path. He purposely shortened his gait to match his companion's.

"How did you find us, if you have no memory?" the old man asked.

Wulf explained.

"What a curious thing," the elder said. "You know the house, but not the family who dwells there."

"How *do* I know the house?" Wulf asked.

"You've been here many times," he said. "Not for some years, however. Not since you and Elen were wed."

Elen was the name of his deceased wife. Wulf's gaze met the old man's. "You are Elen's father?"

"Aye. Edmund MacBain, jeweler."

Wulf allowed that to sink in. It explained the tears of the man's wife, and the dark circles of sorrow that cradled the old man's faded blue eyes.

"I regret that I failed them," Wulf said honestly. He could not picture Elen's face, nor that of their wee lad, Hugh, but he did sincerely regret not being able to save them from the cur who murdered them. The loss of his wife and son was a hard lump in his gut that never went away.

He knew the story of what had happened that night—Aiden had told him everything, answering every question Wulf had with quiet, painful truths. He knew that he'd rushed out of Dunstoras keep, mad with grief, determined to find and slay the bastard who'd murdered his wife and son. And he knew he'd met a group of men down by the loch and come out the loser.

"I've sworn to avenge their deaths, and I will not stop until I succeed."

The old man put a hand on Wulf's sleeve. "It must be difficult to make such a vow when you've no memory of those whom you are avenging."

Wulf shook his head. "It is enough that they looked to me to keep them safe, and I let them down."

The old man sighed. "Such a tragedy. And how does Jamie fare? We've not seen him since he was a bairn."

"He's a strong lad," Wulf said. "He took the loss of his mum and wee brother hard, but he's coming into his own now. He'll make a fine warrior."

"Good, good."

They walked for a while in easy peace, and then Wulf said, "Tell me about Elen."

"She was a good wife," Edmund said. "Orderly. She managed your household by frugal means and still maintained a full complement of servants. And she made you smile. You were ever a serious lad, having to care for your sisters and your mother from a young age."

Wulf halted abruptly. "I have kin in Edinburgh?"

Elen's father shook his head. "No longer. Your mother and eldest sister passed the year after you and Elen were wed. An illness that also took a longtime retainer. Your other sister died in childbed. She was wed to a Macgregor."

"And my father?"

Edmund frowned. "You rarely spoke of him. He was injured in the Battle of Largs, but the circumstances of his death I do not know. All I can say is that any mention of him made you angry. Perhaps because he left your mother without means."

They circled a stone dovecote splattered with bird droppings and headed back the way they'd come. Wulf was grateful for the other man's unique view into his past. His lack of memory, no matter how much the older man might envy it, was a knot in his gut he could not unravel. It prevented him from assuring the jeweler that the memory of his precious daughter would forever be honored—and it prevented Wulf from shouldering the burden of her loss.

"Elen lives on in Jamie," he told the old man. "He is orderly as well, and commands respect from his peers. It might comfort you to know that the lad is faithful to her memory. We laid flowers on her headstone on her name date."

Edmund smiled. "A fine lad indeed."

They stopped before the bright green door of the cottage. Edmund turned thoughtful and then said, "I have something which rightly belongs to you. Give me a wee moment and I'll fetch it."

Wulf waited patiently, and when the old man returned he accepted the small wooden box. Inside were six small wooden horses, very similar to the one Jamie had given him at Dunstoras, but older and clearly worn from use. "Did you make these?" he asked Edmund.

"Your father fashioned them," the old man said. "For you when you were a wee lad. Elen kept them, thinking to gift them to your firstborn, but they were left behind when you took Elen to Dunstoras."

"Jamie's a young man now," Wulf said. "Too old to play with such things."

Edmund shrugged. "Perhaps his son will enjoy them one day."

Wulf closed the lid, nodding.

"Should you return to Edinburgh with young Jamie," Edmund said, "I hope that you will stay with us awhile. I have no sons, and what I have will pass to him one day."

"You have my word," Wulf promised.

The old man smiled, patted Wulf's arm, and then entered the house.

Wulf stared at the green door for a long moment before turning on his heel and leaving the small close behind.

Chapter 7

A handful of cold coins settled into Morag's palm, and she barely restrained a grin as she handed off a half bolt of cloth in return.

"Five shillings," she whispered to her stall companion. "She paid five shillings."

"Aye, and you owe me a shilling eight," he grumbled.

She gave him one of her shillings and dug into her purse for the pence. "But that still leaves me with three shillings four," she said, amazed.

"No need to crow about it," he said. "Adopt a more circumspect demeanor. The other weavers are already looking askance. I've no desire to end up in the middle of another row."

Morag schooled her excitement and tucked the money away. "I've not thanked you for defending me to Master Seamus. It was very kind of you to do so."

He skewed her a hard look. "I did not defend you. I stood in defense of us all." He waved a hand at the weavers around them. "The king's wardrober is an important man, to be sure, but he has no right to say what the weavers' guild can or cannot do."

She nodded. "Still, you have my thanks."

"Accepted," he said, turning away to face a customer.

Morag had sold another half bolt by the time Wulf appeared at the stall. When she spied his head above all others in the street—clearly walking in her direction—her first reaction, as always, was a sigh of admiration. He truly was a braw man. A face defined by sharp but even features, a pair of shoulders wide enough to carry the heaviest of loads, and a strong stride that belied the slight stiffness in his leg. Of course, she was not the only one who noticed. He turned the heads of many a female shopper as he wove through the crowd to reach her.

That, plus the memory of how she'd had to face Master Seamus's accusations without the benefit of his support, added a crisp edge to her words when she asked him, "Where have you been?"

He looked at her without answering, his expression impossible to read. His thumb brushed over her cheek, sending a tiny spark fluttering to her belly. "The sun has painted more freckles upon your cheeks."

Morag scowled. She hated that her skin so easily gave way to such blemishes. And it annoyed her that his compliment softened her heart toward him in an instant. "I'll be more careful to stand in the shade."

"Nay," he said softly. "I like them."

"You may like them all you desire," she retorted. "But I will still do my best to avoid more."

He smiled and glanced at her display. "You've sold some cloth, I see."

"Two bolts," she said happily.

"A very successful day. Shall we buy some food and adjourn to our rooms for the eve?"

Morag bit her lip. There were still a few hours of daylight left, but the volume of shoppers had definitely waned. She turned to her stallmate. "May I pay you now to assure my spot in your stall tomorrow?"

He nodded.

She paid him the tuppence, then swept her cloth into her arms and faced Wulf. "Aye, let's away."

Wulf relieved her of the cloth and pointed down the High Street. "You lead; I'll follow."

Morag celebrated her sales of the day by purchasing bread, wine, and some strips of dried pork for their dinner. Wulf was oddly distant, offering his opinion of her choices when prompted, but saying little else. She waited until they were climbing the stairs at the candlemaker's before commenting on it.

"Is all well?" she asked.

He shrugged. "I am impatient to know what Marcus discovers." Sliding the bolts of cloth to the floor, he opened the door to their chamber and waved her inside.

Morag stopped short. She blinked as she studied the plump new mattress laid across the bed frame. "Lord, please tell me you didn't spend our hard-earned coin on a mattress."

"Is it not a sight better than the old?"

Morag dropped her purchases on the bed and spun to face him. "You bought a mattress?"

"Nay," Wulf said. He grabbed the wine and poured two cups. "I merely shamed the candlemaker into buying one."

Relief poured through Morag, but the moment was fueled by the frustration she'd endured for most of the day, and she lashed out. "Why did you let me think, even for a moment, that you'd bought it? We've no money for such extravagances, and I near expired with fear we'd wasted precious coin."

He downed his wine as she ranted.

"And why did you take our papers with you this morn? Why did you not leave them with me? I doubt the leatherworker had need to see your credentials."

Wulf's eyebrows soared. "Our papers?"

"Aye, our papers," she said, jabbing a finger at the solid muscle of his chest. "Where are they?"

He grabbed her finger and planted a quick kiss on the tip. "Lass, you've clearly found me wanting today. For that, I beg your forgiveness. But do me the kindness of starting the tale at the beginning so that I might fully understand my failing."

Morag sagged, her anger dissolving with his gentle words. "I was nearly hauled off to the bailiff again."

His quiet stare demanded further explanation, and she gave it. The simple act of sharing her misadventure eased her frustration, and by the time she got to the part where her stallmate spoke for her, she managed a smile. "Of course, that was not the biggest surprise."

Wulf broke the bread into several large chunks and handed Morag a piece sopped in red wine. "Oh?"

She ate the dripping bread before responding, not entirely certain she was ready to share what she'd discovered. "He'd sent for Master Parlan, the head of the weavers' guild, and Master Parlan spoke for me as well. Between the two, they set the king's wardrober on his ear."

"Weavers stand up for their own, it would seem." He poured himself another cup of wine.

"Aye." She bit into a strip of salted pork and closed her eyes. "Och, this is a taste of heaven."

"A good man would provide you with such fin-eries on a regular basis."

Her eyes popped open. As she suspected, he was watching her with a faint frown. "You already provide more than I deserve. You are a good man, Wulf MacCurran, but a good man is not in my future. The poor decisions of my past have seen to that."

"Why do you repeatedly suggest I would spurn you because of the past?" he asked. "Have I given you reason to believe such nonsense?"

"Nay," she said, smiling faintly. "You are free with your praise and you show me only honor and respect."

He sat back, a satisfied expression on his face. "Then let us not discuss the matter again." Extending his brawny legs with a ripple of lean muscle, he tipped his wine cup to his mouth and downed a full portion in a single swallow.

Morag enjoyed the sight of him relaxed and half-sotted. The strange air of distance had finally fallen away, leaving him loose and carefree. More like the Wulf of old. The wine added a slight flush to his cheeks and left a warmer than usual glint in his eyes. Perhaps it was the awareness of how easily the day could have gone awry—how very possible it had been that they would have spent the night in gaol instead of reclining on a brand-new straw mattress, but as she stared at Wulf, Morag was convinced she'd never seen him look handsomer.

"Would you kiss me?" she asked of him.

Instantly, the air of carelessness vanished. His gaze sharpened and his eyes darkened with an undeniable flare of passion. But he did not move toward her, or even flex a muscle.

"Nay," he said. When she stiffened with his rejection, he added, "For if I start, I will not stop."

"Would that be so wrong?"

"Aye, it would." He lifted a hand and tucked a loose tress behind her ear. "I care for you, Morag Cameron. And a man does not misuse a woman he cares for."

She arched a brow. "A kiss is misuse?"

He smiled. "You know full well we don't speak of kisses." The smile slid away. "I can't ask you to wed half a man—and without my memories I am but half of who I was."

Hearing the word *wed* fall from his lips tumbled Morag's heart in her chest. Wedding Wulf was a dream she indulged on a regular basis, and his suggestion that it was possible gave her a temporary surge of hope. But whores did not marry knights. "And what if they never return?"

"They must."

She stood up and brushed bread crumbs from her skirts. "Your memories change nothing that is real, Wulf. You are still cousin to the laird, still the finest warrior in his clan, and still father to a lad who needs a steady hand to guide him. Even should your memories never return, you will still be those things."

"I don't deny those truths," he said. "But to forge a new life, I must first settle the old. I must avenge my kin, reclaim my clan's honor, and ensure the ghosts of my past can do you no harm."

"You might yet achieve those goals without your memories." Indeed, Morag was certain Wulf could do so. He was a very determined man. She unknotted her belt and removed it, the wool of her gown now loose against her body.

"I might," he agreed, watching her.

"Or you might regain your memories," she said, lifting the heavy woolen dress over her head, "but never find the man who dealt you those vicious, cowardly blows."

His brow furrowed and his lips tightened. But his eyes remained locked on the sway of her soft linen sark against the contours of her body. "I will not rest until I do."

She shook out her gown and folded it neatly beside the bed. Every movement floated the light material of her sark, sending the linen drifting across her backside and along the curves of her breasts. Breasts that were full and heavy with a longing to be touched. Breasts that were teased by the gentle rasps of linen over their sensitive peaks.

"Vengeance is a hard taskmaster," she said, lifting the hem of her sark to her knees, and then kicking off her boots. "Those who serve him end up alone and bitter."

She glanced at Wulf.

His attention was riveted on the woolen hose covering her lower legs, and she smiled. With a slow, purposeful hand she untied the garter above one calf, and allowed the wool stocking to slip down her leg. A flick of her foot and the material sailed across the floor, leaving a bare ankle and pink toes.

It was not a particularly graceful ankle—her skin was not the pampered flesh of a lady—but the sight of it had a visible effect on Wulf.

His entire mien shifted slightly. He went from relaxed to ready in a single indrawn breath. From casual companion to hungry predator. His awareness of her was etched in every taut muscle and every short breath, and the only thing holding him in check was the bond of his honor.

But Morag wanted that bond to slip.

One day soon, Wulf would awaken with all his memories returned—she was certain of it. And when he did, he would remember all the commitments he had to his old life and all the reasons he could not—and should not—be with her.

He would walk away.

Because that was what men did.

They had their reasons—no doubt valid ones—but those reasons rarely softened the blow. Morag was already steeling her heart for the day Wulf would walk away from her, never to return. But she still wanted tonight. She wanted Wulf just like this, with the flush of hot desire painted on his face. And she wanted all the pleasure that desire promised. She wanted his body next to hers, rocking in a rhythm as old as time. She wanted him to tease her body to the limits of bearable need and then offer her the heavy pulse of satisfaction. She wanted to lose herself in the dream, however brief, of having Wulf for her own.

Morag untied the second garter and slid the stocking slowly over the curve of her calf. His gaze followed the path of her fingers with hot, dark intensity.

Because right now, in this moment, he was indeed hers.

The stocking dropped to the floor.

Perhaps it was the wine. Or perhaps he was simply weary of resisting. Either way, Wulf suddenly found himself in the fiercest battle of his life. He wanted Morag like he'd wanted nothing before—every inch of his skin burned with need. Every muscle ached with want. And every breath begged for the taste of her on his tongue.

If she'd been a different woman with a different past, the battle would have been easier won. But Morag had been sorely used by dishonorable men, and if he succumbed, he would become one of that number.

His heart pounded like a drum in his chest.

She deserved so much more than he could offer her. What other woman could claim to be as bold, as brave, or as gifted? His lovely lass had survived four years alone in the woods, had built her own home out of daub and wattle, and had woven cloth so fine it could attract the attention of the king's wardrober.

Mere words could not define her.

And were she an ordinary-looking lass with a pious demeanor, his honor would play a louder tune. Instead, she had bright green eyes with a hint of laughter always buried in their depths, and a sweet bow-shaped mouth that curved with sinful charm. And her body could tempt an angel into hell.

Shadowy glimpses of her curves taunted him from the voluminous folds of her sark.

He was no angel.

Wulf surged from the bed, caught Morag about the waist, and buried his face in the delicate curve between her shoulder and neck. The room was so small, it was done in a single movement. One step, one touch, and he was lost.

His hands sank into the cool linen folds of her sark until they reached the warm heat of her body. The same warm heat he slept next to each night, that shaped his dreams and lingered in his thoughts all day. He'd never allowed himself to touch more than her face, or an occasional guiding at her back or hands. For good reason. He knew precisely how weak his will would become once that barrier was breached.

His big hands cupped the soft fullness of her breasts, his thumbs flicking across the peaks. Her nipples budded instantly, eager for his caress, and a low moan escaped her lips. And that was all it took to silence the lingering whispers of his conscience. A need so intense it was akin to pain seared through his veins, demanding he take what had been denied him so long, and take it now. His fingers clenched, and with eyes closed, he unerringly found the sweetness of her lips with his.

It was less a kiss than a plunder.

He pressed his mouth against hers, demanding all she had to give. And when she opened to him with a soft mewl, he exulted.

Given free rein after so long under tight control, his muscles flexed with fierce sexual intent. He positioned one knee between her legs, leaned into her soft body, and rocked against the gathered material of her sark. Lost in the haze of his overwhelming need, he didn't register the squeeze of her fingers on his forearm for a moment.

He was being too rough.

Wulf paused. His every breath a ragged draw, his every heartbeat a jolt of raw need, he gentled his hold on her. "Tell me what would please you," he urged as his lips moved along her chin to the soft flesh beneath her ears.

"Don't stop the kisses." She gulped. "Just slow the motions below."

Then she grabbed his chin and forced his lips back to hers. There was desperate hunger and need in her body, too. And he indulged her.

Sliding his hands down her generous hips and over the delicious roundness of her rump, he raised the hem of her sark until it bunched around her waist and the silky smoothness of her bare flesh was his to explore. He took a brief moment to savor the privilege, and then cupped her cheeks and hauled her up his body.

She wrapped her legs around his waist, an intimate hold that nearly undid him. He was already hard and aching, and the press of her feminine heat was almost more than he could bear. Blood pounded through his veins. The urge to take her fast and hard was fierce, but he tempered his desire. Pleasing Morag was far more important than pleasing himself.

But the effort took its toll.

His weak leg quivered with the strain.

Unwilling to risk a stumble with his precious woman in his arms, Wulf closed the gap between her back and the wall with a half step. He bumped the small table as he moved, but with his lips locked to hers and his hands kneading the exquisite curve of her arse, he barely noticed.

Until something crashed to the floor.

It was not the clink of pottery breaking or the dull thud of food falling. It was the sharp whack of wood on wood, followed by the rattle of contents spilling onto the floor.

Wulf froze.

Still breathing heavily, he pulled back from Morag's mouth and glanced down. At his feet, and now at serious risk of being crushed, lay a scattering of wooden horses.

The toys he'd received from Elen's father.

In an instant, the strange events of his day came flooding back, cooling his heated blood. The toys were a sharp reminder of how he'd failed Elen and his younger son, and a vivid reminder of the danger he presented to Morag.

Relaxing his hold on her, he gently lowered her to the floor.

"Why do you stop?" Morag asked. Her voice was husky with passion.

Unable to put his feelings into words, Wulf simply answered, "This is the wrong path." Then he bent, scooped up the toys, and replaced them in the wooden box.

Morag's dissatisfaction tugged at her pretty lips. She ran a light finger down his chest and over the hard muscles of his belly. "How can it be wrong if we both willingly choose it?"

He tucked the box into the bag, burrowing it deep in his clothing. Out of sight, but not out of mind. "I am no longer willing. I have told you that we must wait until I can avenge my family."

Silence descended on the room.

Even Morag's breathing had stopped.

Wulf spun around, realizing the impact of his words. "Tomorrow we will visit Marcus Rose and likely learn the name of our man in black. Then we can return to Dunstoras. All will sort itself out then."

Her eyes were dark pools in the pale, freckled oval of her face. She shook her head. "This is all we have, Wulf. This journey, this room, this moment."

He cupped her chin, rubbing a thumb over the satiny flesh of her lips, still plump from his kisses. "Have faith, lass."

She pulled away, her eyes still sad.

"Time once flown can never be recaptured," she said softly. "Remember that."

Then she pushed past him and grabbed the jug of wine.

Morag waited in the cart while Wulf knocked on the herald's door. Standing all day at the market would be taxing, but she had paid for another day in the weaver's stall and she fully intended to make use of it. Without the fuss caused by yesterday's encounter with the king's wardrober, chances were good that she could sell another three or four bolts of cloth.

Her gaze drifted across Wulf's fine shoulders and down to his narrow hips. She sighed in despair. Sleep had not come easily last eve, even with the help of the wine. How could it, with her body humming with desire and his body occupying a sizable portion of their new mattress?

Wulf knocked a second time but there seemed to be no response.

Morag glanced up at the sky. The sun had already dawned and the pink glow of early morn had given way to a robin's-egg blue. Surely the herald and his wife had long departed their bed?

A grumpy thought settled on her brow.

Unless they had reason to remain abed.

Wulf pounded on the door a third time. To no avail. Not a sight nor a sound stirred from inside the herald's home. Reluctantly, he returned to the cart. "Perhaps they left early for the day."

"Ask the neighbors," she said, pointing to the bothy closest to the herald's. "They'll know."

He frowned at her. "You're not still angry with me?"

Morag chose not to answer his question. She pointed to the neighbor's bothy again. "Be quick. We are wasting my paid time in the weaver's stall."

He stared at her just long enough to let her know that he was calling on the neighbor by his own choice; then he marched across the courtyard.

This time there was no delay. The knock was answered promptly. The door opened, a short discussion ensued, and then Wulf returned.

His expression was suspiciously bland.

"Well?" she asked. "Where have they gone?"

"He does not know," Wulf said. "Nor does he believe they will return."

A short laugh escaped Morag's mouth. "Of course they will return. They have belongings inside."

"Nay," he said, shaking his head. "They packed up a wagon last night and departed. The neighbor says they had the aid of several men. When he tried to ask Marcus what was happening, one of these men encouraged him to go back inside and turn a blind eye."

Gone? "But he has the sigil!"

Wulf vaulted into the seat of the cart and gathered the reins. "Aye."

She frowned. "It was our proof that someone attacked us. We have nothing else."

"Save for the black wolf cloak." Wulf's lips were set in a grim line.

"The trail of the cloak will be much harder to follow," Morag said. "It will be difficult to prove that it belonged to a specific man. Even if we identify its maker, there's no guarantee it is unique. He might have made several similar cloaks."

Wulf turned the cart and headed for the market. "Wolf pelts are not as common as they once were. I'm certain we can find its maker." He tossed her a sharp look. "But you must not make inquiries yourself, no matter how tempting. Leave that to me."

Morag saw worry in the creases 'round his lips. "You think the man in black had a hand in Marcus's disappearance?"

He nodded. "I do. I doubt the wretch will be bold enough to cause you grief in a public market, but you must take care. Is there anyone among the weavers you can trust?"

Morag sat back to consider it.

Trust? Now, there was a curious word. There was definitely a man she could call upon to protect her. But give the man her trust? That was a whole different matter. Her father would help her. She felt quite confident in that. But how did you trust a man who would turn his back on his family and walk away?

"The head of the weavers' guild is very protective of his people," she said. "If I have need, I will beg his assistance."

Wulf nodded, but she could tell he wasn't satisfied.

Morag laid a hand on his arm. "I will be safe. Have no fear. It is you who should be wary."

His eyebrows shot up. "I?"

"You forget," she said dryly, "I was the one who dragged your bloodied body back from the loch."

"I was mad with grief that night. I clearly made an error."

"You were overrun. Even the strongest and bravest of men will be defeated if his enemy is too numerous."

Pulling on the reins, he brought the cart to a halt. Then he turned to her, his expression firm. "I know it is a woman's lot to fear for her man, but you cannot doubt my ability to protect you, lass. Not under any circumstance."

Faced with the squared shoulders and fierce gaze of a very determined man, Morag simply nodded.

He then set the cart in motion again and turned onto the High Street, which was already teeming with shoppers and hawkers. Men bent low under heavy burdens, women carried baskets of food, and lads held armloads of packages. People were everywhere.

"My inquiries will keep me in the market for now," Wulf said. "If you have need, send a lad to fetch me." He pulled up in front of the weaver's stall and leapt to the ground. Offering her his hand, he helped her alight.

Morag studied Wulf as he unloaded her cloth from the cart and set up her stall. By all rights, she should be wringing her hands with concern. If Wulf was right about Marcus's disappearance, there was a faceless madman in the burgh with cause to harm them. But Wulf was clearly the sort of man who was strengthened by adversity. Never before had she seen him stand so tall or move with such surety. Even that night by the loch, when she'd watched him fight eight men, his shoulders had been bowed by grief, his chin low to his chest. But not today. Today his limp was barely noticeable, his muscles flexed with loose readiness, and his gaze took in everything around him.

As Wulf guided the cart around the back of the stall and unhitched the pony, Morag greeted her stallmate and adjusted her bolts of cloth to show the pattern to best advantage. When Wulf returned, she snared his gaze. "A shame you can't carry your sword."

He smiled. "If I can't openly carry a weapon, then neither can my enemies."

A valid point. And a reassuring one. "Might I suggest you begin your queries with the weavers from the Canongate? The black wolf cloak is an unusually fine garment, and they weave brilliant twill for the Aquitaine monks at Holyrood."

He nodded.

"Now, away with you," she said, waving him off. "You're scaring off my customers."

Giving her hand a last squeeze, he said, "I'll return at noontide. Good fortune to you."

And then he sailed into the crowd of shoppers, parting the throng by sheer will. No one stood in his way.

The moment he was lost to view, Morag nudged her stallmate. "I have need to speak with Master Parlan. How can I get a message to him?"

Chapter 8

The weavers from the Canongate had set up a stall next to a baker. Unfortunately, the volume of shoppers visiting the baker did not benefit them—the crush of people vying for freshly baked goods choked the street in all directions and partially blocked the weavers from view.

Wulf used his size and a heavy-browed glare to advantage. He had soon cleared a path to the front of the stall, and he addressed the two men standing behind a table heaped with bolts of cloth. "Good day, sirs."

The two men looked up eagerly.

"Seeking the finest wool in the land?" one of them asked boldly. "You've come to the right place."

Wulf pulled the cloak from the front of his lèine and unfolded it. Only the shoulders were sewn with fur—the bulk of the garment was a heavy wool weave. "I seek the maker of this cloak," he said. "Does it look familiar?"

The man across the table scowled. "We're in the trade of weaving and selling our own cloth, not aiding you in finding another's."

Wulf lifted a loose edge of the fur pelt and pointed to the wool cloth beneath. "So, this is not your cloth?"

The man grabbed a corner of the cloak, rubbing the material between his fingers and peering closely at the pitch-black threads. "Nay, 'tis not mine. This dark a color is difficult to achieve. It would require a talented dyer."

"And where would I find such a dyer?"

The man's eyes narrowed. "Why do you seek the fellow?"

Wulf cultivated an easy smile. "The man who owned this cloak was slain by thieves. We found his body and buried it, but had hopes of delivering the rest of his belongings to his widow. To do so, we must discover who he was."

The man's frown did not ease. "A lot of trouble to see his belongings properly disposed of. Why not simply sell the goods and be done?"

Wulf did his best to look offended. "My own da died on the road. Had not another man delivered his belongings, we might never have discovered what became of him. I simply mean to return the goodwill."

The weaver shook his head. "You're a fool. But

if you're a determined fool, find Mathias the dyer. He's able to produce fine blacks like this."

Wulf nodded his thanks, then flipped the man a denier for the trouble.

Glancing down the High Street, he considered his next move. A dyer would not be manning a stall in the market. He was more likely to have a bothy in the lower part of town, close to where the tanner and the candlemaker lived, but that would mean leaving Morag unprotected. As low as the risk was in the busy shopping area, he wasn't prepared to do that.

So Wulf headed back to Morag's stall.

"Stop that thief!"

He spun around just in time to see a young lad dart past him with a round of bread tucked tightly under one arm. The baker, unable to leave his stall unattended, was hopping up and down, pointing at the escaping thief.

Wulf snared the lad with a quick hand, latching onto the loose cloth at his neck and lifting him clean off his feet.

"Let me go," the boy screamed, kicking.

The lad was filthy, covered in grime from head to toe. He had streaks of soot on his face and dark arcs under his fingernails, but it wasn't the dirt that made the deepest impression. It was the boy's weight. Or lack thereof. Light as down fluff. He was naught but skin and bone.

"Hold," he said sternly to the squirming lad.

The boy grew still and wide-eyed.

Wulf lowered him to the ground, but did not release him. With a gentle push, he forced the lad back in the direction of the baker's stall.

"Thank ye, sir," the baker said. "The constable will take care of this young wretch."

Wulf handed the baker a coin and selected two more rounds of bread from the table. "I'll handle the matter." He pointed to the crowd of shoppers. "You've enough to deal with."

The baker nodded, grateful.

His hand still firmly on the lad's neck, Wulf guided him through the throng and down the street. When they were out of the baker's sight, he halted. He thrust the additional bread into the boy's hands and released him.

"Wait," he ordered, when the scrawny lad made to dash off.

The boy froze.

"I've work for you."

A frown creased the lad's brow. "What sort of work?"

"I'm in need of some aid," he said. "I must leave my lady in the market, but fear she might attract unwanted attention."

The frown deepened. "What would you have me do?"

"Watch her stall for me. Discreetly. And if she

looks to be in trouble, run to fetch me." Wulf eyed the lad's bare feet. "You're remarkably fleet of foot."

The lad scowled. "Not fast enough."

"There's a denier in it for you."

Shock knocked the scowl from the boy's face. "Truly?"

"Aye." Wulf held up the coin. "Even if no one bothers her. Do you know Old Horse Wynd on the north side, down by the loch?"

He nodded.

"Good." Wulf pointed to Morag's stall, which was just visible on the other side of the wide street. "That's the lass who may have need of me."

"And all I need to do is keep a lookout?"

"Aye."

The boy tore off a bite of one of the breads, and sighed with genuine pleasure. "I'll do it."

"Good lad."

Wulf watched Morag discuss her craft with a prospective buyer, her hands mimicking the weaving of threads, an eager look upon her face. Then he patted the boy's shoulder and set off to find the dyer.

"A large man and a dark-haired woman," the blond man confirmed. "They knocked on the herald's door just after sunrise this morn."

Dunkeld poured a cup of wine. "MacCurran?"

"The neighbor said they named themselves Cameron, but the man matches the description you gave me of MacCurran. There are few men of his size with brown hair and a slight favoring of the left leg."

Dunkeld remembered the man well. One didn't easily forget a warrior capable of battling a group of eight men and very nearly coming out the winner. "Any sign of other MacCurrans?"

The blond man shook his head. "They appear to be alone."

"Where are they now?"

"In the market."

He took a deep swallow of his wine. "Wait until there are fewer witnesses and then bury the cur in the ground."

The blond man smiled. "With pleasure."

"Don't underestimate this man," Dunkeld warned. "He is a formidable foe."

The blond man snorted. "He has a weak leg."

"That's what Artan said when our spy returned with news that MacCurran still lived," Dunkeld pointed out dryly.

The blond man drew his sword in a slow, deliberate move. "Not to tarnish the reputation of a dead man, but Artan was not the swordsman I am." He tilted the blade, catching the reflection of the firelight in the gleaming edge of the blade. "A man who has trained with Spanish masters is rarely beaten by a woodland churl, no matter what size blade he wields."

"I care not for the details of how you will defeat him," Dunkeld said darkly. "Do what you must. I will not tolerate failure."

The blond man resheathed his sword and offered a deep bow. "I will bring a full complement of men. The deed will be done; have no fear."

He backed out of the room, leaving Dunkeld to his thoughts.

The grand culmination of his plan was about to unfold, and every heartbeat in his chest sang with excitement. Were it not for his vow to see the MacCurran clan destroyed, he would be humming a victory tune. The end of Alexander's reign was nigh.

His brother's three children by Queen Margaret were all dead, two by Dunkeld's hand. An assassin was on his way to Norway to ensure the king's young granddaughter never set foot on Scottish soil, and come the nineteenth of March, the new queen and her unborn child would fall dead as well.

Poison was truly the great sword of justice.

Dunkeld plunked his cup on the oak tabletop, frowning. The loss of Daniel de Lourdes had been a huge blow. De Lourdes had perished at the hand of Aiden MacCurran a few short weeks ago, while attempting to recover the lost necklace of Queen

Yolande. Dunkeld had spent several wonderful nights at Tayteath with Daniel, and it pained him to imagine his handsome young lover broken and bloodied upon the rocks. But it especially pained him to lose such a valuable resource. The man had been a gifted poison maker. His ability to disguise death in tasty foods had been superb, and his knowledge of unique ways to deliver poison into the body was unparalleled. The king's physician had deemed the deaths of Alexander's two sons to be from unfortunate illness, and no finger of blame was ever pointed. Quite an accomplishment, given that they had been heirs to a crown.

Crossing to the window, Dunkeld threw open the wooden shutter and drew in a deep breath of cool air.

Amazingly, it seemed de Lourdes might aid him from the grave. At Dunkeld's behest, the young man had painted a very potent poison on the back of the queen's ruby necklace—a necklace that Isabail Macintosh had recently returned to King Alexander after locating it at Tayteath. Had the queen's necklace not been out of his hands for several months, Dunkeld would be truly content. It was impossible to know what had befallen it in that time. The poison had been strong enough to slay the former Earl of Lochurkie four months ago. But was it as potent now?

The king intended to gift the necklace to Queen

Yolande on the occasion of her birthday, three days from now. De Lourdes had assured him that the necklace need only lie upon the queen's bare skin for a few minutes before the poison did its evil deed.

But after all this time, would it do what Dunkeld needed it to do?

Hands flat against the smooth stone on either side of the window, Dunkeld peered into the cobbled courtyard of the castle. If the necklace failed, he'd simply find another way to slay the queen. A convenient fall, perhaps. But the necklace was a perfect weapon. Who would suspect evil lurked in such a beautiful gem? If history repeated itself, no blame would be laid. The queen would simply sicken and die. Just like young prince David, young prince Alexander, and the Earl of Lochurkie.

And when all of the king's heirs were gone, Alexander would have no choice but to name his bastard brother as the next monarch, else he would send the country into leaderless turmoil.

It was true that Dunkeld had complicated his plan by involving the MacCurrans, but the lure of crushing his enemy had been too great to resist. Arranging the theft of the queen's necklace while under MacCurran's roof had given him the means to outlaw his enemy while also giving de Lourdes a chance to paint the gem with poison.

All should have worked perfectly.

Except he'd failed to anticipate the actions of two men: Wulf MacCurran chasing him into the woods and spying him hoodless, and the Earl of Lochurkie seizing the necklace and secreting it off to an ally in Baron Duthes's household.

The necklace had been recovered, fortunately, and he had believed Wulf MacCurran dead until this past month. Dunkeld's fingers clawed against the stone as he peered outside. MacCurran clearly thought to reveal Dunkeld's involvement to the king. Why he had waited this long to cause him grief was impossible to know, but his coming to Edinburgh—to the town Dunkeld knew intimately—was a huge mistake.

A mistake MacCurran would pay for with his life.

Morag's father answered her message in person. He returned to the marketplace just before noon, but did not come alone. A young man accompanied him—a swarthy, well-dressed lad who hung on every word the master spoke.

"I had hoped to speak with you alone," she said, as the pair stopped in front of her stall.

Parlan shrugged. "This is my apprentice, Douglas. Where I go, he goes."

She studied the young man's face, trying to decide whether she could risk discussing the cloak in front of him. He was not an attractive lad; his ears were overlarge and his nose had a decidedly bulbous tip. But he had clear, open eyes that held no guile.

Morag leaned in. "I have need to identify the maker of a particular cloth," she said. "But it must be done discreetly. Are you willing to help me?"

Her father frowned. "Of what importance is this cloth?"

Morag chewed her lip. She could lie and give the same story Wulf had given Marcus, but that had not served the herald well. "It is a cloak that once belonged to an assassin."

Her father started, pulling back. "Surely you jest."

"I do not. Nor will I hide the danger inherent in aiding me. If you choose not to help, I will not fault you, but you are my best hope of identifying who made the cloak."

Parlan glanced around him, his gaze darting from face to face in the crowd of shoppers. When his view fell upon Douglas, he paled noticeably. "Dougie, get along back to the loom. We start a new cloth on the morrow. Tie and weight the warp in the pattern we discussed."

"But you said I could see the market."

Parlan's expression changed from that of gentle teacher to uncompromising master. "Go."

The corners of the young apprentice's mouth drooped with disappointment, but he nodded and withdrew, his feet retracing the steps he'd just taken.

Parlan turned his glare on Morag. "Are you mad? How dare you involve me in such a quest?"

"Follow your lad, if that is your wont," she responded. "I ask your aid only because as head of the weavers' guild, you would surely recognize the talents of your best craftsmen."

She did not mention the past; nor did she wield her claim as his daughter. Thinking of him merely as guild master was easier than stirring up those old memories. It meant less anger in her belly, less pain in her heart. And truthfully, she did not want him to think that all would be forgiven if he did her a good deed—her resentment ran too deep for that. He had never once sent word to her after abandoning her and her mother.

She returned his stare, calm and even.

He drew a deep breath and let it out slowly. "Show me the cloth."

"I do not have it," she admitted. "If you are willing to examine it, I will meet you later, in a place of your choosing, to show it to you."

A wave of obvious relief washed over his face. "Meet me at the alehouse in Beggar's Close tomorrow eve. I'll look at it then."

"Thank you, Master Parlan."

He nodded and turned to leave, but then changed his mind. "A woman should not come alone to an alehouse," he said. "It will raise undue attention."

"I will take proper care," said Morag.

Her father departed, and she returned to her spot in the stall. Wulf might not be happy to learn she'd spoken to the master weaver about the cloth, but surely he would applaud the result. And if Wulf had already discovered the maker of the cloth, they need not go to the alehouse at all.

Morag wiped damp palms on the woolen skirts of her overdress. With any luck, the topic of Parlan's relationship to her would never surface in the conversation. Wulf was not the sort to leave a stone unturned or a field unplowed. Given the merest hint, he would soon discover the extent of her sordid past, and he already had cause to pity her. And it was all too easy to imagine him reaching across the table to grab Parlan's throat and demand some form of recompense for his desertion of his daughter.

She blanched.

No. Better that Wulf never discover her secret.

Mathias the dyer was easy to find. There were only a handful of dye houses on the north side, and his was the best known. Wulf ducked under the lintel and entered, his nose immediately assaulted by the sharp scents emanating from the dozen vats laid out before him, at least one of which he was certain contained stale wine.

A man with heavily muscled arms was stirring a vat on the left, and Wulf sought him out. "Are you Mathias?"

The man looked up. "Aye. Who be asking?"

Instead of giving his name, Wulf held up the cloak. "A weaver in the market told me you are the only dyer capable of producing this deep shade of black."

The dyer grabbed a corner of the cloak and peered at the cloth beneath the fur. "Aye, that's my dye."

"This is a very fine garment, crafted by a clothier with obvious skill. The weave is tight and even, and the fur pelts are sewn with great attention to detail. Surely you would remember selling wool to a maker of such finery?"

Mathias stopped stirring. "If you seek to find the owner of that cloak, you've come to the wrong place. I dye wool. That is my trade, and I'm skilled enough to make a fair living. But I do not make note of who buys my wool. I sell a lot of black wool, much of it to traders from Leith, who ship it all over Scotland. There is no way to know who made that cloak, not from its color."

It was the answer Wulf had expected, but disappointment still settled heavy on his shoulders.

If the weaver was not from Edinburgh, the cloak would not be a useful clue to determining its owner. He thanked Mathias for his honesty, and left the dye house. The cool air outside was a balm to his chest, and he sucked in several deep breaths, coughing out the bitter stench of the dyes.

Back to the market.

It was hard to shake the feeling that someone was watching them, that the man in black had thus far been one step ahead of their every move. Wulf's hand sought the rough surface of his staghorn dirk. If the cloak could not be traced to its owner, they would go back to the sigil. He remembered the arms quite clearly and could draw them, if necessary. Such a drawing could not be used as proof, but it would still identify their assailant. So long as the arms were familiar to someone.

Wulf turned down a narrow wynd.

The only person in sight was a solitary man standing at the far end of the lane, but Wulf's hand tightened on his knife. In a town as busy as Edinburgh, no one stood. Everyone had a task, even if it was simply hawking goods from an archway. This man stood in the middle of the wynd, waiting.

For Wulf, presumably.

Wulf continued to walk forward, measuring every step, eyeing every archway for more assailants. Where there was one rat, there were usually more.

The man waiting for him had shoulder-length blond hair and wore the red-and-gold tabard of the king's guard. He was also carrying a sword, which left Wulf at a disadvantage. The arrogant set of the blond man's shoulders and his solid stance told Wulf he was trained to the long blade and would likely wield it with finesse.

To his left, in the shadows of a doorway, Wulf spied a soldier. A glance to the right confirmed there was another on the opposite side. Both carried swords, and both were primed for attack. Wulf's heartbeat slowed and his thoughts settled into the cool calm of battle. Surviving this ambush would require that he set his opponents on their ears. And swiftly. Without taking his eyes off the blond man, Wulf took a quick step to the left, jabbed his knife into one soldier's thigh, and disarmed him. A well-placed pommel strike to the head rendered the man unconscious.

With a short blade in one hand and a sword in the other, Wulf rolled the body into the street, and claimed the doorway as his. The others could come to him.

And they did.

The soldier across the wynd attacked without pause, cutting downward at Wulf's shoulder. When the man was fully committed to his swing, Wulf sidestepped the sharp blade and stabbed his knife deep into the man's forearm.

The soldier screamed and the sword fell.

Taking advantage of the man's instinctive glance at his wound, Wulf slammed the flat of his hilt into the man's face and took him out of the battle. With the odds greatly improved, he kicked the fallen soldier behind him and faced the blond man. This one did not rush in. He trod slowly, his blade held low and loose, his stance ready. There was no weakness in the hold his opponent had on his blade, no anger or fear to leverage. Just quiet, confident amusement.

"I was told you were courageous," the blond man said. "I'm pleased to see that the tales were true. There is no joy in defeating a faintheart."

Wulf did not waste breath on a reply. Why would he care one whit what a scurrilous rat thought of him? His time was better spent considering the man's stance and determining which sword master might have schooled him. Each master had moves he was partial to, and if anticipated, those moves lost power. But the man's stance gave nothing away. If he had studied with a master, he had adapted the moves to his own style, which would make him a challenging opponent.

Wulf had been tutored by a Frankish sword master, and he had honed his skills with the gallowglass mercenaries of Ireland. He knew that much of his past, even though he could not name the men who had instructed him. He also knew that his skills had been tested many times—so many times that he no longer had to think about how he would move or what defense was best in any given situation. His reactions were ingrained, and he was confident that no matter what his enemy did, he could combat it.

Only his lame leg was a true disadvantage.

The blond man smiled. "Shout for help, if you choose," he said. "It's unlikely anyone will interfere." He tapped his tabard with the hilt of his knife. "'Tis the duty of the king's guard to keep the peace."

Wulf's answer was to swing his sword.

The blond man reacted quickly, parrying the cut and sliding away. "You're strong," he said. "Like a bull. Unfortunately, your technique is equally graceless and beastlike. So much wasted effort." He made a lightning-fast thrust, coming within inches of Wulf's chest before being turned away by Wulf's blade.

Wulf weighed his options. The blond man was small and quick, which would cede him the advantage in a long, drawn-out battle. Wulf's leg would not withstand a lengthy encounter. This duel would need to be won with strength.

"It may interest you to know," the blond man said, "that after I slay you, I've been ordered to cut the heart out of your female companion."

A cold lump landed in the pit of Wulf's belly.

Morag would be defenseless against this cur. He could not leave her to face him on her own. No matter what it took, he had to win this battle. But allowing his fear for Morag's safety to take hold of his thoughts would play directly into this man's hands. Fear and anger were not weapons; they were weaknesses. He had failed Elen and Hugh because of his anger and grief. Letting history repeat itself would be a grave mistake. Wulf sucked in a slow breath, pushing aside the maelstrom of his thoughts. Nothing mattered except for this moment, this battle. The time to think of what lay beyond was after this man was beaten.

With his mind cleared, Wulf immediately felt lighter and more able. His shoulders loosened and his muscles warmed. Without effort several moves came to mind, and he selected one. He saw exactly what he would have to do to break through his opponent's defenses. And then he struck.

Power and finesse met speed and agility.

Parry met thrust; cut met slash.

It was a dance of lethal, razor-sharp blades, and Wulf fell back on the reliability of his experience. He'd been here before, in a similar duel, and come out the winner.

Step in, slash, pivot.

Parry, thrust, block.

Wulf hit his opponent hard, slamming the full weight of his large body into every blow. He left nothing behind for later. Pound after pound reverberated up his opponent's blade, and he could see the toll the blows were taking in the grimaces of the other man.

But his foe was not without strategy.

The blond man focused his attack on Wulf's left side, forcing him to lean heavily on his weak leg.

The muscles in Wulf's thigh quivered under the strain, but he ignored the burning pain as best he could. His opponent was also strained. White flesh around his lips and beaded sweat on his brow encouraged Wulf to press even harder. The fury of his attack was such that the air around his blade hummed with the power of his swings.

The blond man gave up a foot of ground, and Wulf advanced.

It was only when he caught sight of the smile on his opponent's face that Wulf realized he'd been lured forward by a ruse of weariness. Two more soldiers leapt forward from behind the wall at his back and he suddenly found himself surrounded.

Chapter 9

Morag sold her last bolt of cloth at an unimaginable profit.

Two tailors had appeared before her stall at the same time, both proclaiming her cloth to be just what they were seeking. The two men bickered over who was the worthiest for some time, slowly driving up the price. In the end, one of them paid a full six deniers for the green-black-and-white cloth. She paid her stallmate his share and pocketed the rest.

Happy with how the day had gone, she sat near the cart quite contentedly, waiting for Wulf to return. That was when she noticed the sandy-haired lad across the High Street. He was slight of build and in sore need of a bath, so she barely took note of him in the beginning. But he remained nearby, watching her surreptitiously from behind a barrel of salted pork.

Each time she caught his eye, he pretended to wander off, but he didn't go far.

Curious, Morag crossed the street and confronted him. "Why are you watching me?"

"I'm no' watching you," he protested.

She crossed her arms over her chest and pinned his gaze with steely purpose. "Is someone paying you to spy on me?"

"Nay," he said. "Course not. What kind of fool job would that be?"

His cheeks turned a furious shade of red, which was visible even beneath the streaks of grime on his face. He did not seem a very worrisome spy, not the sort an assassin would hire.

"Was it a very large man who set you on me?" she asked. "Wearing a lèine and a multicolored brat?"

The flush in his cheeks deepened. "I'm no' watching you."

Morag took his arm. "Take me to him. This very instant."

The boy dug in his heels. "Nay."

She fished about in her purse and pulled out a ha'penny. "Take me to him and you'll earn your coin."

His gaze locked onto the coin. "He'll not be happy that I've been found out."

Aware that the arm she was holding was painfully thin, Morag gentled her grip. "Fear not; he's not the sort to throw his fist about. I'll make certain he knows what a fine job you've done."

The fight drained out of him and he nodded.

"Now show me where he is," Morag urged.

The moment he realized he was surrounded, Wulf leapt back and to the right, thrusting the blade of his sword backward under his arm. The sword went deep into one of the soldiers. Wulf then spun the wounded man around, using the soldier's faltering body as protection. With a quick toss of his dirk, he took down the second soldier, too.

But the maneuvers cost him.

The blond man took advantage of Wulf's split concentration and attacked. His sword sliced across Wulf's right thigh, tearing into the muscle and flesh with ruthless aim.

It took every bit of willpower Wulf possessed to launch himself to the left and save his leg.

The battle was once again one-on-one, but Wulf was bleeding now. The doorway was at his back, his foe pacing in front of him with a satisfied smile.

"I had hoped this would be a challenging duel," the blond man said. "Sadly, you are only half the man I thought you were."

"I feel no shame. Were it just the two of us," Wulf said, "you'd already be lying in the sod."

The wound on his leg was shallow, but a steady rivulet of blood trailed down his leg. Blood loss would soon make his head swim. He needed to end the battle swiftly and decisively, while he still had the strength to make a killing blow. He knew his opponent as well as he would ever know him.

The moment was now. Wulf attacked.

Morag knew what she would see before she turned the corner. The clang of steel against steel and the slither of sharp blades passing along their edges were all too recently played in her ear. She grabbed the young lad by both shoulders, stared him firmly in the eyes, and said, "Fetch help. Quickly now."

The boy took off, but she wasn't convinced he would return. Morag peered around the wattle fence into the narrow wynd. What she saw was chaos. At least three bodies lying in the dirt, and Wulf covered in blood, dueling for his life.

Fearing the sight of her would distract him, she pulled back. She needed to seek help, but where? The castle guard might save him only to arrest him. But surely that was better than watching him die?

She darted across the street and up the next lane. A pair of guards were often standing at the entrance to the north gate. If only she could—

She barreled into a man coming around the corner. A tall fellow with shoulder-length dark hair, blackened mail, and a gold cloak. She nearly lost her footing when they collided, but he put out a quick hand and steadied her.

"Hold, lass," he said gruffly. "Where are you headed in such a hurry?"

Morag grabbed his arm. "My husband has been attacked. Please, sir, I beg you: Help me."

The man took one look at her face and made up his mind. "Show me."

Praying she wasn't too late, Morag lifted her skirts and ran back to the narrow wynd where she'd left Wulf, the stranger running at her heels.

Wulf stumbled, nearly falling to one knee in the blood-smeared dirt. His shoulders sank, heavy with defeat, and he sensed his opponent coming in for the coup de grâce. With a roar of raw determination, he pushed back to his feet and made one final flurry of cuts and slices. But his opponent played it safe, staying just beyond solid striking distance. Clearly he preferred to wait until Wulf was too weak to fight.

With his last thrust, Wulf's boot slid out from under him and he fell heavily, landing prone on the ground. He swiftly planted his sword and struggled to rise, but could not gain purchase in the wet sand. Facedown in a pool of his own blood, he tasted the end.

Ironically, it was his blood that saved him. He caught a brief reflection of his opponent as he swooped in, both hands on the hilt of his blade. When the man was balanced over him, and Wulf was certain the death blow was nigh, he nimbly rolled to one side and thrust his blade upward with great force.

He had the longer reach, and his blade buried itself under the blond man's left arm inches before his opponent's blade hit the dirt.

His opponent's eyes went wide as he realized he'd been fooled.

As always when his blade took another man's life, Wulf felt a moment's pause. He lowered the blond man to the ground and withdrew his sword. Death was never a punishment to be dealt lightly, even when the choices were limited. As the light of life faded from the other man's eyes, Wulf sighed.

He pushed to his feet. His injured leg was still bleeding and he bent to claim a strip of linen from one of the downed soldiers—one of the two he'd struck with his sword pommel. Both men remained motionless and would likely require the services of a healer.

As he tied the linen about his leg, Morag arrived. She fell to her knees at his side, pushing his hands away and taking over the task of wrapping the linen. "Thank God you're all right. I thought for certain I'd be calling for the grave digger."

He leaned against the wooden door and allowed Morag to tend to his wounds. How she had found him, he couldn't fathom. But he was too weary to wonder long.

"Your wife suggested you were about to meet

your maker," a male voice said dryly. "But I see you had matters well in hand."

Wulf stiffened as he met the gaze of a dark-haired man in a fur-lined cloak and brocade tunic. The man's boots cost more than any single possession Wulf owned. How would he explain what had happened to such a man? Especially when the men wore the tabards of the king's guard?

"These men are impostors," he said firmly, hoping surety would lend weight to his tale. "They made no attempt to query me or arrest me."

"Really?" The dark-haired man pushed over the body of the blond swordsman, frowning. "You appear to be right. I recognize this one. A hoodlum recently escaped from the castle dungeon."

"I made an effort to avoid slaying them all."

"So I see," the other man said, as one of the men finally stirred. "Very generous of you, under the circumstances."

Despite the hint of humor he detected, Wulf was still wary. "Wulf Cameron of Braemar," he said, extending his hand.

The dark-haired man accepted his hand with a smile. "William Dunkeld."

"Brother to the king," Wulf added. Once again, a heretofore unknown fact had popped into his thoughts. His memories were truly a strange brew.

Dunkeld shrugged. "I am indeed, but born on the wrong side of the blanket."

Morag finished tying up Wulf's leg and stood up. She offered Dunkeld a broad smile. "A gentleman by any measure tonight, sir. You answered my call without hesitation, and for that I am eternally grateful."

"It is your husband who is the hero, good woman. He defended himself most ably."

Wulf glanced at the five bodies on the ground. "I must make a report to the constable, I merit."

Dunkeld shook his head. "Have a physician see to that leg. I'll fetch the constable and explain what happened. As I said, he'll be familiar with this particular villain and will require little support from you to serve the records."

Wulf frowned. It seemed a miracle to be able to walk away without facing the authorities.

"Truly," Dunkeld said. "Tell me where you are staying, if you wish, and I will inform the constable. If he has need to speak with you, he can seek you out."

Wulf gave Dunkeld the address of their room and thanked him again. Then he and Morag hobbled back to the candlemaker's.

"A fine man, the king's brother," Morag said. "I would not have expected a nobleman to come to the aid of the likes of us."

"Indeed." Before they entered the candlemaker's shop, Wulf ceased leaning on Morag and carried his own weight. "And we are quite fortunate it was he who chanced upon us—few others would have believed the dead men were not the king's guards. But William Dunkeld commands a garrison of the king's guard."

Morag preceded him up the stairs to their room. "They were minions of the man in black, I presume?"

"They did not introduce themselves," Wulf said dryly. "But I'm not a great believer in chance."

"Sit down," Morag ordered as she closed the door. "Let me properly tend to that leg."

"Nay," he said. "I fear it may be time to return to Dunstoras. The cloak cannot be easily traced, and the danger of remaining in the burgh is high."

She put a cool hand on his brow. "Are you feverish? Did you truly suggest we turn tail and run?"

He skewed her a hard stare. His true desire was to continue the search for the sigil. But . . . "Keeping you safe may be more challenging than I anticipated."

"Ah, so you retreat for me? How sweet. You make my heart stir."

She flattened her hand on his chest and pushed. It was not nearly the force required to move a man of his size, but Wulf allowed himself to be guided to the mattress. Seeing her freckled face alive and well, knowing that he had succeeded in protecting her, left a warm feeling in his chest that far outweighed the ache in his leg.

As she peeled back the bloodstained linen and bent over his thigh, he smoothed a hand over her black hair. "You are beautiful," he declared.

One of her eyebrows lifted. "More beautiful today than yesterday?"

"Nay." He frowned. "The same."

She poured a bit of whiskey over the wound, and he grimaced. "Do you find disfavor with my response? Are you vexed?"

"What cause would I have to be vexed?"

A good question. To which he had no answer. He'd barely seen her all day. "None. Yet you seem a wee bit put out."

She wrapped his leg with a clean linen strip, tied it neatly, and then stood up. "You very nearly died today," she said, taking her flint from her purse and making a fire in the hearth.

"But I did not," he pointed out.

"A fact for which I am most grateful," she said. "But I willingly admit the notion of your passing is a distressing one. I am not vexed. I am simply aware that this night might have ended very differently."

"Come here," he commanded her.

She came to him, but her expression was uncertain.

When she stood between his parted legs, he took her hands in his. They were soft and gentle, like the woman herself. Morag made such a fine show of being strong and carefree that even he occasionally forgot that it was all a facade. "Lass, I've vowed to remain by your side the whole of this journey. It will take more than a madman with a sword to make me break my vow. You ken?"

She smiled. All the way to her lovely green eyes.

"The timing of your death is not within your control, Wulf MacCurran. No matter how strong your will."

"I disagree," he said. "You must have faith that I'll not leave you unprotected. 'Tis my duty to see you properly cared for, and I'll not let you down."

"Even if we must stay in Edinburgh another day?"

He rubbed his thumbs over her knuckles, loving the tenderness of her skin against the roughness of his. "Do we have a reason to stay?"

She nodded. "Master Parlan has agreed to examine the cloak. He knows well the work of the weavers in his guild, and he may be able to identify the maker of the cloak."

Wulf's hands tightened on Morag's. "You should not have made any such inquiries. The man in black is clearly watching our every move."

She shrugged. "I spoke to the head of the weavers' guild and I am a weaver. There is nothing sinister in that. We agreed to meet at an alehouse to discuss the cloak."

"Tonight?"

"Nay, on the morrow."

Wulf lifted Morag's hands and kissed the knuckles on one hand and then the other. Remaining in the burgh was risky. Were it only him, he would stay without qualm, but he had Morag to protect. Yet, how could he deny a valuable clue to his enemies' identity?

"We'll stay," he said. "But you'll not return to the market. You must remain at my side."

Sliding to her knees and leaning into him, she closed the gap between their faces to mere inches. It was an intimate pose, and Wulf's blood heated instinctively, forging a fiery trail through his body.

"Remaining at your side," she said huskily, "is not the hardship you imagine." Her lips found the edge of his jaw. The kiss she bestowed on him was sweet, soft . . . and hot.

Wulf swallowed. "What of your cloth?"

"Sold," she whispered, kissing her way to his neck. "All of it."

He closed his eyes and drank in her uniquely feminine scent. Like heather blooms in late summer, it was equal parts sweet and spicy. Need coursed through his body, making him hard. He wanted her so badly, he was choking on his desire.

"What a shame it would have been." Her teeth found his earlobe and she nibbled.

A ripple of sensation ran through him, raising goose bumps on his flesh. "What?" he croaked.

"Had we both died today without knowing each other as we are meant to," she said, her breath hot against his neck.

Wulf released her hands, his palms damp with unrequited desire. There was a truth to her words that he could not deny. They were fated to be together; his gut was certain of it. But so many issues remained to be resolved before he could claim her. . . .

"It might well be my last wish that we lie together," she said. "Would you truly deny me?"

A snort of laughter escaped his lips. "You would sink so low as to claim a deathbed wish?"

She pouted. "I will use whatever means I must to make you see reason. We are neither of us chaste. There is no valid cause to eschew our desire."

Wulf cupped her head in both hands, forcing her to meet his gaze. "Our first time together will be all the sweeter for our denial."

"We've already waited months," she said, grimacing. "The sweetest moment is right now." Pulling his hands away, she pressed a hard kiss upon his lips.

Her frustration was understandable, and he let her have her way for a while. He was just about to push her gently away when her tactics changed. The kiss softened from discontented attack to sensual play. She sucked his bottom lip into her mouth and nibbled on it.

A jolt of intense need went straight from his mouth to his groin.

Her tongue entered his mouth, sliding along his, then dancing away to tease the hot throb of his chewed lip. Wulf's head swam. Every inch of his skin came alive with desperate want. The need to feel her against him, flesh to flesh, was echoed in every pounding of his heartbeat.

"Make me yours," she said on a ragged sigh.

For a moment he resisted. She deserved so much more than a night on a candlemaker's mattress. But in the next breath, he remembered the painful feeling he'd endured in the wynd when the realization had struck him that he might die. Life could be snatched away in an instant. Aye, Morag deserved to know the full extent of his love for her.

"You are mine, Morag Cameron," he said. "And I am yours."

Then he rolled her onto the mattress and seized the moment. If tonight was all they had, he would make it worthy of a lifetime.

As Wulf rolled her back against the mattress and covered her with his hard body, a moan of pure delight rumbled in Morag's throat. The solid weight of him, tempered by his obvious care not to crush her, brought a sweet ache to her heart, even as it fluttered with excitement.

How long had she dreamed of this moment?

Too often to recall. And none of those dreams measured up to reality. Wulf was not a timid lover. He was the man she caught glimpses of whenever he forgot momentarily that his leg was injured and his memories were gone—strong and sure and confident.

He grabbed her hands, threaded his fingers with hers, then forced them above her head. With her body pinned to the mattress, barely able to move, he proceeded to ravish her. The sweet assault on her senses began with her mouth—hot lips fiercely demanding all she had to give—but did not stop there. One of his knees pushed between her legs, and his heavily muscled thigh exerted a firm but gentle dance of pressure against her mons.

A thousand tiny sparks of pleasure shot through her body with every press, and Morag nearly swooned with ecstasy. Her fingers clenched around his and she writhed against the mattress. A yearning so deep it seemed impossible to satisfy bloomed hot and heavy in her belly, and her entire body burned.

She wanted him inside her. Nay, *needed* him inside her. The sweet ache demanded it.

Morag lifted her hips off the mattress, meeting his press with an earthy appeal of her own. Her gown was a nuisance, a barrier between her and a fulfillment that she was desperate to see met.

As his lips left hers and claimed the tender skin beneath her ear, she sucked in a ragged breath and implored, "Unclothe me."

She would have been more specific, but the gentle bite of his teeth on her earlobe stole all rational thought. A mewl of raw need was all she could manage.

But he granted her wish.

Releasing her hands, his fingers adroitly found the hem of her gown, and with a smooth yank he tugged it and her sark up and off. Morag swiftly did the same for him, tossing his lèine aside and running her hands over the naked expanse of his shoulders and chest.

Was there ever a man more finely made?

None that she had seen.

He was not perfection—too many scars marred his smooth flesh for that—but he was an ideal man just the same. Broad shoulders above a muscled chest and stomach that put most other men to shame. All that wood chopping and hiking through the glen had banished the softness he'd developed during his recovery.

Morag's gaze lifted to Wulf's face.

As much as she admired his form, it was his face she loved most. When driven to anger, he could cultivate as fierce a mien as she had ever seen, but at this moment, every sharp angle, every taut muscle, every glint of his gaze reflected desire.

Desire for *her*.

It was not the first time she'd seen desire on his face—he was open in his admiration for her—but it was the first time she'd seen that desire unrestrained. And the unmitigated heat of it thrilled her right to her toes. His eyes were like hot coals.

Morag lay back on the mattress and smiled at him. "Do you like what you see?"

He did not smile in return. "Like? Nay."

She scowled at him. "You lack charm, sir."

Leaning in, he kissed the tip of one breast and then the other. "Adore would come close, but even that word does not do my admiration justice."

Her irritation fell away. "You are forgiven then." She slid her hands up his arms, savoring the hills and valleys of his shape. The ropelike pattern created by the firelight was entrancing. "I'm getting cold. Come warm me."

He slid his body alongside hers, his heat immediately banishing the chill of the air. Their legs entwined without conscious thought, and he picked up a lock of her hair, lifting it to his nose. "Everything about you is bonny, lass. From tip to toe. Even the way you smell."

The light play with her hair sent a thrill down her spine, and Morag shivered with delight. At this moment, with the knowledge that they had survived and the future seeming bright, it was almost possible to believe he was truly hers. She certainly wanted it to be so. Perhaps he was right, and they could find a way to make it work.

She closed her eyes.

For tonight, at any rate, she was going to believe. Tonight he was hers and hers alone. There was no past, no pointing fingers, no shame.

Opening her eyes again, she stared into his gaze.

He ran a finger along her cheekbone and down to her lips. The roughness of his skin was a delightful contrast to her softness, sending another shiver of need coursing through her body. She opened her mouth and encircled his finger, sucking on it. Her tongue dallied with the tip, while her eyes made sinful promises.

A faint smile curved his lips.

"You, lass, are a tease."

She released his finger, and sank her hands into his thick hair, pulling his face toward hers. "Nay, not a tease. Never that." She kissed him hard. "I mean every kiss I give."

He returned the kiss with heated passion and a wild hunger that was barely restrained. His mouth plundered hers, a deeply sensual act that was both a taking and a giving.

One of his hands found her breast, plumping and squeezing the swollen weight until Morag thought she might die of want. Just when the tension in her belly was bow-tight, he transferred his mouth from her lips to her nipple, and Morag squealed.

Her feminine parts grew hot and damp, and she wriggled suggestively against Wulf's thigh. She wanted more. She wanted all of him.

And Wulf delivered. His hand slipped down between her legs, his thumb rubbing circles on her mons while his fingers tested her readiness. The firm swirls of his thumb were masterful. Ripple after ripple of glorious pleasure racked her body, shortening her breath and bringing her closer and closer to the pinnacle of her desire.

Thrashing with need, she gripped the sheets with a tight hand. "Aye, Wulf. *Aye*."

He sank three fingers inside her, even as his thumb continued its teasing play.

And the wave of desire crashed over Morag, sending her reeling. Every inch of her body rejoiced and her feminine parts hummed.

Wulf kissed her gently.

When the ripples subsided and Morag opened her eyes again, he brushed the damp hairs from her face. "I've never seen you more beautiful than this very moment."

She smiled. "Och, now. That's only because you've never seen me swived."

A chuckle broke from his lips. "Are you game, then?"

"Aye. I like a man who finishes what he starts."

He nudged her legs wider apart and gave her a wicked grin. Positioning himself at the apex of her thighs, he drove in hard and deep.

Morag took him fully, wrapping her legs around him as he entered, and lifting her hips to give him all that she had. Heart and soul.

As he was with everything, Wulf was a skilled lover. He wove delight through her as ably as she wove cloth—with a series of smooth, deep strokes that reached some hidden spot inside her and made her body sing. A thin film of sweat broke out on both their bodies as he pumped into her and ground against her mons.

The tension in her belly grew again, promising an even bigger release. Morag urged Wulf on with her heels and soft, eager moans. In perfect unison, breath equally ragged, they met each other stroke for stroke and beat for beat. When they reached the peak, they reached it together. The sound of Wulf's low growl of satisfaction was all it took to send Morag spiraling into oblivion.

As she slowly came back to the moment, Morag snuggled close to Wulf's body. The solid thump of his heart echoed in her ear, and she found true contentment for the first time since her father had deserted them.

Love truly could heal wounds.

Chapter 10

Dunkeld strode down the corridor, his gold cape flapping behind him. MacCurran had not recognized him. There had been nothing in his eyes to suggest hatred or bitterness. But the man had seen him clearly the night the queen's necklace was stolen; he was certain of it.

What kind of devilry was at play?

He had thought the throne room was empty when he entered, but as he approached the carved wooden chair with its lion feet and its seat above the squared Stone of Scone, Dunkeld spied a man standing beneath the fan of halberds hanging on the wall.

A brown-haired man with a cup of wine in hand.

"Your Grace," Dunkeld said, offering a bow.

His brother waved at the side table. "I am indulging in a glass of fine French wine," he said. "Join me."

Dunkeld poured himself a glass. "I thought you were headed for Kinghorn."

Alexander nodded. "I had hoped to depart today, but my council is insisting on a review of the succession plan. The earls descend upon Edinburgh as we speak."

"Are matters not settled?" Dunkeld took his cup across the room and ran a hand over the arm of the throne. "Have they not already agreed that young Princess Margaret is your heir?"

"They have," the king acknowledged. "But with Yolande quick with child, they are eager to name a new heir. One who is already on Scottish soil and not the offspring of a hated Norse raider."

"What is there to discuss?" Dunkeld asked. "If a child is born to Yolande, you will have a new heir."

Alexander nodded. "They fight over who would guide that heir during the minority should I pass prematurely, as my father did."

Our father, Dunkeld was tempted to snap. But he held his tongue, as he'd done for so many years. Because the best reward would be seeing the look on his brother's face when he realized all his offspring were in the grave, and he was at Dunkeld's mercy.

"Fear not," Dunkeld said. "I am, as always, willing to serve Alba."

Alexander's smile faltered. "We've discussed this, William. I cannot name you a guardian of Scotland. The earls are reluctant to see a chance-bairn of my father gain influence over the throne. Had he acknowledged you, it would be different. But he did not."

Hot rage seared through Dunkeld's veins, and his fingers clenched around the arm of the throne. He was the eldest son. It should be he who sat upon the Stone of Destiny, not Alexander. His mother was no serving girl; she was the daughter of an earl. A Comyn. He had been born to her *after* the childless Queen Joan had passed and *before* his father's marriage to Marie de Coucy. She and his father had never been wed, but the pope would have granted legitimacy to him and his sister Marjorie had MacCurran not interfered.

Dunkeld forced himself to release the arm of the throne and turn slowly to face his brother.

"You could sway them, if you chose."

"There is no need," Alexander said. "You already hold a privileged position in my retinue."

Aye. As lackey and bootlicker. But those roles would not satisfy him any longer. "My desire is only to see Scotland avoid the turmoil a lack of clear heir would cause," he said smoothly. "The bickering among the earls prior to your birth was unprecedented."

Alexander nodded and took a long swallow of wine. A sad look passed over his face. "To see two sons in the grave is a blow beyond imagining. I never thought to find myself without a male heir."

Forcing a sympathetic frown to his face, Dunkeld left the throne and walked to his brother's side. He put a gentle hand on his shoulder. "A tragedy, to be sure. But I'm confident Yolande carries a son."

The king covered Dunkeld's hand with his own. "I pray that you are right."

"She is young and healthy. And Father produced a son late in his life. There can be no doubt."

Alexander turned away and placed his cup of wine on the table. "She has brought me back from the edge of despair," he admitted. "Her beauty and grace have enthralled me, and if she delivers a son, I will honor her as no king has honored his queen before."

Staring at the king's back, Dunkeld barely contained a grimace. Alexander imagined himself in love with Yolande, and had spent countless hours in her company—and in her bed. Dunkeld did not see the woman's appeal. Her English was poor, and she was constantly chattering to her handmaidens in French. And she was too thin.

But none of that would matter in a few days.

When Yolande and her unborn child were dead, his brother would turn to him for solace—as he had done upon the deaths of his two sons. That would be the moment to press the issue of adding Dunkeld to the list of successors. Not now.

"We shall all honor her," Dunkeld said, raising his glass. "Long live the king."

It was clear that MacCurran had to die. Whether or not he had recognized Dunkeld, only a fool would allow such an obvious risk to his future to exist. He knew where MacCurran was staying—the man had kindly given him that information—and now it was time to tighten the noose about the miserable wretch's neck. And raise his estimation in the eyes of the king at the same time.

"I have some rather encouraging news, sire," he said. "I've stymied a MacCurran plot against your life. One of the MacCurran's finest warriors has been found hiding in the burgh. He slayed a number of your guards in north town this day, but his arrest is imminent."

Alexander frowned. "Here in Edinburgh?"

"I'm afraid so. Their boldness knows no bounds, Your Grace."

"You serve me well, brother. As always." He crossed the room to Dunkeld's side and laid a hand on his shoulder. "A strong message must be sent to those who would do us injury. A public hanging is warranted, I believe."

Dunkeld smiled.

"I would agree, sire. I'll make the necessary arrangements."

At the first stomp of boots on the stairs, Wulf rolled from his bed and snatched up his sword from the floor. His wound throbbed, but his immediate thought was for Morag's safety.

"Lass," he called quietly. "Rise up."

She sat up, her black hair spilling over her naked shoulders. "What is it?"

"Do as I say, quickly now," he said. "Take the blanket and your gown and go out the window. Move swiftly. Head for Dunstoras and don't look back. You ken?"

Boot steps echoed in the hallway.

Morag surged to her feet and rushed for the window. Although she was rarely without a word of argument, this night she did exactly as he bade and climbed out the window without a fuss. She dropped to the dirt just as the door to their chamber burst open and six armed guards poured into the tiny room.

Like the men he'd fought in the wynd, these men also wore the tabard of the king's guard, but this time no one drew a sword. They merely put hands to hilts and readied themselves for battle. One of the guards addressed him.

"Wulf MacCurran, lay down your weapon. By

order of the king, you are to be taken to Edinburgh Castle, where you will be held until your hanging for crimes against the crown."

He eyed the soldiers one by one and debated his chances for escape.

The captain of the guard accurately guessed his thoughts. "I have another dozen guards downstairs. Escape is impossible. Come quietly, or we will be delivering you to the castle in a shroud."

Wulf laid his sword on the floor and kicked it behind him. Going peacefully would allow Morag the chance to properly disappear. She was a resourceful lass, and with any luck she'd hire a man to take her back to Dunstoras to share the news of his capture with Aiden.

Two guards grabbed his arms and roped them behind his back. They allowed him to slip his feet into his boots, and then they marched him down the stairs and out of the candlemaker's shop.

The candlemaker shook his head as Wulf passed. "An outlaw. I thought myself a good judge of face."

The night was still dark, and although Wulf quickly scanned the wynd for sign of Morag, he saw nothing. He prayed that she'd made good her escape and was now well away from the shop. The candlemaker would not hesitate to call for the authorities if he spotted her.

But where would she go? Whom would she turn to for help?

Wulf closed his eyes briefly.

It would not do him well to worry. Morag had survived years on her own in the woods. He had to have faith that she would find her way to Dunstoras.

Else he would go quite mad.

A gown, a thick woolen brat, and a fat purse. Morag grimaced as she assessed her possessions. A pair of boots would have been nice, as her toes were like ice, but boots could be bought. The door to the candlemaker's shop opened, and she flattened herself against the wall of the neighboring bothy, grateful that the bright March moon cast long shadows.

The soldiers marched Wulf down the street. He stood a head taller than all of them, his shoulders broad and sure despite the lack of brat. Although her fear for his safety was a hard lump in her belly, she was proud of the image he presented as they led him away. Had any prisoner ever looked so fierce and undaunted?

With her bottom lip between her teeth, she watched until he disappeared around the corner. The last bit of warm feeling vanished with him, and she tugged the brat tighter around her shoulders. She had to do something—but what?

It was yet the middle of the night. Good citizens of Edinburgh were abed. She glanced at the door to the candlemaker's shop. Her boots and her spare gown were inside, along with the food she'd bought in the market. The practical side of her demanded she recover those items, but her gut said attempting to do so would be too risky.

The candlemaker would throw her to the wolves if he caught her. He owed her no loyalty. Especially now that he thought Wulf an enemy of the crown. The king was beloved here. As a young man, he'd refused to swear allegiance to the English king, and that had made him a hero to most Scots. The candlemaker wouldn't care that Wulf was falsely accused. Nor would he care that Morag was justly due the belongings left in their room. He would happily sell their goods and pocket the coin.

Were it not for the black wolf cloak, Morag would have walked away from the candlemaker's shop and never looked back. But it was their last clue to finding the man who had murdered Wulf's kin.

She tried to convince herself that the cloak had been confiscated by the guards, but she did not believe it. None of the soldiers had been holding satchels as they marched down the lane. It was still in their room; she was certain of it. But how could she retrieve it?

As she watched, the candles in the window went out. The candlemaker and his wife had returned to bed.

She could not climb back through the window she had escaped from—it was too high above the ground. The only way in was through the front door, but the candlemaker and his wife slept in a bed to the right of the large vats of tallow. Creeping past them would not be an easy feat.

Her feet like icicles, Morag hopped the fence between the two bothies and made her way back to the courtyard behind the candlemaker's shop. The shutters on the window she had escaped from hung open, just as she'd left them—a temptation that called to her.

If only she were taller . . .

A quick search of the courtyard proved there was no convenient ladder lying about . . . but there *was* a rain barrel. Unfortunately, it was half-full of water and beyond Morag's strength to lift. Her attempt only rolled it an inch to one side.

Morag straightened and studied the barrel.

Perhaps that was the answer—walking it instead of lifting it. If she could aim the barrel in the general direction of the window, turn it one way and then the other, she might be able to maneuver it into position.

Morag put her back into the effort.

Tipping the barrel was easier than lifting it, but it was still extremely heavy. It rolled only a few inches each time she tried. Sweat beaded on her brow and dampened her sark under her arms as she labored, but she slowly made progress toward the window.

The good news was that her toes were no longer freezing. The bad news was that the sky in the east had begun to lighten, heralding the advent of dawn. If she didn't hurry, there would soon be witnesses to her raid.

Morag dug deep and found every last bit of strength she possessed. When she was close enough that she thought she might be able to leap from the barrel to the window, she stopped. Her arms were aching and her breath was ragged, but she didn't rest. She climbed atop the barrel, balancing upon the curved edge. The wood dug into the soles of her feet, but she was able to steady her balance with her bared toes. The distance to the window appeared greater than it had from the ground.

But the day continued to brighten.

Morag took a deep breath, eyed the windowsill with resolve, and launched herself into the air. She caught the windowsill with her fingers, and hung there for a moment, quite pleased with herself. Then she pulled herself up—or tried to. Her arms were exhausted from rolling the barrel, and her muscles trembled badly. She managed to pull herself halfway up before her arms gave out, and she fell to the ground.

Morag rested for a moment, her arms hanging loosely at her sides. The eastern sky was lavender now. She didn't have much more time.

One more attempt, and then she'd have to give up the cloak.

Rubbing her arms gently and walking around the water barrel at an even pace, she calmed her breathing. When her arms were no longer feeling limp and weary, she climbed the barrel again and balanced on the edge. Her legs were stronger than her arms. Her efforts would be best served by a hearty push.

Morag bent her knees a little.

In her mind's eye she saw the cloak just inside the room, waiting for her. Next to her boots.

Then she leapt.

This time she hooked her arms over the sill. She freed her feet of her skirts and used her bare toes to help her scale the wall. Combined with her slightly rested arms, it was enough to launch her over the edge. She rolled into the room, taking care not to make any loud noises.

Conscious of the passing time, she swiftly found the cloak—and Wulf's sword, which was lying on the floor, near the mattress. Then she tucked all of their belongings into a bag, stuffed her feet in her boots, and slipped back out the window. With the sword's baldric slung over her back and a heavy bag in her arms, her movements were awkward, but Morag made the best of it. She held the sword tip high as she leapt to the ground. A hint of gloom still held the day at bay, and she darted for the narrow wynd to the left.

Hugging the thinning shadows along the wall, she pondered her next move. There weren't a lot of options. Only one, really—meet her father at the alehouse in Beggar's Close and ask for his aid. But first she needed to hide her belongings and find someone to accompany her to the alehouse.

No small feat, given that she was something of a fugitive.

But she was a Highlander, and challenges that seemed impossible to others were the norm in the north. She grunted and darted across the street.

As long as she was alive, anything was possible.

Chapter 11

Wulf was treated surprisingly well, for a prisoner.

He was given a large cell with a dry floor, a comfortable pallet, and even a small table and chair. A bucket of fresh water was provided, along with a platter of bread and cheese. But it wasn't long before he discovered the reason for his pleasant treatment. One of his guards was quite talkative.

"You're to have anything you desire, within reason," the fellow said, as he handed Wulf a bowl of stew with a spoon. "The rights of a dead man. You're to hang in the public square day after tomorrow."

A chill fell over Wulf.

The day after tomorrow? That was much quicker than he'd anticipated. Two days would not be enough time for Morag to get word to Aiden. There would be no opportunity for his laird to negotiate for his freedom or arrange a rescue.

The hanging was inevitable.

Unless he could break out on his own.

Wulf scanned the confines of his cell. As fine as the accommodations were, the label of *cell* was still accurate. There were no windows or midden chutes. The only way in or out was through the locked door, and that would involve overwhelming the guard.

Worthy of an effort, to be sure.

Because sitting here waiting to die was not an option he could stomach.

Refusing to coddle his injured leg, Wulf paced his cell floor. He prayed that Morag had remained safe, and was even now on her way back to Dunstoras. His greatest regret was leaving her unprotected. The man in black was still a danger, and should any harm come to Morag, Wulf would die a bitter man.

Wulf tested the bars on his cell door. They rattled, but did not come loose. He simply needed a plan to break out, and some luck in leaving the castle. Bribing a guard would have been an option, save he had nothing to offer.

The best option, then, was to use force.

And a moment of surprise.

* * *

It was Saraid who found Morag a place to hide her belongings. The tanner's wee daughter, still grateful for the repairs to her rag doll, helped her bury the bags and Wulf's sword in a patch of old dried grass. The grass lay along a fence in a nearly deserted area of the north side, and Morag was able to hide all of her precious items in the reeds between people passing by. With Saraid promising to stand guard, Morag headed for the market.

Although she now knew several of the weavers quite well, she avoided that section of the High Street. They would not welcome trouble, and in all likelihood they would abandon her at the first hint of impropriety.

But she knew someone with fewer qualms—the young lad Wulf had hired to watch her.

He'd run off without claiming his reward, so her goal was twofold: Pay him what he was owed and make inquiries. It might be a vain hope, but based on how thin the lad had been, she was counting on finding him near the food stalls.

Drawing her brat over her head to hide her dark hair, Morag wandered through the stalls, pretending to shop. She examined neeps and cabbage, carrots and onions, all of which were looking a little thin and limp this late in the season. To ensure she did not draw the ire of the vegetable vendors she parted with a coin for two apples, and another for some hazelnuts. The apples were in sorry shape—bruised and dented—but still delicious. Morag ate one and held on to the other for appearance's sake.

After wandering the market for the better part of an hour, she failed to spot the lad, and Morag gave some thought to other options.

There were few people she could trust. She was a stranger in a strange town and unlikely to gain aid from an honest citizen. If she couldn't find the lad, she'd go back to the north side and look for help of a more scurrilous sort. The woman selling sexual favors might be an ally.

Morag was strolling past a baker's stall for the third time when she caught a glimpse of sandy hair between the baskets of bread. She halted and watched the lad deftly nab a roll and stuff it into the front of his lèine. As he sauntered nonchalantly down the lane, Morag moved to intercept him.

"Hallo, laddie," she greeted him, grabbing his arm before he could run. "You forgot to return for your coin."

He squirmed madly against her hold, but when he realized her grip was firm, he calmed. "I cannot run afoul of the castle guards. Not without ending up in the stocks."

"How did you know they were castle guards? You never looked around the corner."

He shrugged. "No one else carries a sword inside the burgh walls."

Morag held up the ha'penny she'd previously

offered him. "This is yours. You earned it." She tucked it into his hand. "But there's another just like it if you know a strapping lad who can accompany me to an alehouse."

The boy frowned. "What about your man? Did the guards slay him?"

"Nay," she said with a reassuring smile. He clearly felt guilty for running. "They tossed him in the dunny."

"Och," he said. "A shame, that."

Morag tried not to let her fears of what Wulf might be enduring show on her face. Freeing him meant proving him innocent—and the only way to do that was to find the owner of the black wolf cloak. To find the owner of the cloak, she had to meet her father in the alehouse. And to get into the alehouse to meet with her father, she had to avoid frightening this boy. "So, do you know a lad?"

He nodded. "Bran could do it."

"Would you take me to him?"

The expression on the lad's face turned sly. "Your man promised me a full penny for watching you. Pay me that, and I'll take you to Bran."

There was no way to know for certain whether the lad spoke truth or lie, but she had little difficulty imagining Wulf making such an offer—he was a wee bit too generous with his coin—so she nodded. "I'll pay you the penny . . . but only after I've met this Bran."

He wrinkled his nose.

"You've run off on me once before," she reminded him. "I've not the luxury of taking you at your word."

Two bright spots of color flagged his cheeks. "Fair enough. Let's go."

With the morning nearly done and her eventide meeting with Master Parlan swiftly approaching, Morag followed the lad into the seedier streets of Edinburgh and prayed she was not being led astray.

Wulf was seated on his bed, reliving his night with Morag in delicious detail, when he heard boot steps approaching his cell. He leapt to his feet and flattened himself along the wall next to the door. This was it—his opportunity.

A meal at midday was unexpected, but he was ready to seize the moment nonetheless. When the guard entered to deliver the tray, Wulf would overwhelm him and escape. He would need to be quick, as there was usually a second guard in the corridor, but thanks to Morag's tender ministrations his leg was mending nicely.

The boots halted and the grate of a key turning in the iron lock echoed in the cell.

Wulf tensed, ready to pounce.

"Stand where I can see you, MacCurran."

It was a voice he recognized—that of William

Dunkeld, the king's brother. Robbed of the element of surprise, Wulf stepped boldly into the candlelight. He waited until the door swung open and Dunkeld entered. Then he confronted the man. "Why let me go free only to send guards to arrest me in the middle of the night?"

Dunkeld removed his gloves, tucked them into the belt that cinched his dark green tunic, and beckoned to a guard in the corridor. The guard set a flagon of wine and two cups on the table, then departed.

"I took you at your word when I met you in the wynd," he said, pouring the wine. "But I later received a report from a baker in the market who recognized you as Wulf MacCurran, cousin to the outlaw Aiden MacCurran." He gave one cup to Wulf. "Out of concern for my brother's safety, I had no choice but to have you arrested."

Wulf eyed the wine in his hand. "Why are you here?"

Dunkeld smiled. "I was rather hoping you would tell me where I can find your laird."

Wulf placed his cup on the table. "My chief is innocent of the charges made against him."

"A common claim," the other man said. "But the king has declared him guilty, and I am sworn to uphold the king's decrees. Tell me where he is hiding, and I will beg His Grace for leniency. You might yet live to see a new moon."

Wulf stood taller. "You insult me with such a bargain. I will never betray my kin."

"I expected as much," Dunkeld said. "You Highlanders are a proud lot. Willing to sacrifice your life for one another and for your honor. But are you as willing to sacrifice the life of another? That lovely raven-haired lass who begged me to come to your rescue, perchance?"

Wulf's heart turned to ice in his chest. Although if Morag had done exactly as he had bidden and made for the gates, she should be halfway to Queensferry by now. He had to pray that Dunkeld was bluffing. "I compelled her to aid me on threat of death."

Dunkeld eyed him. "Truly? She was very kind for a woman threatened."

Wulf shrugged. "Ask her yourself. I'm sure she'll relate the truth if you but ask."

"I will do that." The king's brother downed his wine. "As soon as we've found her. I've men searching for her as we speak." He waved a hand at the wine. "I'll leave the wine. On the king's orders, you are to have anything you desire these next two days."

"I desire freedom."

Dunkeld threw a half smile. "Anything except that. Were I you, I would consider revealing your laird's whereabouts. I cannot promise my guards will treat your woman with all due respect when they find her."

Wulf's blood raged at the threat, but he kept his expression calm. If even one hair on Morag's head was harmed, he'd tear Dunkeld's body apart with his bare hands. But he could not say that without giving the man greater reason to find her, and that would be a mistake.

"Do what you will," he said coldly. "I will not betray my laird."

Dunkeld nodded. "So be it."

Then he left.

When silence fell upon the cell once more, Wulf grimly did another tour of the room, determined to find a loose brick or a poorly fitting door hinge. Dunkeld might be generous with his wine and comforts, but he was definitely ruthless. If he had the opportunity, he would not hesitate to abuse Morag to get what he wanted.

There was no way Wulf could let that happen.

He would escape this rat hole or die trying.

Bran was nothing like Morag expected. Given his name, she expected a ruffian with hair of a similar shade to her own. But Bran was neither dark haired nor a ruffian.

His hair was a deep gold, like the sun just before sunset, and it was neatly trimmed to his collar. Morag studied him closely as the sandy-haired lad tugged on his sleeve to get his attention. A lean fellow of good height, he stood at the corner of two busy wynds, greeting lady shoppers as they passed and offering to carry their burdens home. Most women denied him, but smiled at his charming chatter. They did not notice him deftly plumb their purses as he plied them with pretty words.

A pickpocket.

Morag tucked her purse well inside her sark. The wretch would not have any of *her* hard-earned coin.

As the young lad tugged again on his sleeve, Bran spun around to face him. "Are ye mad, wee Tim? I've only an hour left before the market is near empty."

Tim pointed to Morag.

Bran's gaze lifted. "And who's this?"

"Morag Cameron," she said, offering her hand. "I have need to hire a companion this eve, and Tim suggested you might be the man I seek."

A slow smile spread across Bran's face as he took her hand. "I'm flattered, lass, but I don't offer my favors for a fee. You're a pretty enough thing. If you but ask, I'm sure you'll find yourself a willing companion."

He held her hand for longer than was proper, and Morag had to gently tug for her freedom. "Not that sort of companion. I need a bodyguard of sorts."

Bran's attention wandered. Two female shoppers were passing by, their arms laden with purchases and their purses hanging at their belts.

"I'll pay three deniers," Morag said.

Bran's head turned, his gaze returning to Morag. "Three deniers? That's a lot of money."

"I need a man who can be discreet and who can swiftly guide me away should trouble arise."

A frown marred Bran's handsome face. "What sort of trouble might there be?"

"Castle guards," said Tim.

Bran's eyebrows soared. He stared at Morag, daring her to deny Tim's declaration, but she could think of nothing to say that wouldn't complicate their arrangement, so she remained silent.

"Where do you need to go?" Bran asked, crossing his arms over his chest. His lèine was faded in color, but clean, and Morag detected no unpleasant odors.

"The alehouse in Beggar's Close."

"I know the place," Bran said, his frown easing. "Not too quiet, not too rowdy. A good place for a private meeting."

"Will you accompany me?"

He ran a thumb along his jaw. "How can I be certain you've got the coin to pay? I see no purse."

"You'll have to take it on faith." Morag flipped Tim his penny. "But I'm a woman of my word. Isn't that right, Tim?"

The lad grinned. "Aye. That you are."

She turned her cool gaze back to Bran. "Do we have a deal?'

He gave her another slow smile. "Meet me in front of the alehouse at sundown. I'll see you get in and out without a fuss."

They shook hands on it and then Morag departed.

Chapter 12

To Morag's relief, as she approached the torch-lit door of the alehouse, Bran stepped out of the shadows. Some of the male patrons were gathered outside, a few of them leering in her direction, and she was decidedly uncomfortable until Bran joined her.

He took her arm in his and tugged open the door. "I've already taken a wee look inside. There are no castle guards to be seen."

Morag threw him a hard look. "You seem to be enjoying yourself."

"Why not?" he responded with a smile. "I've a beautiful lass on my arm, a wee bit of danger in the air, and soon to have a cup of ale in hand. The makings of a fine eve."

"Have you been stealing purses?" she asked.

He gave her a wide-eyed look. "Robbing sotted

merchants with overflowing purses on a night when you've demanded discretion? Of course not, sweetling."

She heaved a sigh. "Cause me any grief and you'll not see a single coin from me."

He winked at her. "Never fear, lass. I have the situation well in hand."

Morag shook her head. Lord save her from overconfident men. "Over there," she said, nodding to a table in the back. A solitary man sat with his back to the wall, watching the door. Even hooded, she recognized her father.

She slid onto the bench opposite him, and dragged Bran with her. "No names," she cautioned her father.

"Aye," he agreed. His gaze scanned the room before returning to her face. "You've my coloring, but your features are your mother's."

"I'm not here to discuss my mother," Morag said sharply. She handed him the cloak. "Look closely at the weave. I need to know who made this garment."

Parlan drew the cloth close to his face. As he examined the material in the smoky, candlelit room, Bran hailed a passing barmaid with a wave of his hand and ordered a pitcher of ale.

"Well?" Morag prompted her father.

"It's a fine twill," he said. "Not all of the weavers in the guild can manage such an even weave, but a number of them can, including myself. There is nothing about the cloth to suggest who the weaver is."

Morag snatched the cloak from his hands. "But how many of them weave cloth this true of color, with this smooth a finish? How many of them sell their cloth to makers of fur-topped cloaks?"

"I do," he said. "As do any of my apprentices who've passed the mastery test. At least a dozen men in all. There may be more."

A heavy sigh tugged Morag's shoulders lower. Not the answer she'd been hoping for. The barmaid thunked a pitcher of ale on the table. "A penny."

Bran held out his hand to Morag. "Pay the maid, sweetling."

She glared at him for a long moment before digging into her purse for a coin. As the maid strode off, she hissed at him. "Order nothing more. My purse is thin enough as it is."

"You can't begrudge a man a cup of ale," he said.

"I can, and I do," she said. "And if you attempt to part me from my hard-earned coin by nefarious means, I shall hunt you down; I swear it."

He grinned. "Lass, we have a deal, and I'll live by it. I've no need to rob you. There are plenty other fish in this sea."

Her father grabbed her hand. "I've heard the man you traveled to Edinburgh with has been arrested," he said quietly.

She nodded.

"Plans are afoot to have a public hanging in the square the day after tomorrow," he added.

Morag's breath caught in her throat. "Nay." She gasped. "Surely that can't be true. There's been no trial."

"He was tried in absentia for treason, along with other members of his clan," her father said, his eyes sad. "Last November."

"But a man has the right to face his accusers," she protested. "How can that be a rightful trial?"

Her father shrugged. "The king defines justice."

Bran handed Morag a cup of ale. "Drink up, lass. You're looking a wee bit pale."

"The day after tomorrow?" she asked, still shocked.

"Aye," her father confirmed.

"But what can I do to stop it?" she asked.

"There's nothing that can be done."

Bran picked up the cup of ale and pressed it to Morag's lips. "I must disagree. There's always something you can do, if you've the stomach for it."

Parlan scowled at Bran. "Who are you?"

Morag took a sip of ale. "He's a—"

"Friend," supplied Bran smoothly. "One with some knowledge of Edinburgh. If you want to avoid a hanging, you've no choice but to set him free."

Hope bloomed in Morag's chest. "Is that possible?"

Bran winked at her. "If you know the right sort

of people and you're willing to pay the price, anything is possible, lass." He turned to Parlan. "I overheard you say you have experience with fashioning cloth. Do you know any tailors?"

"Aye. And I'm handy with a needle myself."

"Very helpful," Bran said. "We'll have need of a disguise."

Her father's frown deepened. "I cannot be involved in this matter. I am a respected man, with many who depend on me."

"So, yet again you would abandon me," Morag said quietly. "I am your daughter, and I require your aid. Can you truly walk away without shame?"

His green gaze met hers.

"I have many regrets," he said. "Perhaps I should have taken you with me, but your mother would not have welcomed that."

"Why did you not stay? We had a good life until you left."

He shook his head. "Dunstoras is a small hold. I could not afford a proper loom; nor could I sell all the cloth that I wove. A burgh was better suited to my craft, but your mother refused to leave Dunstoras."

"I make my living there," she said.

He nodded. "You weave excellent woolens. But I should show you my loom. Then perhaps you would understand."

"Will you aid us or no?" asked Bran.

Morag's father stared at the scarred wooden tabletop for a long moment. Then he sighed and nodded. "Aye, I'll aid you."

"Good," Bran said, leaning in closer. "Then this is what we shall do. . . ."

It was obvious the guards had been warned that Wulf might make an attempt to escape. The evening meal was delivered by two guards, one of whom carried a razor-sharp halberd. Wulf was asked to step into view, but well back in the cell, before they unlocked the door. But the challenge only made him even more determined to secure his freedom.

As he ate his meal, he lay on the bed, walking through several options in his head. He'd barely eaten half his stew when someone quietly approached his cell door. The torches in the corridor flickered as the person passed, but there were almost no sounds of booted feet. Just a slight pad on the wooden floor.

Wulf sat up.

He could see a dark shape through the window of his cell door. Tall and lean, almost certainly a man. "Who goes there?" he asked.

The man didn't answer the question, but he did respond. "Apparently, you're a prisoner of some import. The nephew of a laird, or some such. I'm here to gather your last requests. What final tastes of life would you enjoy before they string you up?"

Wulf surged to his feet. "I need nothing. Begone."

"Don't be so hasty, lad," said the man on the other side of the door. Wulf could see him better now. Golden shoulder-length hair and a firm chin. An unfamiliar face, but the tabard he wore confirmed he was a guard. "They intend to part you from this world. Why not part them of some coin before you go? Request anything at all—a fine meal, French wine, a brocade tunic, or a new pair of boots. Name your desire and I'll see it granted."

"I want nothing."

"Think of those you leave behind. The one who comes to collect your remains. Do you not want her to benefit?"

The image of Morag taking his body home to Dunstoras, walking the pony with a shroud-covered form in the back of the cart, came clearly to mind. Although his intent was to escape, if he failed, would he not want Morag to claim as much as she could?

"Leather boots, then," he said. "And a fur-lined cloak."

The man on the other side of the door chuckled. "That's a fine call, sir. I'll make arrangements straightaway."

And then, as silently as he'd arrived, the man disappeared.

Wulf closed his eyes and pictured Morag the way he always wanted to remember her—lying in his arms, her face flushed with passion, her eyes half-lidded with utter contentment. What a night they'd had. A thousand times more satisfying than the many dreams he'd enjoyed while lying next to her. She had fit so perfectly against him. Her soft body, so sweetly curved and generous in all the right places, had far exceeded his imaginings. But it had been her throaty cries of his name as she found her release that shook him to the core.

For the first time, his name had sounded just right to his ears. He was Wulf MacCurran, Morag was his woman, and they were meant to forge a life together.

But first he had to escape this cell.

Wulf paced the floor, picturing the two guards who'd delivered his meal. The halberd was a formidable weapon, with a sharp ax fastened at the end of a long pole. Compared to a simple pike it was expensive to produce, but very effective in beating back attackers. The long pole kept the guard out of range, and the ax made approach near impossible. The man with the food would be easy enough to subdue. Wulf's size would be an advantage there. But the pole . . .

His gaze fell upon the flagon of wine standing on the table, and the pewter cup alongside it. A cup that was small enough to hide behind his back, and solid enough to break a man's nose.

He smiled.

Now, that might work.

"You said nothing about a wig last night," snapped Morag's father. "How do you expect me to find such an item?"

"Hush," Morag said, nodding to the people around them who'd stopped to stare. The market was very busy as vendors set up their stalls in the predawn gloom, so surprisingly few eyes had turned, but it was enough to alarm her.

Parlan realized his error, and despite the true nature of his anger, added loudly, "No one carries figs this time of year. Expect to be disappointed."

The curious eyes dulled and conversations around them resumed. Morag released the breath she'd been holding. "Assuming we can find a wig, I think it's a fine plan for gaining entry," she said. "But I'm unclear on how I'll escape the castle myself."

Bran shrugged. "There's an element of risk, to be sure. But the king is a renowned family man. If you appeal to him directly, and explain the nature of your involvement, you will walk out of the castle without challenge."

"You are mad," Parlan said. "No one will believe she is an old cobbler."

Bran gave a crooked smile. "Perhaps. But unless you've a better plan, my idea stands. Time is short."

Morag's father tightened his lips and said nothing.

"Let's be off then," Bran said. "You've each got your tasks. I'll find the wig. Meet back here at noontide."

Parlan set off for his workshop, clearly reluctant. Morag grabbed Bran's arm before he disappeared into the crowd. "I understand why I'm doing this, and I understand why my father is doing this, but I don't understand why *you* are willing to risk life and limb, Bran."

He returned her stare. "I'm not the one freeing a condemned man from Edinburgh dungeon."

"No," she agreed. "But you sneaked into the castle last night disguised as a guard to arrange Wulf's last requests, and you're fetching the tools I'll need to appear as a cobbler. What do you gain?"

"Coin," he responded. "You promised me a fat purse."

"You earn good coin here in the market, with little risk. I find myself unconvinced of your reasons for aiding me." And for some reason, Morag knew it was important that she understand.

He peered into her face, then shrugged. "If you must know, then here is the sorry tale. My brother died in Edinburgh dungeon. It happened a number of years ago, and I blame my youth for my lack of conviction, but I had the chance to save him, and I did not."

His cocky smile faltered.

"He was a cutpurse. Like me, but not as gifted. He was nabbed in the market, around this time of year. He was sorely abused by the guards, and I promised I would free him, but I lost my courage. Never made the attempt. Three months later he caught consumption and died."

Morag squeezed Bran's arm. She did not know what to say. She did not condone theft, and she generally believed that those who committed crimes should pay. But such a tale did not reflect justice, and it was hard to see his brother's death as right. "That's how you know the corridors of the castle."

"Aye, and the route to the postern gate." He wagged a finger at her. "Don't think you can swindle me out of my coin because of a sad tale, though, lass. If I earn it, you must pay."

"I'm a woman of my word."

He smiled. "So I've heard."

When the closest guard slid the tray of food onto the table, Wulf struck.

With an aim perfected by months of hunting in the glen, he pitched the pewter cup at the second guard's head, hitting him square in the face. The tip of the halberd dropped and Wulf rushed in. He snatched the weapon from the disoriented guard's limp hands and jabbed the first guard in the gut with the blunt end, robbing him of breath and sending him to the floor.

A solid thump on the head knocked both men out, and only moments after the key had turned in the lock, Wulf was free. He dragged both men across his cell to the pallet, tied them with strips of sheet he'd torn during the night, and gagged them for silence. Best he give himself plenty of time to escape; he had no knowledge of the castle layout, and it might take time to make his way to the outer wall.

With any luck, these two would not be missed until the next meal.

Wulf donned one of the guard's tabards and slipped into the corridor. Lit torches hung in wall brackets every few feet, and he moved quickly until he reached a cross-corridor.

Which way?

He glanced down each of the three possible routes. All he saw were more torches. No stairs to indicate a way out. Choosing decisiveness over knowledge, Wulf turned left and strode down the hall.

Morag's father handed her a thickly pillowed vest.

"Put that on first," he said, his expression clearly reluctant.

The garment added large lumps to her shoulders, back, and chest, making it a chore to tie the closures at the front, but Morag managed. When she was ready, he held up a large dark gray lèine. She lifted the hem and, with his help, wriggled into the wool tunic. She surfaced flushed and hot, feeling like she was swimming in cloth. "Surprisingly heavy, all this."

Her father grunted, but said nothing. Instead, he held her hand as she slid her feet into large men's boots that were stuffed with cloth. Because she could no longer bend enough to reach her toes, he tied the bootlaces. To keep them from falling off as she walked, he tied the last loop around her ankle.

Morag tested the disguise, bending over as much as she was able and shuffling around her father's workshop. "Do I look like an old cobbler?"

Her father scowled. "You look like a fool."

"That," said Bran from the door, "is because the last bits have yet to be added."

He held up two long hanks of gray hair and a satchel of cobbler's tools. Using threads woven into Morag's own braid, they attached the two skeins of gray hair to her head, and then topped the whole outfit with a black hooded cape. Bran belted the satchel of tools over one shoulder and under one arm, and then stood back to assess the final picture.

"Well?" Morag asked. The back of her neck was damp with sweat.

He wrinkled his nose. "Keep the hood low and avoid looking the guards in the eye."

"This will never work," Parlan said.

"It will," insisted Bran. "Deepen your voice, lass. Pretend you're a peevish old man like your da."

Morag practiced walking and talking like an old man until Bran was satisfied, and then she set out for the castle. Certain that her disguise was as shoddy as her father believed, she tensed every time she passed another person. But no one pointed, stared, or shouted fraud, and the longer she walked, the more confident she grew. She walked through the market, right past the weaver she'd shared a stall with for two days, and he failed to recognize her. She even encountered two castle guards who were querying the vendors and passed them by without any bother. She arrived at the castle gate with blisters on her heels, a genuinely cantankerous tone in her voice, and a belief that she appeared to be an old man.

So long as she didn't look up.

"State your business," the guard said.

"Making a pair of boots for a prisoner," she said gruffly.

"Are you now?"

She could hear skepticism in his voice, but she dared not confront him. "Aye."

"I'll have to check with the warden."

Sweat was running down the back of her neck and between her breasts. Her heels were blistered and throbbing. Morag did not need to invent a peevish attitude. "Well, be quick about it. The man swings tomorrow, and boots don't sew themselves."

Then she waited.

Turning left was a mistake. The corridor Wulf chose led directly to the main guardhouse. He realized his error and pulled back sharply before stepping into the room, but he lost valuable time. Retracing his steps to the cross-corridor took longer than he wanted, thanks to the sword wound on his leg, which had scabbed in a manner that made moving awkward, and he was faced with another decision.

Straight ahead or left?

In the brief moment he hesitated, the decision was taken from him. Two soldiers appeared at the far end of the hall to his left. In the brief moment before they looked up, Wulf darted across the open space and down the corridor ahead. He preferred to be out of sight before the pair reached the cross-corridor.

Unfortunately, there were no archways to duck into or shadowed sections of the hall in which to blend. As the boot steps echoed even closer, Wulf was forced to brazen it. With his back to the approaching guard he calmly continued down the hallway. He wore a guard's tabard—with any luck, they'd pass him by.

He heard boot steps pause at the cross-corridor and tensed with anticipation. *Carry on, lads. Carry on.*

But it was not to be.

"You there! Halt!"

Cursing the Fates, Wulf ran.

Today, of all days, the sun decided to make an appearance. Morag stood at the gate, burdened by a thick bundle of clothing on her back and a heavy satchel of tools over one shoulder. The first suggestions of sweet spring weather were untimely.

Morag wiped sweat from her brow with her sleeve, taking great care not to reveal her hands.

What was taking the warden so long? Had Bran been mistaken? Was Wulf not to be granted his last wish for a pair of boots? Was she about to be exposed as a charlatan and a sham? Her feet itched to run. It was all too easy to imagine failure—of being strung up alongside Wulf with the townspeople glaring at her with accusing eyes. Surely if her ruse had been effective, it would not take this long to be granted entry.

Morag swallowed thickly, her throat tight and dry. Despite the powerful urge to flee that cramped her calves, she held her ground. She would never outrun the guard in her unwieldy disguise. Brazening it out was her only real option.

She heard the guard returning, and bit her lip.

"Been a bit of a fuss in the dungeon," he said, "and the warden very nearly denied the prisoner his last wishes."

A fuss? What sort of fuss?

"But word came from the king himself, and the wretch will have his boots. Come along."

Wulf was escorted to his cell. The two trussed-up guards were given a scathing reprimand and sent on their ways before he was tossed unceremoniously into the room. His boot tip caught in the wooden floorboards, and he fell heavily upon his injured leg. Damn his wound. Were it not for that, he might have stood a chance of escaping. But there was no value in bemoaning the Fates. His time was better spent developing a new plan.

He gently massaged his leg around the wound. Despite his rough landing on the floor, the thick scab continued to protect the knitting flesh. He could thank Morag's tender care for that.

He frowned.

Footsteps echoed in the hall once more.

Wulf leapt to his feet. If the opportunity presented itself, he would make another dash for freedom. Or hobble for freedom, as the truth might be. He grimaced. It mattered not. Either way, he had no intention of dying quietly.

"Stand back where we can see you, ya bleeding cur," the guard called from the other side of the door.

Wulf glanced around the cell. There was nothing to throw—all extras had been removed from his cell, including the chains. All that remained was the table, his bed, and his blanket.

He fisted his hands.

If they were his only weapon, so be it.

The key grated in the lock and the door swung open. Two guards with halberds and a third with a sword stood at the entrance. He was about to rush the man with the sword, when a hunched old man with long gray hair shuffled through the doorway.

"This here's the cobbler," the guard said. "He's going to take your measurements and stitch you a new pair of boots. You'll be swinging tomorrow in fine style."

The guard slammed the door and locked it. "Harm the cobbler, and your belongings, meager as they might be, will be given to his family in recompense."

The guards marched off, and silence fell.

As he stared at the bent figure of the cobbler, Wulf relaxed his hands. He had no cause to hurt an old man. "Take the measurements if you must," he said.

The old man straightened and threw back the hood of his cloak.

As a thick black braid and a lovely pale face were revealed, Wulf's heart tumbled to the bottom of his stomach. No!

Morag should be on the road to Dunstoras, not here, where danger lay in store for her.

She closed the gap between them, shuffling awkwardly in overlarge shoes, and reached for his face with both hands. Her fingers were hot on his skin, her touch fiercely claiming. There were many words she could have uttered—he could see a war of choices in her eyes—but she said nothing. Just pulled his head down until his lips met hers.

The kiss began with anger and a little desperation, but almost immediately it softened into a sweet need that blossomed between them. A tear escaped one of her eyes and rolled down to their lips.

Wulf cupped her head and deepened the kiss. He would take the memory of this kiss with him to the grave. Slanting his head, he pressed his lips against hers and encouraged her mouth to open. It was a salty kiss, and sweet at the same time. He would have let it continue for a lifetime, but Morag pulled away.

Raising her hands to her hair, she untied two shanks of long gray hair from her braid. "We must hurry. I have directions on how to reach the postern gate."

Wulf frowned. "How will we escape?"

She shook off her heavy cloak, then bent to untie her shoes. "Not we. *You*. You will depart dressed as the old cobbler. With any luck, the padding I wore will mimic your size and hunching will disguise your height."

He stared at her. "You expect me to leave you behind in my cell? Never."

She straightened. "It is the only way to avoid the noose."

Wulf snorted and took a step back. "You must think me a sorry excuse for a man. When have I ever given you reason to believe I would trade my life for yours?"

Her stare was hard. "My life is not at stake. They will not hang me for your crimes."

He threw up his hands in frustration. "They'll still punish you for abetting my escape. I will not leave you locked in here while I enjoy freedom."

"The risk is low that they will punish me," she said. "I will simply say you coerced me into donning this disguise and aiding you."

Another snort. "Coerced? How?"

She smiled. "You threatened to send the rest of

your evil clan after my family. Promised to see my father slain and his good name forever tarnished."

Wulf blinked. "Your father? What father?"

Morag flushed. "Aye, well, I forgot to mention that. I learned shortly after we arrived here in Edinburgh that Master Parlan, the head of the weavers' guild, is my da."

"Forgot?" he asked, narrowing his eyes.

She waved her hands. "'Tis a long tale, and I've not the time now to share it. We must be ready when the guards return. Suffice to say my da will appeal to the king on my behalf and arrange to set me free. I will not remain in this cell for long."

Her plan, as madcap as it sounded, might actually work. The king was a known proponent of family loyalty, and would likely judge in Morag's favor if she explained that she set him free to aid her father. And Wulf had already done his part to shore up her tale by telling Dunkeld that he'd threatened her life. Still, he hesitated. Leaving Morag behind simply did not sit well.

She grabbed his arm. "If not for yourself, do this for Jamie," she said. "The lad should not have to bury his father alongside his mother and brother."

Her words were quiet, but they struck him hard.

Wulf pictured Jaime standing at the gate as they departed for Edinburgh—alone and resolute. Morag was right. A lad should not have to carry such burdens. And he'd promised Jamie justice, which he had not yet delivered.

"Convince me you'll be safe," he said hoarsely.

"My father is a respected man in Edinburgh, and he'll stand for me," she said firmly. "Live, and you can come to my rescue. Die, and the man in black wins."

Wulf sighed deeply.

Then he peeled off his lèine and exchanged it for the cobbler's tunic.

Chapter 13

Dunkeld grabbed the only thing handy—an inkpot on his desk—and threw it at the guard's head. "Don't tell me how you've failed me," he roared. "Find the woman and find her swiftly."

Ink sprayed all over the guard's face, and the inkpot rolled away on the floor. He did not attempt to wipe the drips away. "No one has seen her since the eve before we arrested MacCurran, my lord. She has not returned to the market to sell cloth, and she has not returned to the candlemaker's shop."

"Not even to collect their belongings?"

The guard's gaze dropped to the floor. "The candlemaker says nothing remains."

"So she did return," snarled Dunkeld. "And you failed to catch her."

The guard frowned. "She has not approached

the candlemaker's shop since we began watching."

"Were you watching the back of the shop, as well as the front?" he demanded.

The guard was silent.

God preserve him from incompetent dullards. "Search the town from one end to the other. Leave no door unopened and no barrel untipped. I want that woman found by nightfall. Now get out!"

Dunkeld sat down at his desk and stared at the arc of ink drops across his parchment. If he couldn't find the woman, he needed some other way to press MacCurran into revealing his laird's location. Some other thing he valued more than his life.

"Sir William?"

Dunkeld looked up. It was the warden of the castle, his lips turned down, his hands tightly clasped together in front of his body. Not the stance of a man with good news.

"What is it?" he snapped.

"I believe we may have found the woman you seek," the warden said. "The one with the black hair and fair complexion."

Dunkeld's eyebrows soared. Not at all the bad news he was expecting. "Wonderful. Where is she?"

The warden could not quite meet his eyes. "She's in a cell in the dungeon."

A grin bloomed on Dunkeld's face. "She's been arrested for some act of vagrancy?"

"Not precisely," the warden said.

Irritated by the man's noncommittal tone and vague explanations, Dunkeld barked, "Spit it out, man. What is your news?"

The warden paled. "The woman is in MacCurran's cell, my lord, but MacCurran himself has vanished. It appears he has escaped."

Everything in Dunkeld's world grew cold and still. It was as if winter ice had flowed through the thick castle walls, doused the blazing hearth, and wrapped around his heart. "Escaped his cell? Or escaped the castle?"

"Both," the warden admitted. "I've had men scouring the castle for the past hour. There are no signs of him."

Rage poured through his veins, melting away his stiffness. He surged out of his seat and around his desk. Grabbing the warden's tunic with two hands, he yanked the man to him, nose-to-nose. "You do not simply lose a prisoner the king has announced will hang on the morrow. You will make His Grace the laughingstock of Edinburgh."

"We continue to search."

"Searching is not enough," roared Dunkeld. "Find him. Spread the word far and wide. I want every citizen of this burgh looking for him." Unclenching his fists, Dunkeld shoved the man away. "I want the woman brought to me. Now."

The warden stumbled, but recovered his footing. "I'm under orders to present her to the king. Her father, Master Parlan, has petitioned His Grace to have her released."

Dunkeld's eyebrows soared. "On what grounds? She abetted a known criminal in his escape."

"He swears MacCurran threatened them, that they had no choice but to aid him."

Utter madness. How could his brother be fool enough to even consider such an argument? "Then bring me the guards who were on duty when MacCurran escaped."

"I've queried them myself, sir. They were the victims of an elaborate ruse."

Dunkeld pinned the other man with a sharp stare. "Do not present me with excuses. I do not accept any reason for embarrassing my king. Unless you are volunteering to serve their punishment, I would be wary of defending these men."

The warden swallowed. "I understand, my lord."

"I hope that you do." Dunkeld returned to his desk and picked up his quill. "The marischal's men will continue to build the viewing platform next to the gibbet. Tell your men it's in their best interest to find MacCurran before tomorrow's hanging."

The warden's eyes widened, but he did not reply. He simply nodded and departed.

Dunkeld looked at his quill for a moment, then snapped it in two. At every turn, the MacCurrans miraculously slipped from his grip and wreaked havoc on his plans.

He flung the remains of his quill across the room.

His brother was no better. The man was too soft to be king. Releasing the woman was further evidence of his weakness. He should have crushed the MacCurrans long ago and proven his might. Instead, he let that lazy lout Tormod MacPherson take over Dunstoras. MacPherson was loyal, but he'd failed to hunt down Aiden MacCurran and his band of traitorous outlaws. Dunkeld gripped the edge of his desk and, with a howl of rage, flipped it over, sending it crashing to the floor.

Relying on others to do a job well only caused grief. Enough nonsense. As he'd done with the theft of the necklace, it was time he took matters directly in hand.

He was the rightful king of Scotland.

He was the one who should determine the lay of the future. And by God and all that was holy, he would make it so.

Exiting via the postern gate, Wulf scaled down Castle Rock to the level ground below. He was now outside the town walls, and with every soul in Edinburgh hunting for him, it made little sense to attempt to reenter. Instead, he made the short trek to Leith, the busy port on the Forth of Firth that served Edinburgh's trading needs.

Down near the docks, where strange faces were the norm due to the constant arrival and departure of ships, he found a room. It was above a fishmonger's shop, and the odor was only just bearable, but it was exactly what he needed—a secluded place.

When he was settled and certain no one had followed him, he sent a message to Master Parlan at the weavers' guild. A few hours later, a gentle knock sounded. Praying that Morag's confidence in gaining her freedom had proven true, he yanked the door open.

The hood pulled low over her face might have hidden her identity from casual onlookers, but it did nothing to fool him. He'd recognize that delicate chin and those full pink lips even in the gloom of midnight. All of his fears for her safety washed away in an instant, and with his heart full, he snatched her into his arms.

As her soft heat melted against him, his lips found hers. Hard and fast and needy. Leaving her behind had been the hardest thing he'd ever done, and even now he wasn't convinced it had been the right decision. He poured all of his regret into his kiss. But the hot blend of their mouths soon made him forget the worry that had eaten at his gut from the moment he left her in the dungeon. She tasted so unbelievably sweet and fresh. Like summer berries warmed by the sun's heat.

He kicked the door closed, scooped her up, and carried her to the bed.

Lowering her onto the mattress, he paused in his plunder of her lips. "Were you followed, do you think?"

"Nay," she said. "There was no sign of any guards when my father collected me from the castle. The king promised me freedom and he's been true to his word."

"I love you, Morag Cameron. Never again shall I let anything part us. Tonight I pledge my troth to you. Every sigh that leaves your lips, every groan that rumbles in your throat, I shall earn. You will cry to the heavens, beg the Lord for release, and find ecstasy in my arms—this I swear. Because only then will I be able to say I am worthy of you."

Her eyes shone with a brightness he'd never seen before and a tremulous smile curved her lips.

He burned the image of her looking just like that into his thoughts, then tugged his lèine over his head and joined her on the bed. For a while, at least, they would hold the rest of the world at bay. Time was theirs, and he intended to make the most of it.

Peeling back the layers of her clothing, he feasted on the sight of her glorious body. So perfect, so womanly, his Morag. Few who met her and experienced her bold, brazen exterior would guess at the soft, gentle soul that lay beneath. But he knew all of Morag, and loved her contradictions. He would have her no other way.

He bent his head and captured the peak of one full breast in his mouth. The first low moan escaped her lips, and he smiled. There would be a thousand more before the night was through, if he had his way. Laving her nipple with his tongue, he gave every effort to bringing her pleasure. He teased that tender flesh into a nub of need and want, determined to hear her scream.

When she was writhing against the sheets, he turned his attention to the other breast. And then to her navel. Burying his face against her belly, he drank in her scent. Every moment of the last four months that he'd lain next to her—wanting her—ached deep in his soul. In a right and proper world, he would have spent those months grieving for Elen, but the world was what it was. He could not grieve what he could not remember. Unfairly, perhaps, he'd gone on to create new memories, and the memories he'd made with Morag were real and vivid and treasured.

Because this woman deserved to be treasured.

It still flooded him with amazement that she'd dragged him all the way from the loch to her bothy—no small feat, given his size—and risked everything to heal him. MacPherson had been combing the glen, routing out MacCurrans, and she had bravely laid claim to him as a Cameron, lying to the soldiers who occasionally stopped by her bothy to search for outlaws. It was a testament to her boldness that they accepted her tale.

Wulf flicked his tongue into her navel.

Sweet, madcap Morag. He'd be dead several times over if not for her bravery.

How could he not love her?

He kissed his way lower, down one hip to the delicate skin of her inner thigh. Then he gently coaxed her legs apart and gave her the most intimate kiss a man can give a woman.

She arched, the small of her back rising off the bed, her hands clenched in the sheets. As his tongue made merry with the nub of her mons, he watched Morag's reaction.

Her eyes were closed, her head tilted to one side. A rosy flush had swept across her breasts and a glow of passion brightened her cheeks. Her guard was down, her defenses crumbled. It was a view of the woman rarely seen, as she had much to defend herself against. Wulf closed his eyes too, holding the image dear to his heart, but respecting Morag's need to always be seen as strong and capable.

Alone with her in their bed, he felt the walls could come down. He would never abuse the trust she gave him here, never hurt her as she feared. But so long as he had her trust he would use it to delight her. Tease her, taunt her, drive her mad. As he did now. Every caress, every kiss, was for her. He coaxed her body to the brink of fulfillment and then watched her scream his name as she came apart.

Wulf kissed his way back to Morag's mouth.

He held her gently to his heart as the ripples slowly eased and she returned to him. It filled him with awe every time he realized this woman was his. With Morag at his side, he could accomplish anything.

Even finding the man in black who could restore his good name.

William Dunkeld stood across the street and stared at the window above the fishmonger's shop. He wore a hooded cloak of dark blue that reached to his boots. It was not a fancy garment. Quite worn and weathered, in fact. He'd stolen it from a chest in the servants' quarters during the supper hours.

His foolish brother had indeed granted MacCurran's woman clemency, moved to misplaced compassion by her tale of being coerced. Dunkeld had lobbied hard to see her remain in gaol, but the king had been swayed by the master weaver, a man who commanded a great deal of respect in the burgh, even from the king's own wardrober.

Now the lass was in possession of a pardon from the king—a document that had driven Dunkeld's pursuit of her into the shadows. His brother would not be pleased to know that he continued to pursue Morag Cameron as a liar and a traitor.

But all was not lost. The woman's relationship to Master Parlan had proven her downfall. It had been an easy matter to watch the guild house for sign of her. He'd known the moment the cart had been readied that he was about to be rewarded, and he had been right. The woman had climbed into the cart and driven off for the gates only a few moments later. Even hooded, he recognized her.

And voilà.

She'd entered this shop and gone upstairs.

If he wasn't mistaken, he had just located the hiding place of an escaped outlaw. Wulf MacCurran was in that room above the shop—he'd stake his life upon it.

Dunkeld rubbed his gloved thumb along his chin. The question was, what to do with his newfound knowledge. He could pound on the door of the constable of Leith and demand the man arrest MacCurran. But he had lost faith in his brother's ability to see justice served.

No, he would not involve the constable. Or the king's guards. This would be best handled by men provided by his brother-in-law, Alan Durward. Englishmen. That way, the English could be blamed if the game went sour. Durward had close alliances to the English crown and was as eager as Dunkeld to see the MacCurrans fall. And as a long-serving ward of the king's door, Durward knew how to be discreet.

Dunkeld eyed the faces of the passing sailors and fishermen. But first he needed a spy. Someone who would keep MacCurran in sight and report on his movements. As an older fellow passed by, his face a little gaunt with hunger, his clothing frayed at the cuffs and neck, Dunkeld reached out a hand.

"My good lad," he said. "Would you care to earn a coin or two?"

Morag woke up with the sun in her eyes. It entered the room through a thin gap in the shutters and inconveniently lay right across her face. She was loath to move, though, with her body comfortably nestled in Wulf's arms, her rump warmly pressed into his groin, her head resting on his muscled upper arm. He was breathing the deep, slow draws of sleep, and if she moved, she would wake him. Given that he'd spent the night working hard to bring her pleasure, that seemed a wee bit cruel.

But that beam of sunlight was truly annoying.

Ever so carefully, Morag extricated her hand

from his relaxed grip and lifted it to shield her eyes. She was reasonably confident she'd done it without rousing him—until she felt him harden against her rump.

"You test the gods waking me so early," he murmured in her ear.

"If the gods are watching us, even they would be weary after our play last night," she said, chuckling. "I doubt they have the energy to smite me."

With an effortless push, he lifted himself on one arm and rolled her beneath him. "Then I'm the better man, because I have the energy to swive you."

She grinned. "I said smite, not swive."

He shrugged. "I hear what I wish to hear."

Leaning in, he teased her lips with a featherlight kiss. It was unusually gentle for her fierce warrior, and remarkably exciting. A velvety rub, a soft press, a flick of his tongue in the corner of her mouth. Morag's sleepy body sprang to attention, her nipples budding and her womb trembling. This was not the heated madness of the night—the ache inside her was more tender and it seemed to stem from her heart, rather than her feminine parts.

Morag returned his kisses with the same tightly coiled warmth. As if the world outside had no meaning and they had eternity to enjoy the passion that stirred within them. She sank her hands into his long brown hair, tipped her chin, and coaxed him to the sensitive cords of her neck. She wanted that eternity. She wanted the promises he offered with every sweet kiss.

So she gave herself wholly to that moment.

They made love again, this time a tender, slow build to satisfaction. Morag couldn't have said how much time passed as they kissed and caressed and teased each other to the peak. Nor did she care. It was magical.

He played her body as if it were a finely tuned harp, every touch a pluck on her heartstrings, every glide over her flesh a shiver-inducing note in a sensual melody. The slow build was powerful. Morag's release, when it came, stole her breath away. The rapture came from somewhere deep and rocked her like never before. Waves of pleasure struck her again and again, pulling a sharp cry from her lips.

"Wulf!"

His release must have been equally euphoric. As he rammed into her with one last, fulfilling stroke, he let out a roar that shook the rafter beams. And when he was spent, he did not roll gracefully to the side as he'd done previously. He collapsed atop her like a rag doll.

A very *heavy* rag doll.

Morag could still breathe, because even in the

throes of his ecstasy, Wulf had the presence of mind to fall slightly to one side. But his heated body was stifling nonetheless, and she gave him a gentle push.

Obliging, he rolled.

"If I die now," he murmured, "it will be as a happy man."

Although a similar feeling warmed her chest, she gave him a mild slap. "Do not say such things. You invite death into our midst."

He opened one eye. "Are you superstitious, lass?"

"I wasn't before I met you," she said. "But now I take no chances."

"Aye, well," he said, pulling her atop his chest, "death will have to get in line. There are others eager to see me in the sod."

She frowned. Amazingly, she'd forgotten that for a few moments. "My da says there's no way to trace the cloak back to its maker. He believes it was made somewhere on the continent."

Wulf opened both eyes. "How is it you never mentioned your da was head of the weavers' guild?"

Her cheeks heated. "'Tis a sorry tale, and I'm not much for sorry tales."

"I should like to meet him. Will I have the opportunity?"

She narrowed her eyes. "What words would you offer him?"

Wulf's gaze met hers, unwavering. "The truth. That if he dares to hurt you, he'll face my wrath."

His determined stand for her, even if a wee bit misguided, warmed her heart. She drew a pattern on the hairs of his chest. "A kind gesture, to be sure. But unnecessary. He's been most helpful since I've been in Edinburgh."

He waited for a moment to see whether she would add more, and when she did not he said, "Then we'll head back to Dunstoras. Neither the arms nor the cloak have borne fruit."

Morag bit her lip. She'd come frightfully close to losing Wulf, and she had a healthy respect for the tingle on the back of her neck that suggested danger still lurked here. But Wulf would not be pleased if she failed to tell him all she knew.

"There may be one last lead to follow," she said.

His eyebrows lifted. "Oh?"

"My da reminded me about the Book of Arms."

"The one Marcus Rose mentioned?"

"Aye. All arms granted by the king and all arms of those permitted inside the castle are recorded there. If we could examine that book, we might find the sigil."

The hint of interest died in Wulf's expression. "It's kept within the castle. We have no hope of setting eyes upon such a book."

She nodded. "It would be foolish for you or me to enter the castle. But I may know someone who could steal the book and bring it to us."

Wulf stared at her. "Surely you jest."

"Nay," she said, smiling. "It will likely cost me every coin I earned from my cloth, but I know a man who can do it."

He frowned. "How do you know such a man?"

She kissed his downturned lips. Then she rolled off him and gathered up her clothing. "It matters not. Are you game or no?"

Wulf surged from the bed, snatched her to his chest, and gave her a hard kiss. "Aye, I'm game, but you'll use none of the coin you earned. We'll use the coin the laird gave me."

Morag smiled. Even better.

"Get dressed," Wulf said. "I want to meet this thief."

Wulf did not like Bran.

He did not like the man's brash, confident demeanor, or his easy dismissal of the challenges of entering the castle. But he especially did not like how close the man stood to Morag, or the slow, deep smiles he regularly bestowed upon her.

"A book is not a trinket or a coin you can easily slip into your lèine," Wulf said. He made no move to claim Morag in front of the other man. She was his, and he knew she would never betray him. "How will you pass the guards with it in hand?"

Bran's gaze left Morag's face and turned to

Wulf. "The game is to direct their attention elsewhere. Coax them into seeing what you want them to see."

"What is the largest object you have ever stolen?"

The other man thought for a moment, then answered, "A horse."

"Anyone can abscond with a horse in the middle of the night," scoffed Wulf. He gave Morag a smoldering look, and she crossed to his side and took his arm.

Bran grinned. "Agreed. But not everyone can walk off with a man's horse in broad daylight."

Skeptical, Wulf merely raised a brow.

The cutpurse dug into his lèine and pulled out a small leather purse. He opened the drawstring and poured the contents into his palm. Five nuggets of gold winked in the mid-March sunlight. "If his eyes were on these, do you think he would be watching his horse?"

"You intend to bribe the castle guards with gold?"

Bran laughed. "These are only pebbles painted with gold, but nay. I've no confidence in the effectiveness of bribes. There's always one honest soul who cannot be bought."

Wulf lifted Morag's hand and kissed her knuckles. "Then be clear. What is your plan?"

"As always," the thief said. He raised his hand and beckoned to someone. "I'll arrange a distraction."

At his signal, a woman carrying several leather-bound books in her arms stepped around the gangplank of the ship and walked toward them. She was rather difficult to miss, especially after she let the brat around her shoulders slip to her elbows.

Wulf watched her path.

The men on the gangplank stopped to stare.

The woman wore a bright green gown with a scandalously low neckline. The mounds of her ample breasts were clearly visible above the books in her arms. She walked past them without stopping, but Wulf's gaze remained on her until Morag jabbed him in the ribs with her elbow.

"How many books was the lass holding?" Bran asked slyly.

"Two," Wulf said decisively.

"Are you certain?" the thief asked. "Are you willing to stake your life on that answer?"

"Three," Morag said, with a note of absolute disgust in her voice. "There were three books."

Bran grinned. "We'd best hope there are no women guarding the castle."

The old sailor met with Dunkeld in a dark wynd between two warehouses. With the setting of the sun, the docks had become nearly deserted, but with MacCurran's luck of late it seemed wise to avoid being seen by anyone.

"A book, you say," Dunkeld said.

"Aye," the sailor said with his cap in his hands.

"And where did this book come from?"

The old sailor shook his head. "I cannot say. One instant the man's hands were empty, the next he held a book."

Dunkeld grimaced. "Was anyone passing by at the time?"

The sailor nodded. "A handful of lads. But if one of them gave him the book, I didn't see him."

"And they took this book into the fishmonger's shop?"

"Aye," continued the old sailor. He held out his hand, palm up.

Dunkeld dropped a silver penny into his hand. "Speak one word of what you've seen, and I'll make certain you can never speak again. Understand?"

The old sailor's gaze widened, but he nodded.

"Go," Dunkeld dismissed him.

When the sailor had vanished into the gloom, Dunkeld walked down the lane to the street fronting the docks and stopped not far from the fishmonger's shop. The shop was closed, but candles burned in the windows, downstairs and up.

What could MacCurran possibly want with a book? Most tomes were written and illuminated by monks, and few people had the skill to read them.

Were he in MacCurran's boots, he would have left the towns behind and returned to the Highlands. The sigil they had ventured to Edinburgh to identify was lost, the herald was dead, and every guard at every gate had a description of his face. What more would the man gain by staying? What more could he discover from a book?

Dunkeld suddenly stiffened.

Unless it was a book of arms.

Dear Lord. There was such a book. William de Keith, the marischal of Scotland, maintained a detailed record with the help of several heralds. It was gloriously illuminated with every arms granted in the kingdom—and the arms of those who had sworn fealty to the king. It was very possible that the arms of Daniel de Lourdes and Artan de La Fleche were recorded there.

He frowned up at the lit window above the fishmonger.

But that book was kept in the castle. Behind high stone walls and locked doors. It was nearly impossible for that book to be the one MacCurran was peering at.

Near impossible, but not *impossible*.

Dunkeld wrapped his cloak around his body and strode off down the street. It was time to make use of his brother-in-law's men. Neither MacCurran nor that book could be allowed to see morning.

Morag turned another page, then sat back. "Och, what does this mean?"

Wulf stared at the illuminated arms in the upper right corner of the page: a tower with a raised sword in the middle. His gut tightened as he noted the large black mark that ran through the image. "Those are—nay, were—the arms of Laird MacCurran. They've been struck from the record."

"But he's been unjustly accused."

"The king does not believe it so," Wulf said heavily. Although he knew the MacCurrans had been outlawed and he had seen the hardship that proclamation had wrought upon his clan, there was something stark and undeniable about the mark through Aiden's arms.

He quickly scanned the other arms recorded on the parchment, then turned the page. There was no sign of that sigil they remembered from their attacker's tunic, and they were three-quarters through the record.

"Keep looking," he said to Morag. "I'll fetch us some food from the tavern."

Morag glanced up. "We'll find it. I'm certain."

"I'll return anon." He bounded down the stairs, nodded to the fishmonger and his wife, who were supping on garvie stew, and left the building. With the moon on the wane the night was dark, and he walked swiftly.

It bothered him that he sought the name of the man in black so desperately that he was willing to risk harm to Morag. A sane man would have packed up the cart and headed for home. But every time he thought of what the man in black had stolen from him, a dark rage roiled in his gut. It did not matter that he could not picture the faces of Elen and Hugh. They'd been his kin, his beloved wife and son. He owed them justice, and the only way to deliver that justice was to find the man who had murdered them.

He entered the tavern and pushed his way through the throng of patrons to the barmaid. An older woman with faded red hair and tired eyes, she barely looked at him as she asked, "Aye, what will it be?"

"Some bannock and honey," he said. "And a pint of ale."

She served him swiftly, if a little brusquely.

Imagining her with a surly husband and ungrateful children, he left her an extra penny and gathered up the food.

No sooner had he passed into the cool night air

than the scent of smoke caught his nose. Not the mild wisps of a cooking fire, but the thick smell of burning daub. Wulf's eyes lifted to the fishmonger's house, and his heart dropped into his boots.

The lower half of the building was aflame.

Tossing aside his purchases, he ran.

Chapter 14

At the first significant whiff of smoke, Morag swiftly grabbed their bags, Wulf's sword, and the book, her heart pounding. She raced across the room and tore open the door to the hallway. Fat plumes of smoke billowed into the room, choking her, and hot air carried the crackle of fire to her ears. The smoke was so thick, she immediately shut the door.

And spun around.

Once again, she was faced with a madcap escape. She flew to the window and hammered against the shutters. They did not open. Dropping her armload to the floor, she tried again. To no avail. The shutters were locked tight, which made no sense. She'd opened them earlier in the day.

But there was no time to dwell on that.

She grabbed up her belongings and ran back

to the door. Covering her nose and mouth with her brat, she braved the wall of gray smoke on the other side of the door. The smoke seemed thickest at eye level, so she bent forward and crept in the direction of the stairs.

Her eyes watered madly, and despite the brat, she coughed as smoke burned a path into her chest. She found the stairs, and, almost crawling, she felt her way to the bottom. It was there that she discovered the body of the fishmonger's wife. Already terrified, Morag took one look at the dirk protruding from the poor woman's chest and moaned.

This was no ordinary fire.

Someone was determined to see her die.

Morag closed her eyes briefly and struggled to regain her composure. She had to escape, and escape swiftly. The fire was raging at both ends of the shop. Long tongues of flame were reaching across the ceiling. If she didn't break free soon, this shop would be her funeral pyre.

But where to go?

Her eyes popped open. Nearby, on this side of the shop, there was a chute the fishmonger used to dispose of the unwanted fish parts. It was narrow, but it should be just wide enough for her to squeeze through.

If she could find it.

Down on her hands and knees, dragging Wulf's sword and their bags, Morag crawled across the wooden floor of the shop. The Book of Arms was large and extremely awkward to carry, and she dropped it several times. Wave after wave of unbearable heat struck her, and beads of sweat ran down her face. The next time the book slipped from her grasp, Morag let it fall. As valuable as it was, she could not lose her life trying to keep it. The bags and the sword were burden enough, and the smoke was suffocating. Were it not for the brat tied over her nose and mouth, she would never have made it.

But she did.

She shoved open the door of the chute, gulping in the cool air. Then she tossed her belongings outside and pitched herself down the chute, landing headfirst in a slippery pile of fish guts. For a moment she just lay there, coughing and wheezing like an old woman.

Then she remembered Wulf.

She needed to find him—and warn him.

With any luck, he was still at the tavern enjoying a pint of ale. Morag scrambled to her feet, slipping and sliding in the slimy fish parts. Brushing off the worst of the gunk, and turning her soot-covered brat inside out, she picked up her belongings and carefully made her way around the back of the burning shop. The back wynds would be safest.

* * *

Several sailors had already begun a line of buckets to douse the fire when Wulf reached the fire-engulfed shop. He stared at the closed shutters of the second-floor window, willing them to open.

"Morag," he shouted.

But the roar of the flames was surprisingly loud, and he couldn't be sure she could hear him. And as he stared at the shutters he realized there was a stick jammed between them, preventing them from opening.

Wulf's pulse began to pound.

He swiftly scanned the faces of the people on the street, hoping that Morag had already left the shop. But there was no sign of her freckled face and long dark hair. He had to go in. But not through the front door. Fire had already overwhelmed the entrance. The iron fish that hung above the door was swimming in a pool of fire, its head glowing bright red.

Wulf jogged around the right side of the shop. The very back of the building had not yet caught fire, and the side delivery door stood half-open. Smoke poured out, but here there were no flames.

He tugged the door wide.

"Morag!" he called.

There was no reply, save for the crackle and snap of burning wood.

Wulf pictured the stairs to the second floor and drove through the smoke in that direction. Half a dozen steps in, he stumbled over a body and his throat clenched. *Dear God.*

No.

He dropped to his knees, feeling with his hands until he found wool clothing and an arm. An arm that was too muscular to be a woman's. Relief flooded him. It wasn't Morag.

He regained his feet and moved forward. The smoke was so thick and the heat so unbearable that he could no longer be sure he was headed in the right direction. But his fear for Morag drove him on. He was about to call her name once more when something slammed against the back of his head. Dazed, he spun around.

Two very large men garbed like seamen stood before him, holding short wooden clubs. They gave him no chance to recover, diving on him. They pummeled him again and again. Wulf fought back as best he could, but the smoke defeated him. As he used his fists to beat back his attackers, he sucked in a deep fiery breath and choked. He went down with another solid blow to his head.

His last thought was a desperate hope that Morag had somehow escaped. Then everything went black.

Morag skirted wide around the back of the burning shop. Although the fire was currently contained to the front, numerous sparks were floating in the air above the wynd, brightening the night. A villager raced past her, no doubt headed for the main street, where a crowd had gathered and the fire-dousing efforts were in full swing. Just as she was about to dart across the dark lane, the delivery door of the fishmonger's shop burst open and two burly men carrying short poles ran out. They paused and bent over, hands on their knees as they looked back at the smoke-filled doorway. Sweat made trails in the soot on their faces.

"He's done for," one of them said, coughing.

"Are ye certain? I thought I saw him move."

The first man shrugged. "If he's still alive now, he won't be for long. The fire will take him."

"Let's go then."

Still coughing, they ran into the lane and disappeared into the darkness.

Morag stared at the door after they ran off. It was possible they'd been speaking about the fishmonger, but her gut said differently. Those men were likely working for the traitorous man in black. And if she was right, there was only one man those men would be after—Wulf.

Had Wulf gone into the shop looking for her?

She stepped toward the door, and then stopped. Her chest was unbearably tight just thinking about going back inside the burning shop. But if Wulf was in there, injured but still alive . . .

Morag whipped the brat back over her mouth and nose.

If he was in there, she had to get him out.

She stepped into the smoke, immediately feeling a blast of heat pulse over her body. Her eyes stung and immediately began to water, but she pressed on. How would she ever find him in this murk?

He would have headed for the stairs had he come looking for her, so that was the best direction to head. Morag sank to her knees and made her way, low to the ground where the smoke was thinner. She moved as quickly as she could, but the route was perilous—chunks of smoldering thatch kept falling from the roof, and occasionally one hit her. Twice she had to kick pieces aside.

A few feet along she found a body.

Her heart raced with hope, but she swiftly determined that the body was too slim and too short to be Wulf's. It was the fishmonger. Her instincts had led her astray. Morag berated herself for being foolish enough to reenter the burning shop. She spun around, intending to exit as swiftly as she could, when she heard a groan.

Halting, she listened carefully. With the roar of the flames in her ears, she might have been mistaken.

Nay. There it was again.

To her left.

Morag turned toward the sound and started to crawl. She moved aside a wooden crate of herring and spied a familiar set of boots. It was Wulf. But just as she moved toward him, a large beam from the ceiling dropped to the floor with a loud crash. One end struck a barrel of fish and the other struck the floorboards. Morag shrieked and pulled back, aware that she'd very narrowly escaped being crushed.

But a burning beam now lay between her and Wulf. The only safe way to reach him would be to go around the barrels of fish to the other side of the shop.

Too far.

And judging from the falling wood from the roof, it was unlikely she had time. The shop was about to collapse. She had to get Wulf out quickly.

Morag looked at her hands.

Bare skin and burning beams did not mix well. She tore several long strips from her skirts and wrapped them snugly around both palms, creating a fat barrier of protection. Then she grabbed the beam in a spot that wasn't actually burning—just glowing with hot coals—and lifted it using every ounce of strength she possessed.

It was incredibly heavy, and Morag found she could pivot it in only one direction. Slowly, breathing in ragged burning breaths, she edged the beam to one side. But just as she lifted it over Wulf's body, the cloth protecting her hands started to smolder.

Morag felt the hot coals of the beam bite into her flesh, and she looked down. She stood right over

Wulf. If she let go of the beam, it would fall on him. There was no choice. Steeling herself against the pain, she took another step and another. The wads of cloth around her hands burst into flame. Morag heaved the beam aside and shook off the burning material.

The skin of her hands was berry red, and the pain was searing. But her job was not done. Morag grabbed Wulf's arm with both hands, and much as she'd done four months ago by the loch, she dragged him to safety. It was only a few feet to the door, but smoke filled her lungs and fits of coughing slowed her down. A section of the roof fell in shortly after they exited, sending a powerful whoosh of smoke and fire into the air.

As the fire consumed more of the shop, the back wynd became busier. Several men appeared with buckets, trying to stop the fire from spreading. Fortunately, their attention was focused on saving the other shops, so Morag was able to reach the wynd wall without notice.

Only when she had Wulf hidden in the shadows did she drop to the ground next to him and look at her throbbing hands. Her fingers were curled like the talons of a hawk, and she couldn't straighten them.

Tears sprang into her eyes as the horrible truth sank in. She might never weave again. How would she provide for herself?

But Wulf was alive. He would return home to Jamie. She had no regrets.

Still wary of being discovered by the men who'd set the fire, Morag cared for Wulf in a barn not far from the fishmonger's shop. She had the coin to rent a room, but chose discretion over comfort. Not that the barn was uncomfortable. It was actually quite pleasant. The hay made a good bed, and the roof protected them from the spring rains. But she had to bury Wulf and herself with hay every time the barn door swung open, and constant vigilance had made her bone-weary.

Well, that and worry over Wulf.

The wounds on his head were deep, but they had started to heal. He had no fever and his color was good. The problem was that after two days, he still had not awoken. And his sleep was not peaceful. He regularly tossed and thrashed in the hay. He murmured words she could not make sense of, often with obvious agitation. When his dreams were especially disturbing she shook him and spoke to him, trying to end the nightmares. The sound of her voice sometimes calmed him, but it never truly broke through the dreams. He slumbered on.

Spoonfuls of vegetable broth were not enough sustenance for a man of his size, and he'd grown noticeably leaner, so Morag took a risk and hired a healer. But it was wasted coin. The old woman offered little advice save to bleed him.

Morag resorted to prayer—and a visit to the market for heartier food. She would have attempted the journey home, but the cart had been lost in the fire, and her pony had been collected by the constable. The discovery of the fishmonger and his wife in the rubble of the shop had caused all sorts of talk.

Fingers had been pointed at Wulf and Morag as the culprits, but fortunately it was decided that since the fishmonger had died without a dirk in his chest, it was he who had done his wife in. Apparently there had been frequent arguments between the two.

Morag sighed with relief when she overheard that tale in the market. She had worries enough without running from the constable.

She parted with some coin to purchase an oxtail, hoping to make a heartier broth for Wulf. By necessity, she also bought a new gown—a dull brown affair to replace her torn and fishy smelling dress. The soot had come out of her brat with a good wash, but nothing could remove the fishy odor clinging to Morag's gown. Not even lye soap.

Packages in hand, Morag sneaked back into the barn through a loose plank in the back wall. The building was a temporary hold for horses shipped by sea, and several of the stalls at the rear were empty. Wulf lay in one, covered in hay.

She brushed away the chaff and checked on his condition. No change. It was too dangerous to make a cooking fire inside the barn, so she set her broth to boil outside. The sky was heavy with clouds, and she prayed the rain would hold off until the soup was done.

She returned to Wulf's side.

His thrashing had worsened, and the hay around him was scattered. Mumbled noises escaped his lips as he turned his head from one side to another, only occasionally forming a recognizable word.

"Elen. No."

Morag started at the sound of his dead wife's name. Not once in all the months he'd lived with her had he spoken that name. Not even in sleep. Her heart ached as she realized he was reliving a memory of his past. The moment she had feared was approaching. As she'd always known they would, his memories were returning.

She laid a curled hand on his shoulder, rubbing her knuckles over his flesh. "Wulf. 'Tis I, Morag. Wake thee up." She uttered the words in a low voice, not expecting a response.

So she gasped when he suddenly opened his eyes.

Then she beamed and threw herself atop his chest. "Och, Wulf, I cannot believe it! I feared you might never awaken."

He stiffened beneath her.

Morag leapt back, worried that some injury yet plagued him. But the expression on his face was not a wince of pain. It was horror. He was staring at her like she'd crawled out of a dung heap.

"No," he said hoarsely. "No."

She put a hand on his forearm. "What is it?"

He shook off her hand and sat up. "No, it cannot be true. It cannot be real."

"What cannot be real?" asked Morag. But in her heart she knew. His memories had not come back slowly, a bit at a time, as she'd expected. They'd come in a rush, all at once.

"You," he shouted, leaping to his feet. He stumbled and stared at his legs—both injured—with a look of utter betrayal. "This. Everything."

Morag got to her feet, trying not to feel as though her heart were breaking. But it was.

He lifted his gaze to hers, his eyes dark and tormented. "Because if this is real, then . . ." He put both hands to his face, rubbing and scrubbing as if he could erase whatever vision was in his thoughts. "No."

But even in the midst of her heartbreak, she ached for him. Because she knew the course of his thoughts. Elen and Hugh and that terrible night in November.

He went completely still. "No."

Then he sank to his knees in the hay.

For the first time since she'd met him, she saw Wulf's shoulders curl in absolute defeat. His head hung low, a reflection of hopelessness that was the very opposite of the man she knew.

"Dear God," he moaned. "Elen. Hugh. It was all real."

But his despair was short-lived. An instant later his hands fisted, and he threw back his head. His face was still dark, but now it was rage that held court—a terrifying, bitter rage that made Morag take a step back.

He surged to his feet, raised his fists in the air, and howled like his namesake.

Most of the shop had been consumed by the fire. The entire front of the building, including the room that had been occupied by MacCurran and his woman, was gone. All that remained was blackened rubble.

Dunkeld eyed the destruction with satisfaction. He halted a passerby and pointed to the ruined building. "A tragedy, that. Was anyone injured?"

The sailor frowned. "I heard it said that a man and his wife perished within. But we've only just docked, so ye might be wise to query another."

Dunkeld nodded.

A man and his wife. That certainly sounded promising. Before they set sail for England his brother-in-law's men had assured him that Mac-

Curran had been slain—but he'd been disappointed by the service of others too often to take them at their word. He circled around to the back of the shop. The damage was not as severe here. A portion of the inner structure remained intact, and it was possible to enter. Rubble had been cast aside, and he could see the two tidier spots where the bodies had lain: one at the base of what was once a staircase, and one closer to the side door. All of it was consistent with the story his henchmen had relayed, and yet, Dunkeld wondered.

Two bodies would not account for the shopkeep.

Three bodies would have made him happier.

To his mind, that meant someone had escaped. He kicked aside several twisted hazel sticks that had once been spars on the roof thatch. There, covered by a thin layer of soot, was a wide drag mark, leading toward the door. Someone, or something, had been dragged out of the shop.

Dunkeld frowned.

Glancing over his shoulder, he spied the wynd behind the shop. Following the feeling in his gut, he left the burned shell of the building and trudged up the lane. The buildings on either side were warehouses, most with locked doors and no windows. Up ahead lay a few homes and a barn. Behind the barn, he could see the thin wisp of a cook fire rising up into the air.

It might be nothing.

Or it might be everything.

Dunkeld trekked up the lane and made his way quietly around to the back of the barn. When he peered around the corner he could see only the fire and a clay pot seated in the glowing coals. So he waited.

And he was rewarded.

A few moments later, a woman exited the barn by pushing aside a loose plank and bent to tend to the meal. A brat was draped over her head and shoulders, and he was unable to make out her features, but having followed her from Edinburgh wearing a similar disguise, he recognized the slim shoulders and curved rump.

It was MacCurran's woman.

Seizing the moment, Dunkeld drew his dirk and dived around the corner. But he was an instant too late. The woman picked up the pot and ducked back inside the barn. The plank swung back into place, leaving Dunkeld staring at a pine knot. He leaned in, trying to hear through the wooden barrier but caught only vague murmurs from within. Snatching the woman outside the barn was one thing. Rushing headlong into a room he couldn't see was quite another. Who knew what lay inside? MacCurran might have called upon aid from his brethren.

He lowered his dirk.

Perhaps it was time to make use of the constable.

"Eat some soup."

Wulf turned away from the bowl Morag offered. His stomach was too tight to eat, his head too full of the memories that were suddenly his again. Memories that were so sharp they left a gaping hole in his heart. The miserable events of the night kept playing over and over in his head.

There had been music and wine and food to celebrate the visit of the king's courier, Henry de Coleville. Sixteen courses, the third of which had been Elen's favorite—eel soup. Wee Hugh had been one of the first to fall ill. Wulf had left the high table to see to him when Elen, too, fell ill. The poison had been virulent, taking hold quickly, and it was only minutes later that he was clasping his wee bonny boy to his chest, blue lipped and lifeless. The memories were fresh, like those moments had happened yesterday, even though he could also remember all the events of the past four months.

A part of him wanted simply to grieve. To let the bitter weight of his memories press him into the earth. Elen had been a good wife and a fine mother. The moment she realized the danger lay in the eel soup, she knocked the spoon from Jamie's hand and sent his bowl flying. She hadn't deserved to die, especially in such a cruel way. Hugh passed so quickly, the wee lad barely knew he was ill, but Elen had known she was dying, and she had reached for him, weeping.

Wulf swallowed tightly.

"I know who the man in black is," he said, his voice rough. "I need a sword and a dirk."

"I saved your sword from the fire," Morag told him.

"Where is it?"

She remained silent, and he spun around to glare at her. "Damn you, Morag. Are you with me or against me?"

Morag stood taller. "I am with you, as I have always been. But I won't applaud your desire to rush into battle without adequate preparation. That's what nearly got you killed down by the loch."

"My wife and son need avenging," he roared. "Would you have me turn my back on justice?"

"Nay," she said softly.

"You have no idea how hard it is for me to stand here, knowing what I know. Knowing that I've had the chance to claim justice and failed to take it."

She stared back at him, frowning. "Who is—"

"In the name of the king," came a loud male voice from outside. "Lay down your weapons and surrender!"

Wulf stiffened.

"The barn is surrounded. Come out peacefully and you will survive another day!"

No. He fisted his hands. It couldn't end this way. Not when he finally had his memories. Not when he finally knew who the man in black was.

Morag grabbed his hand and tugged.

Wordlessly, she pointed to a stack of grain sacks on the opposite wall, and pulled him toward them. Behind the sack, hidden beneath a woven mat of hay, was a trapdoor. He tugged on the iron ring, lifted the door, and stared into the hole. On the ground below lay his sword and the bulk of their possessions. Beyond that, a dark tunnel.

A smuggler's egress, likely leading down to the wharves.

Without a torch, it would be a difficult journey, but surely better than what lay in store for them outside the barn.

Wulf jumped into the hole, then offered his hand to Morag. He closed the trapdoor behind them, pulling the rope that replaced the hay mat as he did so. Then he gathered up their belongings and, with her hand firmly in his grip, led the way down the dark, dank tunnel toward the firth.

In the dark, with Wulf's warm hand wrapped gently around her burned palm, Morag could almost forget the past hours. How many times had he held her like this with fondness in his heart?

But that man was gone. He was no longer her gentle warrior, content to chop her wood and thatch her bothy. She'd seen the last of that quiet man who polished his sword by the fire as she worked on her loom. He no longer wanted her soup, or her advice.

He was once again the Wulf MacCurran who'd ridden after the man who had poisoned his family and fought like a man possessed when ambushed by that man's disciples. He was once again the grieving husband of Elen and father of Hugh.

And in some ways, she was pleased for him.

She had known this day would come, had steeled her heart against it. But her preparations had not been enough.

The look on his face as he'd asked her, *Are you for me or against me?*, had nearly ripped her heart out. She'd always stood for him. From the moment she first spied him at Dunstoras, she'd held nothing but admiration for the handsome young warrior. And the day she'd been shunned, when he had called a halt to the abuse of the villagers and then carried her loom into the woods, would forever be etched in her memories. She had loved him for such a long time.

She could forgive Wulf anything.

Even this.

But letting him go was going to hurt far more than she'd imagined. She could already feel the ache in her heart, and he was not gone yet.

She sucked in a shaky breath.

But before that, she had to stop him from repeating the mistake he'd made down by the loch. Yes, he was grieving. Yes, his family deserved justice. But justice would not be served if he confronted the man alone.

They reached the end of the tunnel, and Wulf shoved open the door. It opened on a rocky shore, just below the docks. As it was noon, the tide was out, and they were able to walk up the beach to the path leading into the town.

When they were once again on even ground, Wulf turned to her. He lifted her hand and stared at her curled fingers. "You paid an unbearable price to pull me from the fire, and my regrets are legion."

"I merely did what I had to do."

He shook his head. "You did far more. I owe you everything, lass. My health, my freedom, and my very life. Were it not for you, I would not be standing here on the brink of avenging my kin. You've done so much for me," he said, kissing the tip of each finger. "I cannot ask more. Pay Bran to accompany you back to Dunstoras. From here I must go alone."

"No," she argued. "Alone is the choice that lost you four months of your life."

He gave her a half smile. "Is that how you see it?"

"Do not repeat the error of that night. Come

back to Dunstoras with me. Tell the laird what you know. Together you can defeat this man, no matter how powerful he is."

His gaze met hers. "The man in black is William Dunkeld, the king's brother."

She had guessed as much from Wulf's earlier comment about failed opportunity. She nodded. "Not an easy man to accuse."

"Especially if you are an outlaw and an escapee from Edinburgh dungeon," he agreed. His face darkened. "But I must see justice done."

"How? He commands an entire garrison of the king's guards, and you are but one man. And any hope of proving his duplicity is gone. I was unable to save the Book of Arms."

Wulf's gaze turned to the burned shell of the fishmonger's shop. Then, without a word, he marched in that direction.

She grabbed his hand, trying to halt him, but failing. "What are you doing?"

He didn't answer, just continued to walk. When he reached the ruins, he began digging through the rubble, unconcerned that several people had taken note of his actions.

"Are you mad?" she asked. "Dunkeld has set the constable on us. We should not be here."

He tossed aside a roof beam and several half-burned planks of flooring. Working swiftly, he soon uncovered the remains of the fallen staircase. Morag pointed to the spot where she'd made the difficult decision to release the book. A blackened heap was all that remained of the fishmonger's mattress, but Morag could see several sticks of wood that had once been a table.

Wulf kicked aside a sheaf of burned thatch and found what was left of the book—the heavy leather binding had not been completely destroyed, but the bubbled black sheets between turned to ash the instant his fingers touched them.

Their last hope of connecting William Dunkeld to the murders was gone. All they had now were Wulf's memories—which would never gain credence while Aiden MacCurran stood accused of the crimes.

Having found what he sought, he turned to leave, but his boot caught a corner of the burned table and it tipped.

Wulf froze, and Morag wondered what he'd seen.

A moment later, she knew. He bent and pulled something from beneath the table. A carved horse. She had saved the box from the fire, but one of the toys must have fallen loose. His hand trembled, just barely, and then he shoved the carved figure into the front of his lèine.

His face was calm—suspiciously so. There was

no sign that he'd been disturbed, but she knew the toy had rocked him. He left the shop and strode into the street without a word.

Morag followed him, but there was a distance between them she couldn't bridge. He looked at her, but didn't really see her—his memories had pulled him to another place and time.

"Send a message to Bran," he said. "He'll see you home."

Even though her previous pleas had not swayed him, Morag tried one more time. "You are not ready. You have not eaten in two days."

His gaze turned west, in the direction of Edinburgh. "I'm more ready than you think. This day has been waiting for me."

Morag wanted to say more, but she held her tongue. He was not hers anymore. He belonged to the memory of Elen and Hugh. There was only one thing he was forgetting.

"Jamie is also waiting for you," she reminded him.

His gaze dropped. "Aye."

"Don't do anything foolish, Wulf MacCurran. Else you'll lose my respect."

He nodded. And then he was gone.

Chapter 15

Holyrood Abbey was an impressive structure. Wulf entered through the twin-tower front and walked down the aisled nave toward the far left bay. The high-vaulted ceiling, glorious stone arches, and fluted pillars nearly stole his breath away—it truly did seem as though God must have had a hand in building such a monument.

In the hours between sext and vespers, only a handful of worshipers were inside the abbey, most on their knees near the Chapel Royal. Wulf sought out the hooded figure near the choir.

"I must thank you for meeting me," Wulf said in a low voice.

His father-in-law did not raise his bowed head. To all onlookers he continued to pray. "How could I deny you? If you have truly found the man who murdered my daughter, then I am honor-bound to aid you."

"My memories have returned. I saw his face."

The old man nodded. "Tell me what you need."

"I cannot enter the burgh," Wulf said. "But I must know the instant this man leaves the city gates."

"Some men never leave the burgh."

"This man will," Wulf assured him. "He is William Dunkeld, brother to the king."

Elen's father was silent. He did not caution Wulf on the difficulties of reaching Dunkeld or try to convince him it was unnecessary, and for that Wulf was grateful.

"Can you help me?" Wulf asked.

"Aye," the old man replied. "A jeweler must cultivate a variety of relationships to acquire the stones he needs. I know a reliable man who can report on Dunkeld's travels."

"Excellent," Wulf said. He told the old man how to get word to him and then stood for a moment in quiet companionship. As the old man turned to depart, Wulf said, "On our wedding day, I planted a sapling yew in the garden of Dunstoras keep. Elen could see it from the window of our chamber, and together we watched it grow from a thin switch to a deeply rooted tree."

The old man lifted his eyes to Wulf's face.

"That yew still stands," Wulf said. "Healthy

and strong. Elen's sons climbed its branches, and so will her grandchildren and great-grandchildren. Long after you and I are but dust in the sod, it will stand."

Tears sprang to the old man's eyes and he put a thin hand on Wulf's sleeve. "May your aim be forever true, lad."

Then he hobbled away.

Dunkeld strode across the great hall, kicking a sleeping hound too slow to clear his path. As the dog yipped and ran off, Dunkeld flung a curse to its sorry parentage.

"Devil-whelped cur!" he snarled.

Several gillies scurried out of his way, no doubt fearing a similar fate as the dog. Dunkeld snatched a candle from a wall sconce and stomped up the stairs to his rooms.

"Fetch me some wine," he ordered his valet when he entered. The fool bobbed his head and rushed off.

Dunkeld plunked the candle on the table and spread the rolled parchment wide. He'd already read the missive twice, but he read it again. MacCurran had escaped the constable of Leith. The wretched cur was a bloody ghost. And now he was wandering free. He could be anywhere.

He pushed away from the table in disgust, allowing the parchment to curl up with a snap. How many times must he gather the man in his grasp, only to see him slip between his fingers? He ought to be long dead. Instead, the man tormented him.

Pacing the floor in front of the fire, Dunkeld struggled to tame his rage. An angry man did not think well. He was capable of crushing MacCurran, but to do so he had to find the man's weakness.

His valet returned with the wine.

Dunkeld snatched it from his hands and barked, "Get out!"

Downing the contents of the cup in a single long swallow, he barely tasted the wine. But it sang through his veins and warmed the cold lump in his belly.

The woman was his only hope.

If he could find her, he could gain the advantage.

Sadly, the last time he'd seen her, she'd been with MacCurran, and if she remained so, his cause was lost. But he'd found her once at the weavers' guild house. The head of the guild was her father. Wasn't it possible she might return there?

Dunkeld closed his eyes, sucked in a deep breath, and let it out slowly.

A good king ruled with equal parts patience and ruthlessness—the ability to wait out his enemy combined with the courage to do whatever was necessary to win the day. He was that man. Those qualities had taken him this far, and if he but held the faith, they would gain him the crown.

He pictured himself seated on the throne, a jeweled crown upon his brow, and he smiled.

To the guild house, then.

By the time Morag traveled to Edinburgh from Leith and forded the line at the gate, it was dark. Her feet aching and her heart heavy, she flopped down on a pile of old burlap sacks.

The more she thought about returning to Dunstoras, the tighter her chest became. What was left for her there? If she could not weave, how would she make her way? And without Wulf, how could she live at the bothy? Every corner of the little house held memories of him now. She would be constantly reminded of the time she'd had with him—a bittersweet memory she wasn't sure she could endure.

Perhaps it would be better to remain in Edinburgh, at least for a time. Until the ache of Wulf's loss was more bearable. Her father had a powerful position in the burgh—and he'd already proven he could provide a measure of safety, even against Dunkeld. Surely if pressed he could find work her curled fingers could conquer?

Morag pushed to her feet, refusing to let her

maudlin thoughts gain purchase. She was a capable woman. She would make her way, just as she'd always done. Curled fingers or no.

She trudged wearily to the guild house door and knocked, but no one answered. It was the supper hour and most people had gone home.

"Are ye seeking Master Parlan?" a passing lad asked.

Morag nodded.

The boy pointed down the street. "He lives in Gordon's Close. Perhaps he'll see you there."

Morag thanked the lad and stared down the street. Safety with Parlan would come at a price. Thus far, she'd kept her relationship with her father as distant as possible. Visiting him in his home would invite a more personal connection—while under his roof, she would be hard-pressed to deny his questions about her mother or the past. Was she ready for that?

Morag sighed. Perhaps she was.

Although her feet protested, the soles throbbing, she set off down the lane. She would need a place to bide the night as well. A guild master would surely possess a hearth large enough to accommodate a guest.

With the aid of another passerby, she found herself in front of a pleasant little bothy with a neatly thatched roof and two shuttered windows. There was a small herb garden in the front, freshly tended and beginning to sprout new growths of thyme and rosemary. Morag tried to picture her father on his knees in the dirt, and failed.

Clearly she did not know the man well.

She rapped on the blue-painted door.

A moment later, the portal swung open, and Morag found herself staring at a slim lass of ten or twelve years. The girl wore a simple but finely crafted gown and stitched leather boots that put Morag's rough footwear to shame. She smiled a pretty smile. "Aye?"

Suddenly uncertain, Morag glanced over the girl's head into the bothy. A number of people were seated around the blazing hearth, soup bowls in hand. One of them she recognized as Parlan's apprentice, Douglas. "Is Master Parlan within?"

The girl nodded and spun around. "Da! A woman to speak with ye."

Morag froze. *Da.*

This was his daughter. Why hadn't she considered that? Her father had not only begun a new career in Edinburgh, he'd started a new family. She stared at the spill of long dark hair falling down the young lass's back and swallowed a sour mouthful of spit. He had never returned to Dunstoras because he'd had no need. He had all he needed here—a new loom, a new wife, and a new daughter.

Her gaze lifted to the lad seated by the fire.

Better yet, he now had a *son*. A lad he could teach his craft to. A lad who would surely become a skilled weaver, because he would have a father to guide him every day, to share all the secrets of fine-cloth making. A lad who wouldn't have to peer at old notes and pray he'd correctly interpreted the ingredients that made the colorful dyes her father was famed for. A lad who wouldn't be forced to use trial and error to discover the art of pattern making, wasting yards of wool in the process.

Morag turned away from the open door and strode off.

A lad who wouldn't stare down the lane for hours, wondering whether his da would ever come home.

"Morag!"

She heard her father call her name but she didn't stop. What a fool she'd been to think there might be a place for her here. Her home was in Dunstoras. The memories might be bittersweet, but they were memories of her own making. She wouldn't choke over them like she was choking right now.

"Morag!"

She picked up her pace, her walk becoming a run.

And then, because her day hadn't yet thrown her every challenge it could, the heavy clouds in the sky finally gave up the rain they'd been threatening for hours. Fat drops to begin with, then a steady stream. By the time Morag passed the guild house, she was soaked to the skin.

Water ran down her face in rivulets, only half of which were rain.

It had been a long time since Morag had let herself weep. The occasional tear, aye. Those were common enough. But great racking sobs that burned her throat and clogged her nose? Not since her mother died.

Perhaps that was why she didn't see William Dunkeld until it was too late.

"Sire, it would be most unwise to travel," de Keith said, as the king strode down the corridor, his chief advisers following in his wake. "The weather has turned quite foul."

"And there are still issues to settle with the earls," the Earl of Buchan added.

King Alexander spun around to face them, his expression angry and determined. "I go to Kinghorn today. There will be no further delays. Do you understand?"

Dunkeld smiled. His brother could be quite stubborn when the mood struck him. And when it came to his queen, the mood struck him often.

"I will not be absent for my lady's celebration," the king said, continuing down the hall to his rooms. "Ready my horse."

"As you wish, sire," de Keith said. He bowed and departed.

Dunkeld and Buchan followed Alexander into his private rooms, where the valets de chambre were waiting with the royal wardrober. As his attendants prepared him for the ride to Kinghorn, the king addressed the Earl of Buchan, the justiciar. "Meet with the earls. Explain my need to depart and invite them to wait upon my return, at my hospitality."

"But their desire is to formally announce Yolande's child as the new heir. Why not simply make that proclamation?"

Alexander waited until his red tunic was replaced by a pale blue one with gold thread running through it. "Until the child is born there will be no proclamation. The maid Margaret will remain my heir until that time."

Buchan frowned. "But, sire, you know the earls are unhappy that your heir resides on foreign soil. Especially Norse soil."

"They must learn to be patient," Alexander said. "In a matter of months Yolande will deliver me a son, and this bickering over nothing will be seen as a waste of time. There are more important matters to attend to."

"Aye, sire," Buchan said, bowing.

"Now go," the king said. "Keep them busy while I ride out of the gate."

The justiciar left the room, and Dunkeld stepped into the light. "The weather is truly hellish, brother. The storm has swept across the city like a biblical torrent, and may very well plague you all the way to Kinghorn."

Alexander shrugged. "So be it. A little rain will not damage the king of Scotland."

"I did not receive notice that you would be leaving this eve," Dunkeld said, plucking a candied plum from the bowl on the table.

"There was no need," the king said. "I am not taking a full complement of guards. Just my four *gardes du corps*."

Dunkeld raised a brow. "Is that wise?"

"'Tis a short journey," the king said, "over friendly territory. There's no need for a show of arms."

"But you are the king," Dunkeld pointed out dryly.

Alexander chuckled. "If you feel strongly that I need more protection, you may accompany me."

It was the invitation Dunkeld had been angling for, and he grabbed at it. "It would be my honor to accompany you, sire. If you would allow me, I would beg a moment to collect a unique gift for Her Grace's birthday celebration."

"A moment," the king granted. "But not much longer. I must be away."

Dunkeld bowed deeply and left the room.

Such an opportunity might never come again. A stormy night, only a handful of guards, and a rocky trail overland to Kinghorn. It had been his intent to poison the queen first, and watch the horror on his brother's face as he realized he was once again without male issue. But slaying a king was a difficult business. Alexander had testers to ensure his food wasn't tampered with, and now that de Lourdes was dead, it would be impossible to poison another object like the necklace.

But throwing him off a cliff?

It was perfect. All he had to do was separate the four guards from the king for a brief moment and startle the man's horse. A slippery trail and the rocks below would take care of the rest.

But he had his guest to see to, as well.

Bringing her along was not his preferred choice, but his only choice. The woman had already succeeded in breaking MacCurran out of the castle—he wasn't about to leave her alone to save herself. Besides, he needed to know what she knew. He could rip truths from her lips as easily at Kinghorn as he could here in Edinburgh. Kinghorn Castle had a delightful dungeon built into the cliffs. No one would hear the lass scream.

Dunkeld skipped down the stairs into the bowels of Edinburgh Castle. He signaled the guard to open the cell, then drew his sword and entered. Why take chances?

She was standing near the back wall of the cell, taking no comfort from the fat straw mattress or the chair provided. He barely recognized her now that she was mostly dry and her hair had been neatly braided. The weeping, defeated woman he had dragged here an hour ago had disappeared.

She met his gaze easily, even smiled when she saw the sword in his hand. Not a kind smile. More of a sneer.

He picked up her brat. His memory hadn't deceived him. It was a lovely piece of wool, woven with brilliant colors and finished to a soft sheen. The queen would be pleased with such a gift.

"Bring this with you," he said. "We journey to Kinghorn."

A frown lowered her brow. "Why Kinghorn?"

"Your place is not to ask questions," he answered, "but to do as I bid. Gather your brat, or weather the storm without it."

She collected her brat.

"You will speak to no one, save to me," he said, leading the way out. The guard brought up the rear. "The tale I have given the king is that you will weave a cloth for Queen Yolande in celebration of her birthday, a design of her own choosing."

They reached the courtyard, where the king's white stallion stood bridled and ready in the gusting rain, along with six other horses. Dunkeld put a hand on the woman's arm. "You will have opportunity to speak with others on our journey. I highly recommend you keep what you know to yourself. My reach is great—especially here in Edinburgh. Cross me in any way and I shall see your father and his family into hell. Is that clear?"

She nodded, but there was no cowering in her eyes, no fear for his retribution.

That gave Dunkeld pause. If she did not fear him, she would be difficult to control, and he did not want trouble. Not tonight. Tonight his focus had to be on his brother . . . and the crown.

"Good," said King Alexander, walking past him into the downpour. "You are here. Let us be off."

The king and his guards mounted, leaving Dunkeld no choice but to follow suit. If he begged another delay to return Morag to her cell, the king would leave without him.

He helped her mount, then leapt upon his own horse.

As they rode out of the castle gate, horse hooves clopping on the cobbles, Dunkeld shed his doubts and settled into a cool, calculating calm. As rain dripped off his hood and the wind snapped the wet edges of his cloak, he smiled.

This was his moment.

Everything he had done thus far had led here. His plan was finally coming to fruition. After tonight, events would unfold swiftly. The king's council would be thrown into turmoil with Alexander's death. They would pray for the healthy birth of Yolande's babe and bicker over who would rule during the minority. The queen would receive her dead husband's last gift—a glorious necklace painted with lethal poison—and Dunkeld would encourage her to wear it at his state funeral.

Dunkeld's smile grew.

Once the babe was dead, the council would send for young Margaret, the Maid of Norway. But Dunkeld had already seen to the fate of the young princess. She would not survive the journey to Scotland.

And in the midst of all the turmoil, he would be the quiet voice of reason. He would step into the breach and make the decisions others were too weak to make. Today the earls turned their noses up at the thought of him wearing the crown, but when all of Alexander's heirs were buried in the ground, and the option was to send Scotland hurtling into political war, they would come crawling to him on their knees. He would be the only remaining blood heir.

They would beg him to be king.

Dunkeld's gaze lifted to the sight of his handsome brother leading their party. Windswept and sodden, he still looked regal on his fine white steed. History would right itself tonight.

Justice was about to be served.

* * *

Wulf ran a hand over the stallion's wet withers, his experienced eye looking for any sign of distress in the rented beast's body. When he was certain the horse was in fine shape, he paid the farmer his coin and promised to return the animal in two days' time.

The stallion was not a destrier built for battle. Nor was it a courser built for speed. It was a heavy stock animal bred to pull a plow, but it could gallop at a fine clip and hold Wulf's weight with ease. It would do.

He was about to vault onto the beast's back when he spied an old man walking down the path in the rain toward him. Not Elen's father, but a familiar face just the same. One he hadn't seen in a number of years.

"Bhaltair?"

The old man looked up. He wore an ankle-length lèine and a dark cloak, and sported a long white beard that reached past his belt. Rain dripped from his sharp nose. "Ah, there you are, lad."

Wulf shook his head. The old druid had lived for years in an old ruin south of Dunstoras keep. To see him here was a surprise. "You are a long way from home. What brings you here?"

Bhaltair patted the stallion's muzzle. "I follow the stars," he said.

"They led you to Holyrood?"

He smiled. "They led me to you."

Wulf tightened the baldric strapped around his chest and shoulder, making certain it was secure, as wet leather tended to stretch. "I've not the time to break bread with you," he said. "I've just received word that a man I seek has ridden out of Edinburgh Castle."

Bhaltair nodded. "You must go."

Wulf leapt up on the horse. "Take care, old man."

"The stars say this is a night of dramatic change," Bhaltair said. "The fate of Scotland will be decided tonight."

Wulf frowned. "Scotland?"

The fate of William Dunkeld for certain. That he intended to change. But slaying Dunkeld should have no bearing on the future of Scotland.

Bhaltair released the horse's muzzle and stepped back. "They head for Kinghorn. This steed will not be fleet enough to give chase. You must travel for Leith, and take a boat around the headland to Kinghorn harbor. In the town, you will find a faster horse to take you into the hills."

Wulf stared at him.

The old man was asking a lot to have him take that route based only on his word. What if Dunkeld was not headed for Kinghorn? On the other hand, Bhaltair was rumored to be a druid—a diviner and mystic of some renown. Wulf's cousin

Niall and the Black Warriors swore they had witnessed him perform magic.

"Taking a boat around the headland on a night like tonight would be perilous," he said.

"Aye," Bhaltair agreed. "But everything you lay value to is at stake. The risks of not taking the boat are far greater."

It wasn't the old man's words that convinced him. It was the flash of lightning that lit up the sky behind him as he spoke. For an instant Bhaltair was perfectly highlighted against the stormy sky, the ends of his long white hair floating despite the rain. As portents went, it wasn't unusual, but it was dramatic.

"Then I'm for Leith," he said.

The old druid smiled. "May your travels be swift and the aim of your sword be true, Wulf MacCurran. Godspeed."

Wulf threw caution to the wind and urged his plow horse into a canter. It felt wrong to leave the old man standing in the downpour, but when he glanced back, there was no sign of Bhaltair. Just an empty path and the outline of Holyrood Abbey.

Trying not to lay meaning on that, he leaned over his horse and rode like a madman for the coast.

It was well past midnight when they reached the cliffs overlooking Kinghorn. The king's party, sodden and miserable, had slowed to a walk. The cliffs were muddy, and it was difficult to see in the driving rain.

Dunkeld kneed his horse to come alongside his brother. "The castle is almost within view, sire. Shall I send the guards ahead to prepare for your arrival? Dry clothing and a cup of hot mead are an absolute must."

"Aye," shouted Alexander, as another lightning strike rumbled through the air. His shoulder-length brown hair was plastered to his head, his beard aglitter with drops of rain. Weariness lay in every line of his face.

Dunkeld had to bite back a smile.

Really, this was going to be too easy.

Falling back, he waved to the guards bringing up the rear. "Go on ahead," he told them. "Announce His Grace's arrival and ensure a proper greeting."

The guards urged their mounts into a canter and rode off into the fog and rain, passing the king and then swiftly disappearing from view. Dunkeld twisted in his saddle to glare at Morag. "Stay here," he said quietly. "I'll return momentarily."

She stared back at him, her expression cool.

Dunkeld felt compelled to add, "Attempting to ride off would be foolish. You are not an accomplished rider and it would be easy to become lost or lose your footing on these slippery cliffs."

Her stare remained cool and hard.

Although he worried she might try to flee, Dunkeld left her behind. He needed a moment alone with his brother, and that moment was far more important than any lass. Even MacCurran's lass.

Encouraging his horse into a trot, he caught up to his brother. Walking alongside him, he waited for the best spot with the steepest drop to the beach below. The horses were already tired and a bit skittish from all the lightning. It wouldn't take much to spook the king's stallion. The beast was magnificent and strong, but high-strung.

"If you had your wish," Dunkeld asked his brother, "what would you have the historians say about your reign?"

Alexander glanced at him. "What a curious question."

Dunkeld shrugged. "I think about our father from time to time, and the legacy he left behind. Would he have been pleased to know that the songs sung about him mostly remember a bairn whose brains were dashed upon a stone?"

The king shook his head and droplets sprayed. "Nay, he would not. But the people favor an entertaining story and the grisly death of the MacWilliam's infant daughter is one that begs to be retold."

Dunkeld agreed. "What story will they tell of you?"

Alexander grinned. "I should like them to remember that I outwitted the Norse and reclaimed the Western Isles. But they might prefer to recall that I once rode to Kinghorn in the middle of a stormy night to visit my new bride on the eve of her birthday."

"Both good tales."

Dunkeld judged this spot to be as good as any. The embankment was especially steep here, and large boulders lay at the bottom. So he palmed his dirk and prepared to jab the king's horse.

Chapter 16

Wulf did not question why a man with a fine bay stallion waited for him when he stumbled from the boat. He was too ill from the turbulent seas to dwell upon it. He simply mounted, threw a coin at the man, and rode off.

Compared to the wild pitching of the boat under his feet, the horse was an easy ride, even in the mud. He passed the castle, a lovely stone hold standing high and proud on the headland, and climbed into the hills beyond. Torches were ablaze at the castle, suggesting the king had not yet arrived, and he encouraged his mount to greater speed.

His challenge would be to avoid the king's guard.

The only logical way to do that would be to lay an ambush along the king's route, and pray for an opportunity that allowed him to attack Dunkeld alone. He found a perfect spot in a small copse of trees along the ridge overlooking the rocky beach, and reined in his mount. The path to the castle led right past him, and even in the driving rain and heavy fog he was certain he would spy their passing.

Waiting proved difficult.

The wind tore at him, rain poured down from the skies in sheets, and his horse churned the ground at his feet into a thick ooze of mud.

But Wulf held to his plan.

And he was rewarded. In between the occasional flashes and crashes of lightning, he heard the rumble of horses cantering toward him. He peered through the gloom, waiting for a glimpse of the riders. Four mounted men tore past him, not a dozen feet from where he was hidden in the trees. All four wore the red-and-gold capes of the king's guard and displayed weary faces eager to reach the comfort of the castle.

Dunkeld was not among them.

Wulf frowned. Neither was the king.

He stared up the path. Elen's father had reported that Dunkeld was in a small party. How many were left to come? His heart thumped a slow, steady rhythm in his chest. For some reason, Bhaltair's odd words at Holyrood were echoing in his head. *The fate of Scotland will be decided tonight.*

Were Dunkeld and the king alone?

And if they were, what did that mean?

The four guards who rode by did not look to be panicked or angry—merely determined to reach the castle. Their pace had been quick but not frenzied. So nothing had happened to the king.

Not yet, a whisper in his head said.

Dunkeld might be the king's trusted brother, but he was also the man in black. The man who had poisoned the king's courier, stolen the queen's necklace, and murdered Wulf's family. His reasons remained unclear, but all of it seemed to revolve around one person—the king.

Was he reading too much into Bhaltair's warning?

Perhaps.

But Dunkeld was not the man King Alexander believed him to be.

Wulf urged his horse out of the trees and onto the path. Not entirely certain what his intent was, he set out across the ridgetop. If he encountered a large group of the king's guard, his hopes of slaying Dunkeld would be dashed. Still, his gut was telling him to ride, so he rode.

Morag's experience with horses was limited to a handful of rides on the back of Wulf's destrier, and this miserable midnight journey across the land. Were it daylight, she might have been tempted to whirl about and make a break for freedom. But not tonight. In the storm she would swiftly become lost.

Staying where Dunkeld told her to stay was not her only option, however.

He and the king had disappeared into the darkness together, and something told her Dunkeld was up to no good. Morag knew nothing of court intrigue or political maneuvering, but she knew a lot about liars and deceivers. Men who swore devotion with one breath and demanded a shunning the next. And she knew Dunkeld should not be alone with the king.

Morag prodded her horse with her heels and sent a prayer skyward.

Now would certainly be a fine time for Wulf to appear.

Wulf was nearly upon Dunkeld and the king when a flash of lightning revealed them riding along the ridgetop. The wind was howling and the rain was lashing sideways, so the king's head was down, buried beneath the hood of his cloak. He did not see what Wulf could see—Dunkeld's hand raised, the shining tip of a dirk aimed at his horse's flank.

Wulf shouted a warning, but the wind carried it away. And in a flash, the world went dark again, the king lost to him in the darkness.

Wulf spurred his horse forward, praying he was mistaken. He'd seen them for only a moment. Perhaps he'd only imagined the dirk in Dunkeld's hand. But he feared the worst. Dunkeld was a madman—his continued persecution of Clan MacCurran was evidence of it. If he was bent on doing harm to the king, he would be difficult to stop.

He rode furiously toward the king, hoping he could reach him in time.

Another lightning bolt lit up the night sky, and Wulf peered ahead.

The pair on the ridge was much closer now, but what he saw this time shot an icy spear into his gut. Morag, on a horse, colliding with Dunkeld. No sign of the king or his fine white steed. What was Morag doing here? Why was she not safe with Bran, making preparation to return to Dunstoras? The world went dark again, and Wulf raced toward the battle on the cliff top.

Morag was no match for Dunkeld.

Time passed too slowly, the only sounds in his ears the horse's labored breathing and the pounding of its hooves on the muddy ground. And then suddenly they rose up out of the mist and rain—Dunkeld and Morag, no longer on horseback, but slipping and sliding in the mud. Dunkeld's fist swung. Wulf saw Morag's head snap back, and she fell heavily to the ground. In the blink of an eye, his past and his present collided. Despite his grief over his lost wife and son, he loved Morag. More than life itself.

A rage like he'd never known filled his heart, and he drew his sword.

"Dunkeld!" Reining hard, he leapt off his mount. "You black-hearted wretch. Prepare to meet your maker."

The man in black glanced up, took one look at Wulf's face, and grabbed for Morag's hair. He hauled her to her feet and laid his sword to her throat. "Come no closer, or she dies."

Morag's head lolled against her captor's shoulder, her eyes half-closed. Her left cheek bore the rosy red imprint of Dunkeld's fist, and Wulf had to stem a rush of hot anger. "Is that how a prince does battle, Dunkeld? With a woman as his shield?"

Dunkeld backed up, edging closer to his skittish mount. "I can't speak for princes," he said. "But it's how wise men do battle."

"Traitors and craven curs, perhaps," Wulf said. "But not wise men."

A faint smile settled on Dunkeld's lips. "Shall we let history be the judge? I suspect that when I reach Kinghorn Castle and inform the queen that Wulf MacCurran has murdered her beloved husband, it will be you who is seen as a craven cur, not I."

Wulf pointed the tip of his blade at Dunkeld's

heart. Rain spattered on the polished steel and ran down the edge in a stream. "You mean *if* you reach Kinghorn Castle."

"Nay, I mean *when*." Dunkeld dragged Morag back another step. "You and I both know that should you make a single move toward me, it will take but an instant to slit your woman's throat. I will not hesitate. She will die in your arms, with her blood on your hands."

Wulf refused to let that chilling image surface in his thoughts. Morag would not die.

Not this night. Not while he still had breath in his body.

"A meaningless threat," he jeered. "I care naught about the woman. I am here for vengeance. You poisoned my wife and son at Dunstoras, and tonight you pay the price."

Doubt flickered in Dunkeld's eyes, but even as Wulf watched, he shook it off. Water spraying, he took a determined step toward his horse and reached for the dangling reins. "Four months is a long time to delay vengeance."

"I was injured," said Wulf, scowling. With Dunkeld's blade so close to Morag's tender skin, there was no room to free her. He needed an opening. "Your reprieve ends now."

Wulf tensed, ready to strike. The best opportunity would come when Dunkeld leapt upon the horse, but Wulf would need to be quick. The cur would slit Morag's throat and toss her aside before he raced for Kinghorn; that was a certainty. He had nothing to gain by letting her live.

Wulf got his chance.

Thanks to Morag.

She chose that moment to open her eyes with a gasp, and stiffen in Dunkeld's grip. Her sudden movement startled Dunkeld, and the sharp sword against her throat drooped. Only an inch, and only for an instant, but it was all the opportunity Wulf needed. He pounced.

The length of Dunkeld's weapon was his downfall.

Wulf struck the tip of his opponent's blade with a powerful downward whack, taking the sharp edge away from Morag's neck. She did the rest, ducking out of the man's hold and scurrying away. Once he knew she was safe, Wulf let the slow burn of impending justice flow through his veins. This bastard had murdered Elen and Hugh, and quite likely the king. There was none more deserving of death than he.

His muscles warm and loose, Wulf attacked.

Dunkeld was no weakling. He had spent a lifetime with a sword in his hands, but he was not the warrior Wulf was. Wulf felt as if he had been born with his blade in his hand. The fit and weight of it in his palm were perfect, and every swing came as natural as breathing.

But it wasn't an easy win.

The rain and the mud made the duel a challenge for both men. Wet hands and slippery footing played havoc with their aim and stole power from their hits. Neither of them scored a single slice in the first few minutes of engagement. Dunkeld's strategy was defensive—he parried and blocked far more often than he attempted a strike. But Wulf's intent was to take the man down. His movements were spare to conserve energy, but he leveraged every true opportunity.

Men without honor made difficult opponents, however.

Dunkeld was willing to sacrifice anything to win, even his horse. Just as Wulf swung his blade, his opponent ducked to the left and tugged on the reins. The horse stepped into the arc of Wulf's swing, and he had to swiftly adjust his aim to avoid decapitating the creature. As it was, the edge of his blade clipped the animal's shoulder, and it squealed in pain. Not a serious wound, but enough to cause the horse to rear up, flailing its front hooves.

Wulf stumbled back, one foot sliding wildly in the mud.

Dunkeld took advantage, attacking Wulf's sword arm with a vicious slice.

His ploy might have succeeded, save that the cur neglected to factor in Morag. From somewhere behind Wulf, she lobbed a great glob of mud at Dunkeld's face, hitting him just above one eye. Half blinded by the dripping ooze, he swung wide of his target, and Wulf was able to regain his footing.

Dunkeld swiftly wiped his face with his sleeve and snarled at Morag, "I'll see you into hell for that, you ill-favored jade."

"Not if I see you into hell first," she shouted back.

She certainly did her part. As Wulf attacked with the strength of his sword arm, she continued to pelt Dunkeld with mud. But the villainous wretch barely took note after the first hit. His attention was locked on Wulf, his determination to triumph written in every tight line of his face.

"No MacCurran will best me," he vowed. "Not Duncan, not your laird, not you."

Wulf said nothing.

"I am the rightful king of Scotland, and I will wear the crown."

"You are a traitor and a maligner," Wulf contested. "You will *never* wear the crown."

Dunkeld lashed out with his blade, the tip catching the sleeve of Wulf's lèine, slicing through the sodden material with ease. But he drew no blood.

Wulf held his blade loosely in front of his body, the tip high, waiting for the right moment. Rain dripped off his nose and chin, and his hair was plastered to the sides of his face, but none of those discomforts burrowed into his thoughts. All that mattered was the occasional narrowing of Dunkeld's eyes, and the slight tensing of his muscles before he made a move. Wulf knew the instant Dunkeld decided to feint and stab.

And he met the man's attack with an attack of his own.

Their blades collided and slithered along their edges, sighing in the rain.

Only one blade met its intended target. The other passed to the right of Wulf's face, narrowly missing his ear. Wulf felt his sword strike true, felt the resistance that told him he'd made the right call. Dunkeld's face registered shock, his eyes wide, his lips slack.

The man in black dropped to his knees in the mud, releasing his weapon.

"Nay," he said softly. "This not how it should end."

"You brought the end about yourself," Wulf said. "You betrayed your king."

Dunkeld's gaze dropped to his chest, and his hands wrapped around Wulf's blade. "I will still win."

Wulf frowned. How did dying upon another man's blade constitute a win?

A crooked smile lifted one side of Dunkeld's face. "If I cannot wear the crown, then neither shall any child begat of my brother. They are all doomed. I've seen to it."

Wulf grabbed Dunkeld's shoulder. "What have you done?"

Dunkeld laughed, and choked on his blood. "Everything."

Wulf squeezed hard. "Tell me what you have done."

But Dunkeld had retreated into his own thoughts. When Wulf let go, he fell to the ground, smiling. His eyes were unfocused, staring sightlessly into the darkness. "So beautiful she'll look . . . in death."

And then he died.

Wulf stared at his nemesis for a long moment, watching the rain splatter on his pale face and pool in the mud around him. He had hoped this death would bring him peace. That the memories of that night in November would lose their sharpness once the man in black was gone. But the ache in his chest was as painful as ever.

Morag slipped her hand into his and hugged his left arm.

"We must find the king," he said, threading his fingers with hers.

She pointed to the edge of the cliff where the turf was churned into a muddy bath. "There. I fear it will not be good news. Dunkeld stabbed the king's horse in the flank, and the frightened beast tossed the king from his saddle. It followed him over the side a moment later."

They peered over the ridge, hoping to spot the king, but there was only darkness. The mist and rain made it impossible to see more than a dozen feet down, and the bottom was much farther than that.

"Stay here," Wulf said, brushing a kiss over her knuckles.

He handed her his sword, then leapt over the side and slid a way down the embankment. He reached a boulder that hung over a steep drop, and there he paused. "Sire! Can you hear me?"

He listened intently, but there was no answer. Just the wind and the rain and the low rumble of thunder over the sea. Unable to descend farther without losing his footing, Wulf climbed back up the embankment.

At Morag's raised brow, he shook his head.

"How will we explain what has transpired?" she asked. "Dunkeld was right. If we bring our tale to the castle, no one will believe us innocent. They will accuse us of murdering the king."

He nodded. "We will take Dunkeld's body back to Dunstoras and let the king's guard retrieve His Grace. If he is alive, they will find him in the morn, after the storm has passed. If he is dead—"

"But that's not right," she cried. "They might simply believe he lost his way."

He frowned. "It eats at my gut that Dunkeld will never be seen as the murderous traitor he was, but I see no way to cast blame upon him. He was the king's beloved brother. We are the only ones who know the truth."

"Perhaps he carried something in his possession," she said, turning to look at his horse. "Some document that outlines his plans."

"He'd have to be a fool to pen such a document," Wulf said dryly. "And Dunkeld was anything but a fool."

"We cannot give up so easily." She carefully approached Dunkeld's injured mount, using soothing words and slow movements. It was still trembling badly, but it allowed her near. "Are you not worried about the words he uttered with his last breath?"

"Even Dunkeld cannot reach beyond the grave," Wulf said.

"But he implied his evil deeds were already afoot."

That he had. And dying men had no reason to lie.

She scooped up the reins and gently stroked the horse's muzzle. "There now, laddie. The worst is done. Let me have a look at that wound."

Wulf crossed to the horse, and while Morag cleaned the sword graze on its shoulder with the sodden corner of her brat, he went through Dunkeld's bag. As he expected, there were no incriminating documents tucked inside. But he found something else—the gold-and-ruby necklace that had been stolen the night Elen and Hugh were slain. Queen Yolande's necklace. His gut churned as he stared into the velvet bag. If it was possible to hate an object, then he hated this necklace. It lay at the root of all his troubles.

He was tempted to throw it over the cliff.

But it was extremely valuable. The king had commissioned it as a gift to his bride on their wedding day, and at its center lay a large heart-shaped ruby. A rare gem that might well be the king's last gift to his beloved queen.

Morag leaned over his arm, peering into the velvet bag. "It's beautiful."

"It is," he agreed. Then he frowned. Beautiful.

What had Dunkeld's last words been? *She'll be so beautiful in death.* Had he been imagining the queen wearing this necklace as she died? It surely could not be a coincidence that he had it in his possession. But what harm could a necklace do?

Wulf shook the bag, listening to the jingle of fine gold links.

The necklace had been part of Dunkeld's plan from the beginning. All the death and destruction he had wrought could be traced back to the night in November when it was stolen. But what had he hoped to gain? Had his intent been to tamper with it in some way?

If so, how?

The pale blue face of his young son rose in Wulf's thoughts. The necklace was not the only common thread in Dunkeld's mad plan. Was it possible to coat a necklace with poison? If so, it would be a terribly effective weapon. The queen would drape the gem around her neck thinking it a glorious gift, only to sicken and die—her babe along with her.

Alexander's line would die with that babe, just as Dunkeld predicted.

He lifted the velvet bag over his head and prepared to throw it.

"Wait," Morag said, grabbing his arm.

"He poisoned it," Wulf said hoarsely, the image of wee Hugh vivid in his mind.

"Aye," she agreed. "He likely did. But if he did, that necklace is your way back into the good graces of the crown. Let them find it and the black wolf cloak amid his possessions. They will hearken back to Laird MacCurran's tale of a man in black and give new weight to his testimony. Tomorrow we will surrender ourselves to the castle with our tale of Dunkeld's treachery and beg them to test the necklace."

Wulf lowered his arm. "A fine plan, if the necklace is truly poisoned."

"There's only one way to know that," she said slowly, shaking her head.

"I must touch it," he said, realization a heaviness in his chest.

"Nay!"

Wulf brushed a raindrop from Morag's chin. "We need to know the truth."

Morag grabbed his hand. "This is madness. If it's truly poisoned, it could kill you!"

"I'll hold the necklace for the briefest of moments." He peered into her green eyes, begging her to understand. "There's no other way to be certain, lass. And we need to be certain. Our fate—and the fate of our clan—depends on proving Dunkeld duplicitous."

Morag shook her head. "Don't ask me to agree. I can't."

Her disapproval was evident, and Wulf knew he would not sway her. But he also knew that if they hoped to clear the MacCurran name and live a life without the constant fear of arrest, he had no choice. Tipping the bag, Wulf emptied it into his palm, then immediately poured it back into the bag.

"Why did you do that?" Morag said, aghast. "Are you mad?"

He tucked the velvet bag into Dunkeld's pouch and quickly washed his hands in the rain. "If I sicken, we will know it was poisoned."

"And if you die?"

He pressed a hard kiss upon her lips. "Tell me that you love me, and I'll die a happy man."

"I love you, Wulf MacCurran, but that was a witless thing to do." Her tone was angry, but Wulf could see that she was genuinely frightened. As was he. He gathered her against his chest and planted a gentle kiss atop her wet head.

"Had there been any other way," he said, "I'd not have touched the wicked thing. Leaving you is not my desire."

A mild wave of nausea crested over him, and he released her, stepping away. Even in the pouring rain, he was suddenly stiflingly hot, his mouth dry. A second wave hit him, this one harder, and he bent over, retching onto the turf. Dear Lord, it had been only a moment since he touched the necklace. His gaze met Morag's.

"I think we have our answer," he whispered.

Then he dropped to his knees, overwhelmed by weariness. And an instant later, he collapsed face-down in the mud.

Morag rolled Wulf over on his back, shocked by the swift advance of the poison. His skin was already burning hot, his cheeks flushed. Desperate to protect him from the rain, she glanced around. The only trees in view were a league in the distance—

too far to drag him. All she had were the three horses and their cloaks.

They would have to do.

She walked each horse to one side of Wulf's prostrate form, then draped the cloaks over the saddles, tying the corners with the reins. It was a flawed arrangement—water leaked in almost everywhere—but it shunted the bulk of the downpour away from Wulf. She huddled in the tiny lean-to and held Wulf to her chest. During the night he went from hot and dry to shivering and restless and back again. At one point he was so still and pale that she put her ear to his mouth, checking for breath. Fortunately, he was indeed still breathing.

Midway through the night, the storm broke.

The wind gentled and the rain eased to a light drizzle. With the skies calmed, Morag finally allowed her eyes to close. But not for long. The end of the storm would bring soldiers from the castle searching for the king, and she and Wulf had to be gone by the time they arrived.

When she awoke from her doze, Morag had the sense that something had changed. But the night was still dark and the horses still stood quietly beside her. It was only when she touched Wulf's cheek that she realized he was cool to the touch and breathing the long, deep breaths of an effortless sleep.

She shook him gently. "Wulf?"

He opened his eyes, and Morag nearly wept with relief.

"How do you fare?" she asked.

"I live," he said, struggling to sit up. "So I'd say I fare well. We should be off. If we are spotted by the king's guard, our efforts will be for naught."

"Are you certain you are well enough to travel?"

He pushed to his feet. "Aye. My belly heaves and my legs tremble like an old man's, but I can sit a horse easily enough."

She unfastened their cloaks from the saddles, and attempted to mount her horse. The blasted creature kept shuffling, and she couldn't get a leg up. Wulf clasped her about the waist and lifted her into the saddle.

"When we return to Dunstoras, I shall teach you to ride," he said.

Morag stared at him, a warm feeling in her belly. They had not spoken of their return, not since Wulf had regained his memories. He would return to his old life; she knew that much. But might he visit her from time to time? Might he actually teach her to ride?

"I should enjoy that," she said happily.

He hefted Dunkeld's body over his horse's shoulders and then vaulted smoothly into his saddle, displaying little of the trembles of which he complained. Pointing to the dark outline of trees to the west, he said, "We'll head back the way you came and pray for a little more rain to dull our trail."

He set off, and Morag followed.

Chapter 17

Wulf's heart was heavy.

From the distant trees, he and Morag watched the guards retrieve the king's body from the beach below the ridge and head toward the castle. It was apparent from the solemnity of the group that he had not survived the fall.

"Had I not stopped to waylay Dunkeld, I could have saved him," he said.

"Had you not stopped, you would have met the king's guards as they rode to the castle," Morag reminded him. "You would never have reached the cliff, and Dunkeld would yet be alive."

"Bhaltair warned me that the fate of Scotland rested on my actions, and still I failed."

Morag put a hand on his arm. "What more could you have done?"

He shook his head. "I know not. I only know

the king is dead, and I was not man enough to prevent it."

Wulf turned away from the procession on the ridgetop and watched Morag. She collected her brat from the bushes on which it was drying, and tied it about her shoulders. Her fingers were still stiff and curled, but they had regained some flexibility. The sacrifices she had made on his behalf humbled him beyond measure. He did not deserve so fine a woman.

"This plan to ride into the castle is a little mad," he said. "I cannot ask you to accompany me."

She smiled. "I do not go because you ask it of me. I go because I love you."

He closed the gap between them in a single fluid step and cupped her face in his hands. "If the queen is not swayed by my tale, it may mean the gallows."

She covered his hands with hers. "I was a member of the king's party, a weaver brought along to fashion a gift for the queen's birthday. The guards will know me. My words will lend weight to yours."

Wulf kissed her. Slow and hard and deliberate.

"Let us save Scotland together, then," he said.

Wulf hid Dunkeld's body in the hollow of a fallen tree. If all went well at the castle, he would reveal its whereabouts. If his explanation met resistance, it would be better if the body was never found. Morag could vow that Dunkeld had run off, which would leave some measure of doubt regarding the events of the night.

They mounted their horses and left the trees. Crossing the cliff top, they passed the patch of mud that marked the loss of the king, and with solemn faces they rode down the path to the castle. The portcullis was lowered, despite the early hour of the day. Armed guards met them at the gate, denying them access.

"Begone," the guards said. "The queen sees no one today."

"I come with word of a plot against the crown," Wulf said boldly. "I need not speak with the queen, but I must have an audience with the king's *gardes du corps*."

His forthright demand set the guards on their heels. They looked at one another, confused about what to do. But Wulf had no time to waste. He had to tell his tale before the queen had opportunity to touch the ruby necklace.

"Fetch one of the *gardes du corps*," insisted Wulf. "Now."

"And who are you to make such a request?"

"Tell the king's bodyguards that Wulf MacCurran, champion of the outlawed Laird MacCurran, is at the gate."

That got the result Wulf sought. One of the guards took off for the main door of the castle at a run.

They did not have long to wait. The young sentry returned with a mail-clad knight bearing the tabard of the king's guard. The knight eyed Morag before giving Wulf his attention. "Whatever games you play, MacCurran, this is not the day for it."

"I am aware that the king has perished."

A thunderous scowl darkened the knight's face. "Be careful what words you toss about."

"The king's brother had a hand in his death," Wulf said.

"You lie!"

"Dunkeld is the one responsible for the theft of the queen's necklace. He wore a black wolf cloak the night de Coleville and my kin were murdered, a cloak that I believe he still possesses."

The knight drew his sword. "Why do you trouble us with this crazed tale? Today of all days?"

"Because the queen's life is in danger." Wulf held up his hands to show they were empty of weapons. "Slay me if you must, but first hear me out. The gold-and-ruby necklace the king intended to gift the queen has been poisoned by Dunkeld. You cannot allow her to touch it."

"A necklace cannot be poisoned," scoffed the knight.

"Test it," dared Wulf. "But beware. The poison painted on its surface is potent."

"You are mad," denounced the knight.

"It was potent enough to kill the Earl of Lochurkie

when he touched it." Wulf had no proof the earl had been killed by the necklace, but it was possible. The man had been poisoned while in possession of the wretched thing. "If you value the queen's life, and the life of her unborn child, you will search Dunkeld's belongings immediately and confiscate it."

The knight stared at him.

Then he pivoted on his heel and stalked off.

"Were we successful?" Morag asked quietly.

"Perhaps," he answered. The door to the guardhouse swung open and a dozen armed soldiers spilled out. They marched toward the gate. "Or perhaps not."

Wulf and Morag were dragged from their mounts and led into the castle at pike-point.

The inside of Kinghorn Castle was an opulent space. Arched ceilings, marble floors, and massive tapestries that covered whole walls surrounded them. The great hall was lit with hundreds of candles and a huge hearth that roared with a well-fed fire. Everywhere they looked there were cushioned chairs and carved tables. But the high table that would normally have seated the royal family was today serving as a resting place for the king of Scotland.

His body had been washed and garbed in silks.

His brown hair and beard shone golden in the candlelight.

Next to the table, on her knees with her veiled head bowed in prayer, was Queen Yolande.

Wulf and Morag stood silently, witnesses to her grief. Today was her twenty-third birthday, but instead of celebrating with joy, she was enduring the tragic loss of her husband. A slender woman given to wearing fine satin weaves, Yolande made no attempt to disguise the slight roundness of her belly. She was indeed quick with child, as the rumors had suggested.

The queen genuflected, then rose to her feet with the help of her spiritual adviser, the royal chancellor William Fraser. She turned to face them and waved a slender hand to indicate that they should advance.

With Morag's hand clasped tightly in his, Wulf stepped forward and bowed deeply.

"Your Grace."

"You may rise," she said, her French accent thick.

When Wulf's gaze lifted to her face, she said, "My guards say the necklace is indeed poisoned. Had I laid it upon my skin, I would now be dead."

Wulf said nothing.

"How do I know it was not you who poisoned it?" she asked.

"The clan MacCurran has always been loyal to the crown, Your Grace. The night your necklace was originally stolen, my wife and wee bairn were slain, felled by the same poisoned soup that killed de Coleville. My laird has always maintained that the culprit was not a MacCurran, but a man wearing a black wolf cloak. A cloak that William Dunkeld has been known to possess."

She nodded. "Such a cloak was found with the necklace."

"The king gave Dunkeld his trust, Your Grace, and he was betrayed."

"You think Dunkeld had a hand in my Alexander's death?"

"I do," he said.

"Why should I believe you? Dunkeld was a faithful brother to my husband. You are the champion of an outlaw."

"Was he truly faithful?" Wulf shrugged. "He had everything to gain from the king's death. Especially if every other heir to the crown was dead. What do the MacCurrans gain by the king's death? Nothing. Men without power do not change the fate of a nation, Your Grace. Bastard brothers to a king, on the other hand, can change everything. Ask the king's guards who sent them back to the castle, leaving the king alone. Was it me? I daresay not."

"But how can we be certain he had a hand in this? Dunkeld is nowhere to be found."

He shrugged. "Rats will run, Your Grace."

The queen tipped her head toward Morag. "And

you, madam? My guards have informed me that you are the daughter of a respected guild master and that you rode with my Alexander and his brother this past night. Tell me what you witnessed."

"I saw Dunkeld stab the king's horse in the flank."

Yolande shook her head. "What reason would he have to do such a thing?"

"I believe that Dunkeld aspires to wear the crown himself, Your Grace. He sent the guards ahead to the castle so he could be alone on the cliff with the king. And now the king is dead. Does that not say everything that needs to be said?"

"Perhaps."

"Surely the injury to the king's mount can be verified?"

Yolande glanced at the captain of her guard, and he nodded.

"It appears the horse did suffer a wound such as you describe."

Wulf saw Morag's shoulders straighten. "I am a mere weaver, Your Grace, and I know my word cannot stand against that of a nobleman. But I swear to you that what I saw is true. Dunkeld attacked the king."

"It will be up to the Guardians of Scotland to officially rule on Dunkeld's guilt," Yolande said.

"But I am satisfied that I know the truth." The queen wriggled a ring from her middle finger and held it out to Wulf. "You have proven yourself a worthy champion this day, MacCurran. Take this ring as a sign of my gratitude."

"Thank you, Your Grace."

She turned, intending to walk away.

"If I may, Your Grace?"

She paused.

"If you believe Dunkeld guilty, a pardon of my laird's crimes would not be undue," he said carefully. "If you have the power to influence such a thing, I would beg that favor."

She faced him. "I cannot return his lands. They have been forfeited."

Wulf nodded. "I understand."

"But I can speak to the council regarding a pardon. I'll see it done immediately."

Wulf bowed deeply.

As the soft swish of her satin skirts over the marble floor faded away, he straightened. Morag rose, too, and he grinned at her. This moment held a magic that the death of Dunkeld had not. His clan no longer had to hide. They were redeemed.

The moment they left the hall, Wulf grabbed Morag about the waist and spun her around until they were both a little dizzy.

"Are you ready to go home, lass?"

* * *

They did not immediately set out for Dunstoras.

Morag begged for an opportunity to return to Edinburgh, and Wulf could not deny her. Especially when she told him her reason.

"You cannot solve all the ills of the world," he said, shaking his head.

"True enough," she agreed. "But I can solve this one."

The first real test of the queen's influence came at the cow gate. When he broke out of Edinburgh Castle, all the city guards had been given his description and told to slay him on sight. But he was no longer a wanted criminal. And his possession of the queen's ring was enough to convince the guards at the gate of his new status.

They scowled, but made no attempt to detain him.

Morag sighed with relief and led them into the busy market on the High Street. She spied young Tim hiding between the breadbaskets at the baker's, and swiftly nabbed him. "If you continue this way," Morag scolded him, "you'll end up in the stocks."

He shrugged. "I've been worse places."

"Maybe you have," she acknowledged. "But I'll not sleep a wink for worry if I leave you to fend for yourself."

She handed him to Wulf. "I pray this works out."

He smiled at her. "Tim has nimble fingers and

small hands. He's young enough to be swayed from his thievery, and he'll make a fine jeweler's apprentice. Elen's father will see him well cared for; have no fear." Then he marched the lad off toward the east gate.

Morag shopped while she waited for Wulf to return.

As she wandered the stalls, apples and bread and nuts went into her bag and coins went out. She would miss the easy availability of fruit when she got home. There were no orchards in the glen, and berries were usually gone by the first frost.

"Morag," called a voice.

She stiffened, but did not turn. She had nothing to say to the man. Instead she continued to peruse the offerings of the vegetable vendor, pretending she had not heard her father call her name.

"Morag," he said, much closer to her now.

She paid the vendor for a small sack of hazelnuts and tucked them into her sark.

He grabbed her arm and forced her to turn around. "Listen to me."

"Nay," she said. "Whatever your story, it is of no interest to me. I grew up without a father, and I am a better person for it."

"You cannot believe that."

She glared at him. "I do."

He let go of her arm. "I made a terrible mistake. I admit that. I should never have left."

"There was no mistake. You simply started again. Everything new and fresh."

He raked a hand through his raven-black hair. "There was nothing simple about it. I loved you, and I loved Jeannie. But I let my pride dictate my choices. I wanted to be respected and admired for my skills—lauded for my brilliant weaves. I thought such accolades would make me happy. I was wrong."

"Do you think I care what makes you happy?"

"No," he admitted with a short, bitter laugh. "But my regrets run deep. The image of you standing in front of the bothy, watching me walk away, still haunts me. I betrayed you that day, and for that I am truly ashamed."

Morag shook her head. *No.* She wasn't ready to forgive him.

But deep in her gut she was still that little girl waiting for her father, and it stirred her to know he clung to a similar memory. So she offered him a tiny opening. "I am bound for Dunstoras this morn, and it's unlikely that I'll find myself in Edinburgh again."

He stared, digesting her words.

"Perhaps someday I'll find myself in the glen," he said carefully.

She softened just a bit. "Perhaps."

Then she walked away. If he truly did come to Dunstoras, she would meet with him. In time, with repeated meetings, there might be ground on which to build a friendship. Beyond that, she couldn't commit.

She glanced down at her hands.

Especially as she would be finding a new way to make a living.

Wulf purchased a pair of palfreys with the coins Aiden had given him. It took them only three days of hard riding to reach Dunstoras Glen. Without the cart, they climbed swiftly into the hills and avoided the badly rutted roads. For Wulf, the journey was uneventful and tranquil, but for Morag it was exhausting.

He saw the weariness creep into her face and regretted driving her so hard.

But home and all its memories beckoned. When he reached the crag overlooking the glen, and the keep's pale gray tower appeared through the trees, a thrill of familiarity rippled down his spine. He'd grown from boy into man inside that keep, training at the knee of his uncle Duncan. He could picture every face now and remember every name.

Aye, some of the memories were bitter. But most were not.

He urged his mount forward, picking his way down the rocky path to the floor of the glen.

"We're almost home," he said encouragingly to Morag, as he tugged the reins left.

"Nay," she said.

He glanced back. "What's wrong?"

"This is where we part ways," she said. She pointed down the glen to the right. "My bothy lies in this direction, the keep in the other."

He frowned. "We must make our report to the laird."

"You can do that," she said. "Every bone in my body aches, and my bottom is chafed raw. I'm certain he will forgive my absence."

"But you will miss the celebrations."

"You can tell me all about them at a later date."

He turned his horse around and trotted back to her side. "That simply won't do. It is your effort that we should be celebrating."

She sighed heavily. "You make this more difficult than need be."

He arched a brow. "I am not the one who is being difficult."

"Go, Wulf," she said tightly. "Go home to your son and your cousins and your honorable life."

"Do you not love me?"

Morag smiled sadly. "I surely do. I've loved you since those days of old when you helped me build my bothy. But love is not enough, Wulf. It cannot change the past. The villagers of Dunstoras believe me a harlot and they will always see me thus."

He stared at her for a long moment, then edged his mount closer, until their knees were brushing.

The thoughts running through her head were dark, judging by the shadows in her eyes. And she was bone-weary, barely able to sit up in the saddle. Quite beyond reason.

He snagged her about the waist and hauled her effortlessly into his lap.

With her snug in his arms, he turned the horses toward Dunstoras. That she failed to protest his actions was testament to how weary she was. Indeed, she slumped back against his chest, taking shelter in his warm strength in a way she rarely did.

"We will have words about this," she said darkly.

"I look forward to them," he murmured in her ear. If he had his way, there would be many conversations with Morag, shared over a lifetime. Aye, there would be challenges ahead—the grief he felt for Elen and Hugh was still fresh and painful, and the villagers held deeply seated beliefs about Morag's promiscuity. But if they faced the future together, he had no doubt they could weather all of what lay ahead.

His horse picked its way along the trail, the midday sun beaming through the trees. Morag's mount plodded along behind. The sounds of spring were everywhere—in the twitter of dunnocks in the trees, in the leaf buds beginning to swell on the branches, and in the gambols of red squirrels searching for mates. Even in the long, mournful wolf howl that reverberated through the glen.

Morag shifted in his arms.

"There hasn't been a wolf in the glen for years," she said, frowning.

"I've seen them in the hills," Wulf said. "But they tend to avoid the more frequented areas."

"If they've returned to the glen, I'll have to bring my goats into the bothy at night to keep them safe."

Wulf did not respond. He had hopes that Morag would abandon her bothy and come to live with him in the keep—but it was too early to ask that of her.

They ducked beneath a low-hanging bough.

As Wulf straightened in the saddle, he spied a man standing in the trail ahead. An old man with a long white beard, a bright green cloak, and a long hazel walking stick. Bhaltair. Spying the old druid stirred all the uneasy thoughts Wulf had about the night King Alexander had perished.

He halted the horse.

Despite the druid's urgings to ride hard and fast, Wulf had failed to reach the king in time to prevent his death. And that failure weighed heavily on him. While it was true that he'd had no knowledge of Dunkeld's intent to murder his brother until that fateful moment upon the cliff top, the lost opportunity still nagged at him.

If only he'd gone straight to the cliffs instead of waiting in the woods . . .

Bhaltair raised a hand in greeting. "Hail, Wulf."

"Have you returned to the glen for good?" Wulf asked. The old man had a large sack tied to his back, a wooden bowl hanging from its drawstring.

The old man nodded. "I will make my home in the auld broch once more."

Unsure what news the druid might have heard, Wulf said, "The king perished at Kinghorn."

Bhaltair nodded, a faint frown on his brow.

Giving voice to his regrets, Wulf added, "I did not place proper weight upon your words that night, and the fate of Scotland was sorely impacted."

Bhaltair's faded blue eyes met his gaze. "You believe you failed?"

"Did I not?"

The old man shook his head. "You averted disaster. Had you not confronted William Dunkeld and put an end to his treachery, the future of Scotland would have been a mere shadow of what it is destined to become."

Wulf frowned. "Was Alexander's death foretold?"

Bhaltair shrugged. "The stars are never that easy to read, lad. All I can tell you is that the events of that night played out as they should. Scotland's current path may be a turbulent one, but it is a necessary one. Our nation shall define itself by the days to come."

Wulf's gaze lifted and he looked to the west, toward the auld broch. Deep in the tunnels beneath the ruin lay a treasure the MacCurrans had been tasked with protecting for centuries—the crown and sword of the last king of the Picts, Kenneth MacAlpin. Wulf remembered everything now, including the hiding place of the treasure.

"And what role will the treasure have in the days to come?"

Bhaltair smiled. "You know the answer to that as well as I. The legend says that the crown and sword will one day be needed by the true king of Scotland."

"That suggests all the other kings were false."

"Nay," said the old druid. "The Stone of Scone assures that all who are crowned upon it are true, but one king will need the MacAlpin treasure to firm his claim on the throne—and that king will shape Scotland's destiny for an eternity."

"You are remarkably certain of that," Wulf said dryly, "given the vagaries of the stars."

Bhaltair tapped his walking stick in the dirt several times. "I listen to more than the stars."

Morag yawned and snuggled deeper into Wulf's embrace. Reminded that their journey was near an end, he saluted Bhaltair with a respectful nod, then said, "We have two possible heirs now—Yolande's babe and the young maid Margaret—so I suspect the future you describe is still some way off. I'll bid you adieu."

Bhaltair stepped aside to let him pass. "Give my regards to the laird."

Then Wulf spurred his horse into a canter and raced up the glen to the gates of the keep. Although she must have had questions about Bhaltair, Morag waited until they had ridden beneath the portcullis before she uttered a single word.

"Need we stay long?" she asked, glancing about the close with a frown.

"Be prepared to spend the night," he answered. He had some convincing to do. But first he needed to speak with Jamie. Wulf slid down from his mount, and then cast about for a glimpse of his son. He spied the lad over by the stables, mucking out a stall. Aware that Morag longed for respite, he removed his brat, folded it, and laid it over the top of a nearby crate. Lifting her down from the horse, he gave her a quick kiss on the lips. "Sit for a while and rest. I've a promise I must fulfill, and then we'll find food and wine."

Morag favored him with a hard stare, and then flopped down on the crate. "If I am tossed from the keep while you are gone, I will not return."

"You will not be tossed from the keep," he said. "I sent word of our victory."

"Your victory."

"Nay, *ours*. Have faith in me, lass." He kissed the top of her head, dug into his bag, pulled out the box of carved horses, and crossed the close to the stables.

Jamie looked up as he approached, and Wulf met his gaze easily.

"The man in black is dead," Wulf said briskly. "I promised you his name, so I will tell you he was William Dunkeld, bastard brother to the king." He opened the box, took out the silver locket and the newer toy horse, and offered them to his son. "I also promised to return these."

Jamie took the two items, staring at them for a long moment. Then he said, "Now Mum and Hugh can rest peacefully."

Wulf nodded. "Aye."

Then he folded Jamie into his arms and gave him a short, decisive hug. No awkwardness, no needless effusiveness, just a quick shot of genuine affection. "And because you're still a wee lad, I've brought you a box of toy horses."

He gave him the box.

Jamie frowned. "I don't play with toys."

Wulf smiled. "I know. As I recall, you were never a lad given to playing with toys. Hugh was the one who enjoyed such games. I suppose you'll have to find some other use for them. Planning battle strategies with your uncle Niall, perhaps."

Jamie stared at him for a moment, and then his eyes widened. "Da? Are you back for real?"

"Aye," Wulf said. "I'm here. Let's take a walk."

Eyes closed, Morag tipped her face to the sun, enjoying the warmth of the bonny spring day.

"Good to see you've returned unharmed," a feminine voice said.

She opened her eyes to find Isabail Macintosh standing before her. "My lady."

Isabail's gaze dropped to Morag's hands and she frowned. "I spoke too soon, I see. What happened?"

Morag thrust her curled hands into the folds of her gown. She did not need pity from the lady of the keep. "It's nothing," she lied, hopping down from the crate.

Isabail took her arm and led her across the busy close. They dodged a man carrying a sack of grain, and stopped in front of the kitchens, where a woman with a long red braid was tending to one of the gillies. A wave of hot air from the open door struck Morag, and she sucked in a deep breath, savoring the scent of baking bread.

"Do you remember Ana Bisset?" Isabail asked her.

"The other woman who was with you the night you rode for Tayteath?"

"Aye," Isabail said. "And a healer of some renown." She tapped the redhead on the shoulder.

Ana smeared unguent on the gillie's burned arm and then turned.

Isabail tugged one of Morag's hands free of her skirts. "What do you make of this, Ana? Can anything be done?"

"Och," said Ana, cupping Morag's hand. "A very bad burn this was."

Morag shrugged off the sympathy. "It doesn't hurt," she said.

"Not anymore," agreed Ana.

"Well?" demanded Isabail.

Ana's expression turned thoughtful. "How long ago did this happen?"

"A sennight ago," Morag explained.

Ana exchanged a look with Isabail. "It might be possible to mend them. I can't promise success, but it would surely be worthy of the effort."

"Indeed it would," said Isabail. "Morag is a talented weaver, and her hands possess a skill we'd be sad to lose." She tossed a look at Morag. "Are you a superstitious lot?"

"A bit," Morag admitted.

"A blindfold might be in order then," Isabail said, smiling broadly. "Go with Ana. She'll tend to your hands in one of the rooms upstairs."

A blindfold? Whatever for? Morag looked at her hands, suddenly hopeful. If the healer could increase the stretch of her fingers, it would be a miracle. She followed Ana up the stairs to the solar she'd entered on her last visit. Ana sat her in a chair in front of the fire and fetched a pail of water.

"Prepare yourself," Ana said. "My healing skills are truly a gift from the gods."

Then she closed the door and the healing began.

Chapter 18

Wulf returned to the crate to find Morag long gone.

He queried everyone in sight, but no one had seen her for some time. Not since Lady Isabail had happened by. He slowly scanned the inner close, praying that his reluctant lady hadn't made a dash for the gate.

"Did you lose something?"

He spun to face his cousin Aiden, who was coming down the wide steps to the castle tower. He nodded. "A brave lass who does not deserve to be shunned by the laird."

His cousin smiled. "Does she have raven-black hair, a dark blue gown, and a multihued brat?"

"Aye."

"If she accomplished even half of what your message credited her with, consider her unshunned.

I would be honored to call such a capable woman kith." Aiden nodded toward the heavy oak door above him. "She's inside, but I wouldn't enter just yet."

"Why not?"

"She's a wee bit upset over the healing she's received from Ana."

Wulf frowned. He didn't like the sound of that. He pushed past his cousin and surged up the steps to the door. His eyes struggled to adjust to the dim interior, but the sound of Morag's voice was easy enough to follow, and he had no difficulty recognizing the sweetly feminine curves on the woman to the right.

"A warning would have been appropriate," she snarled.

"What warning could I have given?"

"Anything," shouted Morag. "You cannot simply do such things without notice. How am I to make peace with healing that involves strange swirls that run down your arms and heat that comes without a fire?"

"How are your hands?"

Wulf blinked and the shadowy shape to the left became a lovely redhead wearing a forest green gown.

Morag held up her hands—which to Wulf's amazement were no longer curled or leathery. "They are fine. I don't deny that."

The redhead shrugged. "My job is done, then."

Morag glared at the other woman with such disdain that Wulf feared for Ana's life. He stepped forward and snagged Morag's arm. "Thank you, Ana," he said to the healer. "Morag is grateful, truly."

His dark-haired beauty held on to her anger for a brief moment longer, then offered Ana a rueful smile. "He has the right of it," she said. "I am indeed most grateful. A wee bit disconcerted, but assuredly delighted with the results. I will weave again, thanks to you."

Ana gave Morag's shoulder a light squeeze. "I am pleased I could help."

As the healer walked away, Wulf took Morag's soft hands in his and lifted them to his lips, one at a time.

"Lass, you didn't wait for me."

Her gaze swung toward him, and her eyes softened. "I saw you take a walk with Jamie."

He nodded.

"Is all well, then?"

"Between him and me? Aye. Between you and me? Perhaps not."

Her eyebrows lifted. "Oh?"

He tugged her toward the stairs. "Come with me."

She came, albeit a tad reluctantly. Up the stairs they climbed to the very top floor and then down the corridor to the door at the end. Wulf pushed open the door and escorted Morag inside. It was a small room, little bigger than the bed that stood within its four stone walls. But it had its own hearth, a tiny table, and two chairs. Sweet-smelling rushes were strewn upon the floor, and a tray of bread and cheese was warming by the fire.

"Whose room is this?" she asked.

"Ours," he replied.

She blanched. "You mean the room you once shared with your wife?"

"Nay. This is a different room. One granted to you and me alone."

She shook her head. "Nay."

"Aye," he insisted. "The laird has granted you leave to stay."

"Truly?"

"I know you fear that the villagers will not accept you, but in time they will. Four years have passed since you were banished. There are many who barely remember why you were cast out. Those who still do will soon replace the tales of old with new stories of how you freed me from Edinburgh dungeon." He pulled her close and kissed her gently. "Even Jamie has no issues with your presence. He knows that my feelings for you do not replace the feelings I had for his mother."

She looked at him. "But you still grieve."

"Aye," he admitted. "And I will for some time. But that does not mean I do not love you."

"Are you certain?"

He took her hand and splayed it on his chest, right over his heart. "As certain as the heart that beats within my chest. I loved Elen. She was a fine woman and a devoted mother, and I shall always hold her memory dear. But you and I have found each other in the darkness time and time again, lass. I'm not a great believer in destiny, but I do believe we were meant to build a life together now."

Morag's eyes glistened. "Can we truly weather the comments of viper-tongued gossips?"

"Aye, we can. So long as we stand together."

He bent and scooped her off her feet. Ducking under the bed hangings, he laid her atop the plump feather mattress. Her lovely raven locks spread out over the pillows, and her multihued brat acted as a foil for her pale, freckled beauty. "This was the way I imagined I would take you," he said gruffly. "With the honor and attention deserving of a wife. Will you wed me, Morag Cameron?"

She pulled him down on the bed beside her. "Only if you promise to occasionally resurrect a strong, simple warrior by the name of Magnus."

"I am and always will be that warrior," he vowed. "The warrior whom you rescued from near death, the warrior who loves to watch you weave, the warrior who is blessed to love the bravest woman in all of Scotland."

She smiled.

"Now kiss this warrior," he demanded.

And she did. Slowly, deeply, and passionately.

Morag set aside her fears about the future, and kissed Wulf with all the love she'd held for him since the beginning of time. It would not be easy enduring the gossip. But building a bothy in the woods and carving a life from the wilderness hadn't been easy either. Yet, with Wulf's help, she had survived that challenge and grown stronger from it.

With his help, she would survive this, too.

She opened her mouth to the insistent press of his, and she drank of his passion. Although each and every intimate moment they'd shared had been a delight, this kiss was sweeter than any before—because she no longer felt like he'd be snatched away from her. The past had ceased to haunt them. Time was no longer their enemy. The future lay whole and bright before them, and she intended to make the most of it.

His hand found her breast, his thumb grazing over her already taut nipple.

A moan escaped Morag's lips.

Dear Lord. He knew just how to touch her, just how to bring her alive. In an instant she was ready for him, hot and wet and welcoming. A familiar tension—the most exquisite ache she'd ever known—was building in her belly, and she desperately wanted to feel him inside her. To hold him as close as a woman could hold the man she loved.

"Show me the stars," she whispered.

"Every night for eternity," he promised.

And then he kissed her. Slowly, deeply, and passionately.

Epilogue

Wulf knocked on the iron-hinged door and waited for a response.

When the door swung open, he was greeted by the laird, who was attired in a simple linen lèine belted at his waist. "Did you bring it?"

"Aye," Wulf said, handing Aiden the swath of brightly colored cloth.

His cousin stepped back into his chamber and shook out the folded cloth. He studied the pattern with a thoughtful expression. "She designed this just for me?"

"Aye." It had taken Morag weeks to design and weave the cloth. Determined to craft something unique and special for the laird, she'd spent countless hours at the loom, sometimes discarding a whole day's work as she sought perfection. The finished cloth was a vibrant mix of blue, green, white, and red, which Morag assured him were meant to capture the beauty of Dunstoras: blue for the waters of the loch, green for the forest, red for the mountains at sunset, and white for the winter snows that graced the glen in January.

Wulf thought her view of Dunstoras was perfect.

It was a fine piece of weaving, and the laird seemed pleased.

"Will you wear it?" he asked.

Aiden grinned. "I will indeed."

"Best you hurry, then," Wulf urged him. "Else you'll miss the entire celebration."

Aiden's grin fell away. "She would not dare to begin without me."

"Your wife is a woman unto herself," Wulf said. "She bade me remind you that Dunstoras still officially belongs to her, and that if you disappoint her by being late, she will do what she must."

Aiden swept the brightly hued cloth over his shoulder and pinned it at his throat with a heavy silver brooch. "Vixen," he muttered.

They descended the stairs together, passed through the empty great hall, and exited into the close. Summer was but a whisper away, and the vines that clung to the tower were flush with new green leaves. The sun shone in a rare all-blue sky, its warmth giving many a waiting villager reason to fan themselves as they waited silently within the castle walls.

Wulf glanced about, found the freckled face of Morag, and tossed her a reassuring smile. She'd feared the laird would not like her gift. An unfounded concern, but even after a month of living in the keep, she was still a little nervous about her acceptance.

With a quick point of his finger, Wulf drew Aiden's attention to the woman standing before the door of the kirk. Isabail's white-blond hair was braided down her back and entwined with gold thread—the same gold thread that decorated the neckline and hem of her midnight-blue gown.

"Your lady awaits."

As Aiden strode across the close, Wulf found his way to Morag's side. "He's pleased."

She smiled. "Good."

Aiden reached the kirk and smiled at Isabail. "My apologies for being tardy."

"Only you could be late to your own wedding and expect forgiveness," Isabail said without rancor. "What cause had you to be delayed?"

He took her hand in his and brushed a kiss over her knuckles. "I am but a foil for your beauty, lass, but the occasion demanded I don something special."

She touched the finely woven brat about his

shoulders, then lifted her gaze to glance at Morag. "Truly a beautiful design, Morag. I think I will have one made to match. A wife should show her allegiance to her husband in every way possible."

All eyes turned to Morag, and she blushed furiously. "I would be honored, my lady."

There were smiles from several of the villagers, and others nodded approvingly. The tension that had held Morag's shoulders tight the entire morning slipped away, and she relaxed against Wulf's arm.

Wulf's gaze drifted across the faces of their invited guests—William Comyn, Robert le Brus and his young son, and the royal marischal, William de Keith. Great men, all instrumental in guiding the fate of Scotland. All vying for positions of power during the upcoming royal minority. Having them present for Aiden's official wedding was a moment none could have imagined just a few short weeks ago.

Now all was forgiven.

Aiden's arms would be added to the new Book of Arms the marischal had commissioned, and his son would inherit the title of laird. Dunstoras had remained in Isabail's hands, but it had been agreed by all that any children of their union would inherit the keep, too.

Wulf's gaze moved to the faces of Bran, the cutpurse, and Morag's father. Two people who'd appeared quite unexpectedly for the wedding. He wasn't entirely sure Bran was a welcome addition to the castle, even though the man had proven himself worthy of some respect in Edinburgh. He'd warned Aiden to keep a close eye on his valuables. As for Parlan . . . Wulf had taken the opportunity to deliver a few choice words about the true measure of a man.

Wulf's hand sought Morag's.

It would be Ana and Niall's turn next. A wedding in midsummer.

He and Morag would wait until the first harvest. She wanted to make her own gown, and a special brat for him, and he was a much more patient man these days. Truly content.

Or he had been until this morning. Bhaltair had come to see him, talking about messages in the stars. Something about risks to the new monarch and stirrings in England.

Wulf lifted Morag's hands to his lips.

But those were worries for another day. Today he intended to celebrate.

Continue reading for a preview of the next sweeping historical romance in the Claimed by a Highlander series,

WHAT A LASS WANTS

Available from Signet Eclipse in May 2015 wherever books and e-books are sold.

Cambuskenneth Abbey near Stirling Castle
September 1286

Caitrina de Montfort scurried down the darkened corridor of the abbey, a candlestick gripped tightly in one hand and a bowl of lemon brine herring in the other. The queen had awoken in the middle of the night with a fierce desire to eat fish. Given that Her Grace was only weeks away from birthing the future king of Scotland, Caitrina had happily volunteered to fulfill her request. But the timing was inconvenient. And a wee bit disquieting. The graceful stone columns and carved oak crucifixes she admired by daylight were havens for eerie shadows at this hour.

A shiver ran down her spine as she passed an unlit archway.

The circle of light provided by her flickering candle barely held the gloom at bay. Perhaps it would have been wiser to rouse one of the maids. The chambers provided to visiting nobles were in a separate tower of the abbey, more than a scream away from the sleeping quarters of the Augustinian monks—

Caitrina grimaced and slowed her pace to a more ladylike walk. *Dear Lord*. Why did she insist on letting her foolish imaginings give wings to her feet? What reason would she have to scream? Monks lived here. These were hallowed halls. She had nothing to fear.

She climbed the stairs to the third level and turned down a hall lined with several doors.

The queen's quarters were at the far end—a grand set of rooms that included an antechamber, a stone hearth, and a large platform bed. Just beyond the iron-studded door ahead, a pair of armed soldiers stood guard, protecting the queen and the half dozen women who served her.

Safety was a mere twenty paces away.

A faint smile was curling her lips when a hand snaked out of the dark. Big and strong, it grabbed her by the throat and slammed her against the stone wall. She attempted to shriek, but the only sound that escaped her lips was a strangled whisper. Her candlestick toppled to the wooden floor and the flame was snuffed out as it rolled, leaving her in the dark of night with a hot-breathed monster.

Heart pounding, Caitrina squeezed her eyes shut.

"You," growled the monster, "try my patience."

She recognized the voice, but it was no less monstrous for its familiarity. Giric the Bear—henchman and loyal knave to Edward Longshanks, the king of England. Even with her eyes closed, she could see his large, misshapen left ear and the puckered scar some failed assassin had drawn upon his cheek.

"Every move the queen makes must be reported."

Caitrina attempted to respond, but his hand was still too tight, still choking her efforts to breathe.

Hearing her sputter, he eased his hold, and a sweet rush of air filled her chest. He leaned in close. "If the queen shares a meal with the abbot, you tell me. If she eats haggis instead of venison, you tell me. And if she chooses not to return to Stirling Castle for the evening, you tell me. *Every* move. Am I clear?"

"'Twas a belated decision," Caitrina said hoarsely. Miraculously, she had managed to hold on to the bowl of fish, and she cradled it to her chest. A flimsy barrier to be sure, but a strange comfort nonetheless. "She felt poorly."

"Were she already confined, as a woman of her station ought to be, such discomfort could have been avoided."

"And had her husband not perished on the eve of her birthday," Caitrina said, "she might well be resting at Kinghorn, instead of seeking out every holy monk in the land. But she is convinced the unfortunate timing of Alexander's death is an ill omen, and she fears for the soul of her unborn child."

Giric shook his head. "She's a madwoman. All the more reason that I should know what she is about."

"I'm in service to the queen. I cannot be sending a messenger every hour."

"It is King Edward you must please, not that French bitch." Something feather-soft slid along her cheek. "Honor the bargain you struck with him. Find a way to make him happy."

Caitrina swallowed. "I have given him every insight into the queen's affairs that I am privy to. My only lapse has been this delay."

"A delay that might have had serious consequences." Giric tucked the soft object into the neckline of Caitrina's gown. "Fail us, and you lose the land the king has promised you in Skye."

"I have not failed."

The hand about her neck tightened again. "I will be the judge of our success," he snarled. "Not you. Make your reports with more diligence, or you will not enjoy the consequences."

Her family might have fallen out of favor with Edward Longshanks, but noble blood still coursed through Caitrina's veins—her grandfather had been the Earl of Leicester and her grandmother had been the daughter of a king. Allowing Giric to believe she was without power would be a mistake. She opened her eyes. Her attacker's face was only inches away, and she could vaguely discern the rippled flesh of his scar. "I am cousin to the queen. Punish me without just cause, and I'll see you hang for it."

The Bear snorted in her ear. "You and your sister are the spawn of an excommunicated murderer. Who do you imagine will leap to your defense?"

His words sparked a bitter fire in Caitrina's chest, and she struggled against his hold. "He was not a murderer. My father simply did what honor demanded. He avenged his kin."

"There was no cause for vengeance. Your uncle and grandfather died on a battlefield. Henry of Almain had his throat cut in a church."

"You paint Henry as an innocent," she said. "But he was not. He stole Leicester's colors and then slaughtered every man who flocked to his banner."

"King Edward does not tell the tale the same way."

"Of course not. Henry was obeying Edward's orders!"

Giric's thumb pressed deeply into her throat. "I do not care to debate the past," he snarled. "All that matters is the babe. Do as I say, or your dreams of redeeming your family honor will die. Understand?"

Caitrina's arguments vanished along with her air. She nodded.

"Is the birth imminent?"

She shook her head.

Giric eased his hold again. "The midwife in my employ suggests it could be anytime in the next fortnight. I must know the moment she is confined."

Caitrina's gut knotted. What need would Giric have for a midwife? She had been spying on the queen for several months, and she knew King Edward's interest lay in the bairn—the future monarch of Scotland. But what was the king's ultimate intent? "The monks have offered the queen the hospitality of their fine manor at Clackmannan. We travel there on the morrow."

"Good."

"I assume that once the bairn is born, I will be free to leave the queen's retinue and take up residence in the new hold the king has promised to me?"

A short silence followed her question.

Finally, he released her and stepped back. "You may leave when your task is complete."

"And when is that?"

"After you snatch the babe and bring it to me."

Caitrina stared at his murky outline, her stomach heaving. Steal her cousin's babe? The only child Yolande would ever have with her now dead husband? "No word was ever said about me stealing the bairn. I was asked to spy, nothing more. I cannot do such a thing."

"Did you truly believe a bit of spying would be enough to earn you a title and a hold in Scotland?" the Bear jeered. "Surely you are not so witless as that."

Head spinning, Caitrina slumped against the stone wall. If not witless, then certainly naive. It all made a terrible sort of sense now—why King Edward had approached her in the first place, why he'd offered the perfect prize for spying on the queen, and why Giric had taken her sister into his care. This had been their plan all along. Her sister wasn't being protected by Giric. She was his prisoner. God only knew what horrors

Marsailli was enduring at this mongrel's hands. At ten and five, her sister had developed into a willowy beauty with a gentle soul. She would not fare well under abuse. But Edward Longshanks cared nothing for the lives of innocent young lasses—he cared only for his own plans.

And those plans included hammering the Scots into submission in any way he could. He was determined to rule Scotland one way or another—even if that meant snatching Yolande's new bairn. *Dear Lord*. "Kidnapping the heir to the throne of Scotland will be no easy feat."

"You are cousin to the queen," he reminded her.

"Cousin or no," she protested, "what you ask is impossible. The bairn will never be alone."

"Find a way," he said softly. "Or lose everything you value."

Then he took another step back and disappeared into the darkness.

As his footsteps faded and silence took over the corridor, the stiffness in Caitrina's shoulders eased. Echoes of the Bear's threats still rang in her ears, but she darted for the big oak door at the end of the corridor with the bowl of herring clasped to her bosom like a stolen treasure. She'd been gone far too long. The queen would be weak from hunger.

Inside the antechamber, the two armed guards draped in red-and-gold tabards stood silent and purposeful, completely unaware of the incident in the corridor. Not that they would have come to her defense had they known—they were members of the royal *gardes du corps*. They would die before leaving the queen's side.

She pushed on the inner doors and entered.

A waft of soft heat from the fire greeted her. Five ladies-in-waiting, clad only in their white linen night rails and silk slippers, were loosely gathered around the huge platform bed in the center of the room, chatting in quiet undertones.

Gisele de Noyon, the mistress of the robes, scurried to her side. She snatched the fish from Caitrina's hands, irritation evident in the deep creases on her brow. "*Mon dieu!* You lazy wench. Did you stop to stare at the moon? Martine was right. I should have sent a maid."

"The kitchens are on the far side of the abbey," Caitrina reminded her.

But she need not have bothered. Gisele had already spun about and sailed for the bed. The heavy velvet draperies hung open on one side, revealing the young queen reclined upon a sea of embroidered pillows. A broad smile spread across Yolande's face as she spied the fish, and she eagerly accepted a silver spoon with which to eat. She had the spoon poised above the bowl, about to partake, when she suddenly lifted her gaze and stared across the room.

"Caitrina," she called, "come."

The informal summons earned Caitrina a glare from Gisele. Ladies-in-waiting were typically addressed by their titles, and the queen rarely strayed from that etiquette. Except with her cousin.

Avoiding the censure in Gisele's eyes, Caitrina crossed to the bed with as much speed as decorum would allow and curtsied. "How may I serve you, Your Grace?"

"Lady Gisele has assured me that no food would be brought to me without being tasted," Yolande said, gently caressing her rounded belly with her free hand. "But I need to hear that assurance from your own lips. For the sake of my prince."

Her fears were not groundless. Some months ago, a fiend had attempted to poison the queen and her unborn child—and very nearly succeeded. "You have my word," said Caitrina. "I woke the cook, and he tasted the fish himself, right before my eyes."

Satisfied, the queen dipped her spoon into the bowl and scooped up a small portion of the flaky fish. Yolande's eyes closed briefly as she savored her midnight meal. "Perfect," she murmured, after the mouthful was consumed. Then she emptied the bowl in a series of delicate but eager bites.

Gisele removed the bowl to a side table, and one of the other ladies offered the queen a lavender-scented cloth to wipe her lips. Now replete, the queen laid her head back. "I wish to rest."

Caitrina was about to step away when the queen's eyes popped open and she grabbed Caitrina's hand. "Tomorrow, we will talk, my little cousin. You have been a true comfort to me these past months since my Alexander's death."

"I live to serve you, Your Grace."

"We will require a lady of the nursery," the queen said, her eyelids drooping, "someone who will put the needs of the new prince above all else. You have proven your loyalty time and again, and I can think of none better to entrust my babe and his future to."

Caitrina felt, rather than saw, the stabbing glance from Gisele. "Would you not wish to appoint a woman with more experience, Your Grace? A woman with children of her own?"

"Nay," the queen said, allowing her eyes to close on a soft sigh. "An unwed woman is best. The lady of the nursery should have no other claims on her attention." She released Caitrina's hand. "But we will speak more on this tomorrow."

Bowing deeply, Caitrina stepped back.

The other ladies closed in, tucking the sheets around the queen and lowering the drapes.

Lady of the nursery. How incredible. She'd never imagined the queen would honor her with such an appointment. Especially now. If Yolande had any inkling of the conversation in the corridor, she'd have Caitrina wrapped in chains and thrown into the dungeon. And rightly so. Disloyalty and treason should never be rewarded, no matter how fine the intentions were.

With her heart beating a heavy march, Caitrina reached into the neckline of her gown and pulled out the feather-soft item Giric had tucked there. It was a lock of hair, bound with a piece of hemp. Gleaming, nut brown hair with a slight curl.

Marsailli's hair.

It had been hacked roughly from her sister's head, the shorn edges uneven and varied in length, and Caitrina's throat clenched tight. A rather obvious threat: Steal the bairn, or your sister will suffer. Giric probably intended the hair to be a mild warning, but the sight of it stabbed Caitrina deep in the chest. It was one thing to shear a man's hair, but a woman's? Giric might just as well have laid her cheek open with a blow or broken her nose. Her sister's beauty would be marred for some time to come.

And to think she'd willingly handed her sister over to him.

What a fool.

Caitrina lifted her gaze to the queen's bed. The ladies-in-waiting were blowing out candles and returning to their pallets. As fearful as she was to defy the Bear, the time had come for action. She could not allow Marsailli to remain in that wretch's clutches. Nor could she bring herself to steal Yolande's precious babe.

Nay.

She must find her sister and determine some way to outwit Giric.